JOAN

MW01016406

THE
DUCKLING HOUSE

A Primer of Humour and Hope
LARRY SCOTT

 FriesenPress

Suite 300 - 990 Fort St
Victoria, BC, V8V 3K2
Canada

www.friesenpress.com

Copyright © 2019 by Larry Scott
Jacob Dewey, Illustrator
First Edition — 2019

All rights reserved.

No part of this publication may be reproduced in any form, or by any means, electronic or mechanical, including photocopying, recording, or any information browsing, storage, or retrieval system, without permission in writing from FriesenPress.

The characters in this book are inspired by the author's life expereinces but are fictional and resemblance to anyone living or dead is coincidental.

ISBN
978-1-5255-5775-0 (Hardcover)
978-1-5255-5776-7 (Paperback)
978-1-5255-5777-4 (eBook)

Fiction, Humorous

Distributed to the trade by The Ingram Book Company

For Radar
(1986-2017),
the parrot companion who
inspired me.

1
The Parrot Has Landed

"HELLO." THAT'S MY entire human vocabulary. At least that's all my owner has ever heard me say. Not bad for someone who has no vocal cords. I am a noble parrot, and my name is Captain. Alas, my life has been reduced to that of an enslaved feather duster in the home of a rather dysfunctional humanoid. No offence to others of the human species; however, you tend to be invasive critters that threaten to consume the planet through self-serving behaviours.

Aside from the invasive and dysfunctional caveat, I have nothing against the opposable-thumb crowd inhabiting artificially made environments like this house. I am told that chimpanzees and gorillas also have opposable thumbs, but they are not the subject of my rant because they are not one of their homo sapiens relatives interrupting my afternoon nap. This distinction belongs to others, whose names shall remain temporarily unknown to you.

Likewise, monkeys may be the skateboarders of the rainforest canopy, but they don't use their opposable thumbs to operate chainsaws, bulldozers, or guided missiles, and they don't make me do dusting in this madhouse that serves as a sanctuary for dis-placed humans. I don't wish to be accused of being indiscriminately prejudiced against the entire human race. Some of its members are harmless, albeit myopic. As with many things, it's the few who give the many a bad name.

I only take umbrage at the one thumbie in charge of #217 Orkney St. in Victoria, BC, and the various hangers-on who gather around him, like moths drawn to a flickering flame in the velvet darkness of an August night. I guess even moths need an abode. Calling this abode a "house" is like calling the Amazon River a wandering stream. All manner of human reprobates pass through here. Some linger, like the last patrons when the bar is about to close. At least at the bar someone eventually sweeps the rabble out the door.

The appalling lack of entrance standards for this clapboard haven can be attributed to one Stanley McFadden, the somewhat aged owner and manager of Shady Shingles. The only normal occupant of this aptly named domicile is a reluctant yours truly. Need I explain more? No, but I will.

Every story has two sides. In this quaint city of Victoria on the edge of reality, there are two realities—mine and Stanley's. My deluded owner will try to convey the impression that he is master of his domain and servant to none. He is not alone among seniors in believing this about himself, all evidence to the contrary. Humanoid seniors believe the fantasy that age is just a number. In reality, it's their days that are numbered. Mammals and birds take solace in this fact. That being said, I hope my human stays around long enough to keep feeding me.

I know of Stanley's fantasies from decades of overhearing conversations between him and gullible visitors, as well as his animated monologue when talking on the telephone. The verdict is still out as to whether someone is actually on the other end of those conversations. He thinks parrots are gullible, but we know a thing or two. I hear about distant relatives, erstwhile friends, and bill collectors. All of them except the latter are probably wistful figments of Stanley's highly utilized imagination. Stanley's view of the world is not overly tinged with reality. Perhaps he watched too many episodes of *Star Trek* as a boy.

Reality begins and ends with the airspace in and around my cage. As befits its importance, my cage occupies centre stage in front of the best window in the house. It looks into the front porch, which is also lined with windows. My window has needed cleaning for the past twenty-five years, and I have added this task to Stanley's list of "Things to Do Before He Dies." Meanwhile, I have a prime, albeit smeared, view of both the porch and the chestnut-canopied street outside and all who pass under its branches.

The view in the other direction from my cage is decidedly less inspiring. Stanley says we have a living room. It looks more like a pawn shop that is in danger of failing. While I am not an expert on human habitation, I would hazard to guess that the coffee table is supposed to have four legs, not three and a half. The stump of what was the fourth leg sits balanced on several books stacked beneath it. The books are university textbooks with which his lordship could never quite bear to part. They complement the amber fir floorboards quite nicely.

Likewise, the couch may have once graced a Victorian villa in James Bay, but its intermediary resting place on a rainy boulevard did nothing to enliven its appearance. All its get up and go has long since got up and went. The tweedy fabric once had a vibrant plaid pattern, but now its worn threads only hint at former glory. Stanley says the couch "has character."

Victorians like leaving their orphaned furniture on the boulevard in the belief that someone from somewhere will somehow treasure said piece and carry it away. Apparently, there are more Stanleys out there. In the case of our tattered couch, the price was right. I am intimately acquainted with this stubby-legged beast because I am the only one equipped to dust under it. Stanley sets me down behind the couch, and I crouch under it as I take the most direct route back to my cage. Since I have a long tail, it swishes from side to side when I walk, snagging humongous dust bunnies as I go. These creatures proliferate in the dark underworld beneath the couch until I drag them forth into the light of day. Stanley takes away the prisoners, and I presume they go to either a firing squad or the vacuum cleaner. In any case, my reward for a successful mission is a Red Flame grape. We all do what we gotta do. And Stanley knows I am addicted to seedless red grapes.

The forlorn couch is not the only piece of wounded furniture within my view. The common theme of our household decor is that Stanley is not one to pass up bargain-priced furniture—or bargain-priced anything. Since the house is so shaded, it lacks an abundance of light to illumine the wallpapered hallways or the half-timber ceilings of the living and dining rooms. A cracked aquarium once held fish and now is the home of a faded artificial orchid. Stanley had to rescue the aquarium because it only cost three dollars. The fake orchid came later.

The dining table is a further example of this economic strategy. I understand the human convention is to have a solid table of sorts. The alleged purpose of such technology is to provide a suitable surface where thumbies can place their dishes and cutlery while eating. Parrots have moved beyond this primitive technology. Why use a knife and fork when we're born with a powerful beak and eight good claws?

In Stanley's dining room, a plastic tablecloth is draped over a sheet of plywood, which is nailed on top of two crates. His lordship refers to this rather rustic oddity as a "temporary improvisation" while he researches an appropriate period piece. This euphemism might have worked for the first couple of months, but we are now into the second decade of research. Translation: Stanley has not yet found something suitably cheap enough at any garage sale in the neighbourhood. The boarders pretend not to notice the odd nature of our table, probably for fear that the rent might go up if they do. Their fear is well founded.

This primitive dining arrangement also has the effect of discouraging any would-be dinner guests from coming back more than once. All who dwell here are required to accept Stanley's explanation for the house's ramshackle furnishings as a sign of his commitment to recycling. He's not cheap; he's saving the planet.

Even my cage is the recycled abode of a flighty cockatiel. I know of her only by inference, but I gather she flew the coop one day when her bird sitter left the patio door ajar. Silly bird. She escaped into the "freedom" of a Calgary winter. Those Australian genes might have accounted for her cockatiel yen for adventure, but they didn't do much for keeping her warm in the frigid climes of the Canadian prairies. "No worries, mate" indeed. She may have been the first and only cockatiel to become a flying popsicle.

Stanley is not one to allow unused accommodation to go to waste. In his pecuniary logic, an empty bird cage begs to be filled. I would like to think he procured a palace at great cost for my comfort, once the blessing of my presence was assured. In reality, he got the cage at a garage sale while visiting Stampede City, and I was an afterthought.

Apparently, many well-loved children started out as an afterthought, so I don't consider myself too hard done by. I could have ended up with worse: I could have become the resident mascot in a fried chicken outlet. As it is, I am happily ensconced at Shady Shingles as the resident den mother for a flock of ducklings that happen to have human features. The advantage of supervising humans is they don't shed, and most are toilet trained. If this is karma, then I must have been an evil raptor in a previous life. Maybe I shredded the Easter Bunny and carried off baby koalas from their mother's arms. I spend long days looking out the window of Shady Shingles, so I have time to think of these things. Fortunately, no one knows my thoughts—except you.

A parrot supervising a household of humanoid delinquents has a challenging life. I have to feign interest in the various household inhabitants who stop to seek my counsel. Some think I will be entertained if they talk to me in baby language and ask if somebody named Polly wants a cracker. Haven't they heard of the low-carb diet? And why would I take Polly's food?

Alternatively, the humans rush by because they believe they have someplace important to go. Apparently, there are other life forms "out there," and the brave or foolish ones venture forth from Shady Shingles to wage battle against whatever. I know this only by hearsay. I have no intention of going with them. My cage and its immediate environs are reality enough.

The top of my cage is always left open, probably in hopes that I will fly away. Stanley occasionally remarks on the cost of feeding me; one would think that birdseed and distressed fruit are right up there with rare metals stocks and West Vancouver real estate. Flying the coop is not seriously an option given that "out there" is populated by eagles, hawks, bored cats, and golden retrievers. I have no desire to be retrieved by any drooling canine. No, I stay because of this incontrovertible bit of wisdom: nothing is so bad that it can't get worse. What worse would look like is hard to imagine, but I'm sure it's possible. This is not only my motto but one that apparently has shaped the psyche of Canadian voters. At least that's what Stanley says every time an election rolls around.

Back to reality and how one approaches this delicate subject. Unlike Stanley, who is an unfailing optimist in denial of all life experience, I am a realist. Make that a realist parrot prodigy. There is no point in being just ordinary. If I wanted to be ordinary, I would dye my feathers grey and become a pigeon. Come to think of it, Stanley would make a great pigeon. Maybe that's the bigger reason why I stay. Stanley is a reincarnated pigeon who needs me. God knows he couldn't cope on his own. This theological insight is offered free of charge. Feathery guardian angels are not readily available, and it is divine providence that I have assumed the role. This has been my temporary vocation for the last twenty-five years. Everyone needs a gig, and sometimes we are chosen rather than being the chooser.

Of late I have come to suspect that Stanley is greatly lacking in appreciation for my gracious and indulgent presence. Every morning when he eventually gets around to whisking the cover off my cage, I'm here. Everyone else flees the household before he can enlist their help in one of his dubious projects. Undoubtedly, it is a source of great comfort that Stanley's faithful avian guide has not abandoned him. Organizing my food, changing my cage papers, showering me with a water bottle spritzer, and vacuuming the floor, which I have carefully decorated with seed husks, peanut shells, partially eaten grapes, and orange pulp—all that gives his meagre life focus and purpose. I am only too glad to perform this service for a creature in need. Despite all this effort on my part, I detect moments when Stanley is not only distracted but unappreciative of my talents. Now that I consider the matter, this failing may have begun early on when he named me Captain. Clearly, I should have been called Admiral in recognition of my leadership role on the good ship Shady Shingles.

I am told that my ancestors were kidnapped by Alexander the Great from Nepal, Afghanistan, and other nearby regions. This would explain why thumbies refer to my kind as Alexandrine parakeets. I prefer the Latin name, *Psittacula eupatria*, because it sounds more noble. Alexander brought my ancestors back to Persia with him, and from there they ended up in Europe and beyond. Although I am many generations removed from that first kidnapping, my genes are Asian. To this day I have an unquenchable hunger for freshly cooked rice. Too bad rice has the letter "r" in it. Parrots and all Asian people would happily vote to remove the letter "r" from the English language. As with many great ideas, this one will likely go unrealized. It's right up there with self-peeling bananas.

On balance, it's not so bad being a captain. If only I were not the chief officer of a leaking ship. And if only Stanley were a good navigator. But this is the hand I was dealt. And so, we carry on. The art of carrying on is greatly underrated. Carrying on in the face of adversity is actually the veil of hope. You can write that down. It will come in handy later. Parrots only repeat what they hear, so I can't claim credit for this pithy insight. But I can't quite remember who I heard it from. Elephants don't forget. Then again, parrot brains are not as big as elephant brains, are they? So, I'm allowed to forget. Maybe I'll remember later.

Have you ever noticed how the present has a way of catching up to later? Dewy-eyed parents sitting at graduation ceremonies know this. So do long-lived parrots. Maybe even Stanley will learn that fact if I give him enough time. A certain thing will catch up with him for sure.

2

Ducklings Can Need a Helping Hand

I UNDERSTAND THAT you have spent some "getting to know you" time with my feathered companion, Captain. I don't know about him, but my life as the long-suffering proprietor of Shady Shingles has turned out differently than I planned. I am a duckling helper.

In fact, the word "planning" dropped out of my vocabulary some years ago. Planning seems such a strong and definite word. Granite is strong and definite. So is winter in Winnipeg. Planning my life has been more like nailing Jell-O to the wall or awaiting the arrival of the VIA transcontinental train—something wistful and highly tentative. Of course, one must have sympathy for a locomotive and its coaches ebbing their way across Canada's seemingly infinite wilderness. The railbed is shared with interminably long freight trains, mudslides in the Rockies wreak havoc with timetables, prairie blizzards obliterate the tracks, and mother ducks with ducklings must cross the railbed in northern Ontario.

You may think I made that last one up, but once I was on a pre-VIA passenger train crossing northern Ontario . . . forever. The already crawling train stopped completely at one point. When I somewhat impatiently asked the conductor why, he explained that a mother duck was trying to get her ducklings across the tracks. The offspring had tumbled down into the cavernous space between the two rails but couldn't scale the second rail and reach mum, who was offering urgent encouragement from the other side. A brakeman had to get out and help the fuzzy little beasties over the rail, so the train could continue on its way. No doubt the duckies were marching off to become coyote hors d'oeuvres, but at least we saved them from the maw of the diesel dragon.

Why a transcontinental train could be moving so slowly as to be able to stop for mallard daycare is a mystery best left unaddressed. Remember, this is Canada, and every day someone feels called to help ducklings and their directionally challenged mothers cross the tracks to safety. Little did I realize at the time that my own life would evolve into intermittently helping ducklings cross railway tracks. Not all ducklings are easily helped, and not all ducklings are birds.

I didn't start life as a duckling helper; I stumbled into the role. For the last thirty years, my temporary vocation has been land-lord, with a sideline in creative inventing. By some unexplained quirk of fate, none of my inventions has led to prosperity or fame. Earning a living has regrettably intruded upon that creative side of my psyche. Still, being born in 1951, I have managed to reach my golden years. The only thing missing is the gold. Curiously, I have more silver on top than gold.

In particular, the culmination of my journey thus far involves oversight of Shady Shingles—a three-storey rooming house with seven bedrooms and a distinguished lineage. The mortgage that came with it is not so distinguished, although the loans manager at the bank assures me that we are due to be business partners for a long time yet. The loans manager is a cheery chap. He keeps asking about the state of my health. I infer that it is not only our friendship that prompts his concern for my longevity . . . and my ability to keep paying before I die. He has to fund his holiday trips to Bali somehow.

Some people are born to greatness; others have greatness thrust upon them. And then there's me. I simply had a house thrust upon me in early middle age, and I have postponed greatness until I can do something about the house. I am sure greatness is just waiting around the corner, but for now, I am making do with keeping up Grandma's house. Grandma Vi lived here for sixty years and managed not to make a single improvement for the entire time. Had my grandfather stayed in the picture, the situation might have been different, but he decided not to come back from World War I. Perhaps "decided" is not quite the right word. The decision was made for him by a piece of German shrapnel. His remains rest anonymously on some former French battlefield near Arras. These days I make war on invasive rodents that see this house as a prize to be taken. I would yield the battle if they had a bit of cash to offer, but it's my luck to be under siege from impecunious rodents.

In the language of realtors, my house has great potential. One must stress this fact when offering real estate for sale. Potential is a relative thing. When actually living in said real estate, one must pray that none of the potential hazards translates into actual disaster. Shady Shingles has a mixed record with regard to disasters. For now, let us stress its historic character. Indeed, a reliable source attests that it has a long history of many characters living here. My next-door neighbour, Mary Alice Macdonald, is the reliable first-hand source. She can recite a litany of apparently unforgettable occupants of our house, at least those who inhabited it after fate brought her to Orkney Street.

I spent a year one afternoon listening to Mary Alice go down the list. She began with her arrival from Cape Breton in 1946 and moving into the house next door with her late husband, Malcolm. She was twenty at the time. Once we got past the woes of growing up in the Great Depression, the following decades seemed to fly by. All those eras included Mary Alice's friendship with Grandma, whose given name was Violet. Mary Alice was the only non-family member to call her Vi. It seems they presided jointly and, for the most part, amicably over the affairs of the neighbourhood. Grandma was the senior matriarch of Orkney Street, and Mary Alice has been happy to carry on the torch as her successor. I refer to her as the Dowager Empress. I would caution you not to use this appellation in her presence. You may infer that she is a lovely lady with a heart of gold but not prone to humour or outbursts of moderation.

Mary Alice towers over her domain at five foot nothing. What she lacks in height she more than makes up for in portly gravitas. Her steely grey eyes can penetrate the minds of lesser mortals at a glance. A rounded face much weathered by time and the sun adds to her stately presence. I have seen no evidence that she ever commanded a parade square, but her ramrod posture and sonorous voice indicate she would have been up to the task. Mary Alice has never let her standard fall to wearing slacks. A wardrobe of full-front aprons sets off whatever dress she has on, and the total effect screams "serious matron." They know how to produce those in Cape Breton. In this regard, she and Grandma shared common cause.

In the latter decades, after my mother, Shelagh, married my father, and my uncle Alex immigrated to California, Grandma rented rooms to university students, new immigrants, and people she decided to adopt. The admissions screening to Shady Shingles was a carefully orchestrated interrogation in which she and Mary Alice would invite the prospective tenant for tea. To the unsuspecting eye, they were simply two slightly doughty old ladies who might have been covering a secret lesbian relationship. In reality, they were the presiding matriarchs of Orkney Street, exercising their prerogative to determine who should reside in their realm and who fell short. That was the real agenda of their innocuous tea parties.

Grandma greatly valued Mary Alice's opinion. This must have been a fortuitous blessing because Mary Alice has always had an opinion on virtually everything. You should conclude correctly that Mary Alice came with the house. Into everyone's life a little affliction must fall in order to build character. Mary Alice is one of my principal sources of character. She can appear in my kitchen at any time of the day or night without notice, and she often does. I don't recall ever telling her where the key to the front door is hidden or that she should feel free to drop in anytime. This protocol was established with Violet in the spring of 1933. Since I share the same genes as Grandma, and I clearly want to honour her memory, it is an indelible clause of Magna Carta that the same key protocol remain in place.

I once tried starting an oblique conversation with Mary Alice about the importance of boundaries in inter-human affairs, but you can guess how successful that was. Somehow, we ended up discussing the need to repair the blackberry-lined fence between our properties. Mary Alice said she would check to see what fencing might be on sale at Home Depot. "Don't worry, Stanley. I'll look after it for you." Fortunately, I was not in charge of the Allied team in negotiating the Treaty of Versailles, or we might all be speaking German today. As with World War I, some battles are not worth fighting. It's better to have Mary Alice in my trench than to have her in the trench across the battlefield—or in this case, across the fence.

If there is one thing that Victorians love, other than sending pictures of spring flowers to their Winnipeg kin in the dead of winter, it's getting something for free. Mary Alice reminds me that it would be a mortal sin to pay three dollars for a half pint of blackberries in the store when they can be had for free. Mary Alice knows the theology of these things because she's Catholic, and Catholics have cornered the market on mortal sin and guilt. This may only be a skeptic's point of view, but one generally does not challenge Mary Alice's assessment of religion, politics, or who has the best price on canned tuna this week.

I remember when my neighbours were elderly. Now I'm one of them. How did that happen? When I first heard the line that Victoria is a city where old people go to visit their parents, I chuckled. I started coming here to visit not my parents but my grandmother. Clearly, I was motivated by a deep sense of compassion for a beloved relative in her sunset years. And I lived in Saskatoon. In January, sensible Saskatoonians look for beloved relatives who live in warmer places.

You can infer that I am a born optimist but not so delusional that I believe everyone must bloom where they're planted. If you are planted in Regina or Rimouski, there is little chance of you doing much blooming in January. You can give thanks that at least you were not born in Edmonton. Beyond that it's good to take stock of your situation and be prepared to move.

Moving to Victoria in 1988 was not so much a lifelong ambition as an accident of fate. My grandmother dying, and leaving her house to her only grandson was fate. In the mid-1970s, after Mum was gone, I visited Grandma more often—not just in January. Growing up in Saskatoon, I didn't know Grandma very well because we lived so far away. Visits were exotic adventures, involving a long car ride to the coast with my mother. I looked forward to getting to Grandma's house. She made scrumptious sugar cookies, and the giant chestnut tree in front had a rustic swing suspended from one of its lateral branches. Those are two great reasons to visit a grandma when you are six years old.

Later, I realized that the house got its name because the chestnut canopy shaded both the roof and the street in front. Its shingles were indeed shaded and, therefore, trimmed liberally with moss. Anything that stands still in Victoria will get covered with moss, given enough time. I have personally experienced moss starting to grow on me while waiting for a transit bus to turn up.

The house itself is either fate or karma. Some would say it's more an accident waiting to happen. But the house is in that monarch of provincial capitals, Victoria. (Well, I suppose Regina is a monarch too, but for heaven's sake, it's in Saskatchewan.) I always thought Victoria was like some starlet from the past who came out for one too many curtain calls, and the audience was already leaving. American tourists come to Victoria eager to see England without the English. The fact that the early Europeans were largely Scottish-born employees of the Hudson Bay Company is conveniently overlooked. Locals are happy to be perceived as English by American visitors, as long as they leave behind American dollars. Ideally, I would like to recruit American tourists to become tenants and pay in American currency. I have put in a request for such a business plan to my financial consultant and spiritual confidante, Captain.

At first glance, you might think Captain is the strong, silent type. He does stand around a lot, and he hasn't said a recognizable word in my presence since the spring of 1978. By the way, that was "hello," in the voice of his first owner. Owner number one apparently got Captain when he was a fledgling, and she became his first love. He was uttering that melodic hello when I first met him at Birdy Bordello. The manager of said establishment tried to teach him something more engaging, for customer appeal, but Captain was resolute in his commitment to a one-word vocabulary.

I save my speech for intelligent life forms. You just think I can't speak.

Like other visitors to the store, I was going to pass him by and admire a chatty Amazon who could rattle off a number of cute phrases. But before I got out of range, he uttered his "hello" in an unnervingly human voice but without moving his upper and lower beak. Later I learned that parrots don't need to move their mouths to talk the way we do. Instead of lips and teeth shaping sound, they have a syrinx, located between the voice box and the bronchial tubes. This little gismo channels air, and a parrot's thick tongue further shapes the air flow through its beak.

Parrots imitate human sounds in captivity because they view us as part of their flock, and the sounds are a way of bonding with the flock. Captain had bonded with his first owner, so he spoke in her voice. She was his first human after he was adopted from the local breeder. With the passing of time and the lack of reinforcement from that original alto voice, he would stop saying his mournful hello. When people ask the inevitable question, "Does your parrot talk?", I say, "No."

I'm not tongue tied. I'm just waiting for somebody worthwhile to talk to.

I never intended to buy a parrot that day in the store. I had just wandered in to do some research on what kind of pet bird might be suitable for Shady Shingles. It helped that I had already acquired a slightly used cage. Perhaps there was a slightly used budgie or

15

cockatiel out there that would fit into it, and then the cage wouldn't go to waste. The average lifespan for a member of Captain's parrot type is forty years. That realization did not come to me until later.

How long do humans live? I hope I don't have to train another one. This guy has been a slow learner.

At the time of "just maybe I'll buy him," I was intrigued by Captain's penetrating gaze and long flowing tail. His black eyes are very bright, and he tilts his head slightly, as if he were considering something deeply while looking at me. At first, I suspected Captain had a drinking problem because of his deep burgundy nose and his swaggering walk. Then I learned that all Alexandrine Parakeets have burgundy beaks, and all parrots walk with that comical swagger because their knobby knees bend the opposite way from ours. Captain also has a distinguished air that comes from a ring of pink and black feathers around his neck and a burgundy badge of feathers on each shoulder. The rest of him is a light green, except for a slender yellow tail that is longer than his entire body. His feathered mantle has a suffusion of yellow that glows when the sun shines on him. At other times, it is invisible.

When I asked about the bird's name, the clerk thought he had been called Cedric. That struck me as a totally unsuitable name for a parrot. I don't imagine it would be a big hit for a little boy on his first day at preschool either. "Cedric" didn't seem to respond to the name, so I didn't feel too guilty about calling him Captain instead. He already had the uniform, and I could picture him on the shoulder of a drunken sailor. Little did I know that Captain could handle any drunken sailor or any uppity landlord, with nary a feather ruffled.

Thus began the cross-species relationship that has guided the helm of Shady Shingles through many stormy seas. The crew has sometimes been less than sterling, and stormy seas were not our planned course. People generally don't choose stormy seas. Everyone sets out when the sea is calm, the sun is shining, and Shangri-La is but a day's sail away. At least that's the impression that BC Ferries gives when advertising its service to Vancouver Island from the mainland.

Like immigrants of old, passengers may have to mortgage their soul for a one-way ticket and not be able to return home. But the allure of Shangri-La (Victoria) is so persuasive that potential customers abandon all reason and come anyway. Sometimes the goal is so tantalizing or so essential that they just leave it all behind and strike out for the horizon. I'm sure that's what the mother duck thought when she left the nest with her brood on the way to some nearby pond or river. Instead she inadvertently led them onto a railbed that they couldn't climb over, risking them succumbing to the noonday sun, diesel dragons, or passing predators.

You may meet some ducklings who seem to be heading the wrong way. Sometimes it's best to leave ducklings be and not rescue them. At other times a helping hand makes the difference between life and death. My life plan was not built around ducklings or being a helping hand. Fortunately, life is not about the plan. It's about how we respond to whatever comes our way instead. It's also about who accompanies us along the way, perhaps with a stopover at Shady Shingles.

3
Rooms to Let

IT MAY COME as a great surprise to you that there was a time before Craigslist and Kijiji. At least it will be a surprise if you are a Millennial—that demographic of people born around 1980 who entered adulthood at the turn of the twenty-first century.

My more recent tenants have come from the Millennial crowd, and they find Shady Shingles on one of the online services. As an early Baby Boomer, I have come to realize there is a gap between me and Generation X, which is the succeeding generation. This little fault line expands into a chasm when I talk to Millennials, also known as Gen Y, who are the generation after Gen X. Admittedly, we rarely talk—they text me from their rooms when I remind them that the rent is due or they want to complain to me that the Wi-Fi is too slow. My standard response to such complaints is that the Internet could be faster if I covered the cost of the necessary upgrade by raising the rent. This cause-and-effect lesson seems to transcend the generations, and the texting duel ends. Thank God, because I hate texting. Surely our opposable thumbs were designed with something better in mind, like holding a dessert spoon or pushing the remote on the TV. My doctor says my proficiency with these utensils will prove my undoing. I digress.

I only found out that I needed to list my vacancies on Craigslist or Kijiji by consulting with my IT specialist, Liam. He's ten years old, four feet tall, has pencil arms, and lives three houses down the street. Florescent green Nikes complete his look. The boy is not exactly under a legal IT contract, but he turns up after school at the front door if he thinks his ancient neighbour might need rescuing. My needing digital rescuing is a fairly frequent state of affairs, so a random visit by Liam is bound to be close to the mark. He can be bribed to part with his expertise by my giving him gluten-free jujubes and a personal audience with Captain.

A Liam visit has to be cleared by dispatch, which involves a text to his mom at home. I have this one down pat by now. "Liam is here. Can I borrow him for ten minutes?" Apparently, a visit with Captain has virtual pre-clearance, but this involves going into someone else's house, so a certain protocol is required. This is, after all, the twenty-first century, and even grandfatherly neighbours are not immune from parental scrutiny.

The answer comes back. "It'll cost you, you know. Send him home when he becomes a pest."

I dare say even Liam's parents recognize that he is a force to be reckoned with. Indeed, the real danger is that Liam would wear out a frail senior citizen if he were allowed to stay too long. I'm happy to play the fragile senior citizen card whenever I can. It requires less and less acting as time goes on.

Liam and Captain have a certain rapport. Liam stomps into the living room and parks himself just under Captain's gaze. "School was boring today. Mr. Parker yelled at Jennifer. Alex sat on my lunch bag, and we had a fire drill, but there was no fire. It's only Tuesday, and I can't wait till Friday."

Captain tilts his head and yawns. *Go away, kid. You're using up all the oxygen.*

This is not unlike his response when I practice my Toastmasters speech on him. It must be parrot body language to signal rapt attention. If only we knew what went on in that feathered brain. Or maybe it's a blessing we don't.

Since Liam's allotted visiting time is short, I know to haul him away from Captain and get my IT request in quickly. Exploitation of child labour can be rewarding. I came to this conclusion when, on one occasion, I lamented aloud that it was getting expensive to list my vacancies in the newspaper.

"You do what, Mr. McFadden?"

Sensing we were on the edge of a Liam soliloquy, I headed him off. "I phone up the newspaper, and I tell the lady to put my standard ad in the 'rooms for rent' section of the classifieds."

I couldn't decide if his astonished expression was from disbelief that I knew how to operate my cell phone or that I had a phone used for talking rather than scrolling. For a ten- year-old, he has the teenage eye-roll down pat. I shudder to think what his expression will be when he becomes an actual teenager. His parents are in for a ride.

"Mr. M, students, and regular people don't buy newspapers. They look for stuff on Craigslist or Kijiji. You don't even have to pay to put your ad there."

I wasn't sure about the rest of his market analysis, but the part about not having to pay certainly piqued my interest. Liam knows how to reel in a customer.

"I can show you how it all works, but I'm a little hungry just now." Hint. I went for the jujubes while Liam took up his station at my computer in the living room. In a flurry of little fingers, he brought up the right website and showed me where to type my ad.

"You mean people pay to live here?" Liam queried with a distinct tone of adult skepticism as I pecked at the keys. Precious child. I'm not sure if he thought I was a magnanimous benefactor who just happened to give away rooms or he was simply incredulous that anyone would pay money to live in such a place. Either way, his introduction to reality had to start sometime.

"Yes, Liam," I replied with measured kindness. "It is indeed the way of the world that most people have to pay for where they live. People who live in my house pay rent."

Actually, that was more wishful thinking than a summary of what reliably happens; however, I didn't want to burden Liam with too much fiscal reality in one dose. Rent dodgers are a pest species with which IT specialists of tender years need not concern themselves.

"But at my house I don't pay any rent. And you don't make Captain pay rent, do you?" Liam sounded alarmed at the prospect of such a tragic injustice.

Captain raised his head from a slumber pose. *You have no idea, kid. I pay big time.*

Sensing the discussion could intrude into supper time, I tried to wrap things up. "Well, Captain is a parrot, and parrots don't pay rent. You are a child in your parents' house, and they pay the rent for you, sort of. That's part of the parenting deal."

This has always been sufficient rationale for me not to have children. No doubt Liam would perceive the argument differently. Lest we descend further into the irrational world of family finances, I ushered Liam toward the door with his jujubes.

"Bye, Mr. M. Try not to mess up your computer too much. I might have to raise my rates."

Captain's head followed our progress. *Polly wants a scotch. Give the kid the candy, and maybe he'll share some with the bird.*

It was midsummer when I made my entrance to the world of online classifieds. Within a few days, I had a sprinkling of replies, mostly from college or university students wanting a room for September. Some wanted more details about the size of the room, available storage, distance to campus, and so on. Others asked if the household was vegan, omnivorous, vegetarian plus, gluten-free, nut-free, and so on.

While my mother had run Shady Shingles as a boarding house, it was in an era when people ate whatever she provided, and they ate it at the time she put it on the table. My business plan has, of necessity, been modified. People's tastes and preferences are so individualized, and they come and go at such varied times that I quickly changed the setup to be a rooming house. People have access to a couple of shared fridges, and they use a common kitchen. Generations of tenants have informed me that my kitchen is very common indeed.

The house has upstairs bedrooms, but they are not suites with kitchenettes. Only the downstairs kitchen has the upgraded wiring for heavy appliances. Otherwise, Shady Shingles clings to the vanishing glory of the Victorian era. That's an indirect way of saying too many appliances plugged in will lead to a blown fuse. Shady Shingles has not yet reached the age of breakers.

Millennials are used to electronic apps for everything, and they expect everything to work instantly. Putting Millennial tenants in a Victorian house requires much on-site education and no small amount of ominous threats from a live-in landlord. This orientation to reality comes across more effectively when delivered live with the appropriate voice inflection. In other words, I yell, as required.

When a prospective tenant in Kamloops or Lethbridge answers my ad online in July, I don't get to meet them in person until they move in on September 1. So, I resort to references, demonstrated literacy in an email, a hefty damage deposit, or just gut reaction. It's hard to say who takes the greater risk in such ventures, the tenants or me.

The fact that I could actually meet Pierre in person was perhaps the best selling point for accepting the bearded man as a renter. He wasn't a student, and he was looking for a room because he had recently divorced and was "in transition." Pierre didn't elaborate, but I assumed that meant he wanted something relatively low cost until he decided where his work or his domestic life might take him and what was left after alimony payments.

Given that he looked to be in his early thirties, he was obviously a little older and more mature than a first-year university student wanting to party. That was one consideration. A little grey had crept into his cropped beard, and his left eye twitched every now and then. I suspected he was on the fast track to aging, although he still had an athletic walk and energetic hand gestures. Physical appearance is one aspect of a first impression. One also wonders how a prospective tenant is going to pay the rent. Pierre had a nonchalant demeanour and a glib delivery, aided by his Quebecois accent.

"Hey der, Monsieur Stanley. Me, I am self-employed in da h'auto business. I am a successful businessman like you, no?"

I guess I am self-employed in the housing business, so it didn't seem a far stretch to accept Pierre's self-description. He also pulled out a roll of cash to indicate he had the first month's rent and a damage deposit. I immediately concluded that the auto business must be more lucrative than the room-renting business. At least I hoped so.

"Yes, Pierre, I'm glad to see you've come prepared. I was going to say I don't take cheques, but you're one step ahead of me. Now there's just the little matter of references."

Pierre twitched, and his confident air faltered briefly. "Well, you see, that is too 'ard for me. I did own a house in Sooke with my Claudette. We were together then, but now she has dat house, and I need to live here. The women, they are temperamental, no?"

If he thought his estranged wife was temperamental, I couldn't wait until he met Mary Alice. For the time being though, I decided to keep that nugget to myself. So much for following the approved method of checking references. I would have to take a chance on what kind of character Pierre might really be. Gallic charm must count for something. Or not.

Where was Mary Alice when I needed her? I could see how she and my grandmother had used their combined instincts to form a discreet impression of prospective renters. In the moment, the only other confidante to rely on was Captain. My feathered protégé was clearly observing the entire scene. Pierre strode energetically over to the cage and waggled his finger through the bars.

"Salut, little green pigeon. Are you da friend of Pierre?"

Captain recoiled, his eyes pinned with alarm. *Back off, furry face. I'm not interested in being your friend or your dinner!*

Pinning is a process where a parrot rapidly expands and contracts its pupils—a kind of eye flashing. The behaviour can be a sign of happiness, contentment, excitement, curiosity, or aggression. Pierre had gotten too close too soon, but being a non-parrot person (NPP) he just thought the birdie was being cute. To Captain, it looked more like Pierre was trying to break into his cage and mug him with his index finger. Parrots are a bit paranoid that way. On the other hand, paranoid parrots probably live longer than trusting parrots. All this would be lost on Pierre. Clearly, auto experts are not automatically avian experts.

"Captain is a bit shy with strangers," I said.

"Does he talk?" Pierre asked innocently. This is the standard question that everyone asks when they know I have a parrot. The assumption is that I would want to have a parrot because it can talk like a human, therefore making it more valuable than a bird that just makes bird sounds. If I wanted a photorealistic painting, it would make more sense to take a photo than to hire a painter to do what is already available from a good camera. In the same way, if you want another creature to act and sound like a human, get a human. Slavery is currently out of vogue; therefore, the approved way of finding someone capable of human speech is to make a friend, marry, or have children. Sometimes those possibilities overlap. Depending on the relationship, the quality and frequency of human speech may vary, but you will be in the right ballpark.

"Captain doesn't much care for fingers. You might step back a bit." I reserve my most patient tone for idiots and small children.

Owning a parrot is cheaper than committing to marriage or parenthood. But if you crave human speech from someone who knows what they're saying, try the Internet, not the pet shop. There are no guarantees, but the odds are definitely more in your favour if you hook up with an actual human. And I should add that no life decision comes risk-free.

At the time of Pierre's visit, Captain had long ceased uttering his plaintive "hello," reserved for the woman who first owned him. Pierre was at least doing a credible job at feigning interest in my pet. I decided to give him the benefit of the doubt. "Captain once talked a little, but his preference is for young women."

"Hey, hey! He's my kinda guy!" Pierre said.

I decided not to mention that I was gay. Or that Pierre sounded too desperate to be alluring to young women. Or that Pierre's enthusiasm for young women might explain his recent divorce. I charge extra for romantic coaching, so I did not volunteer these insights to my Gallic visitor. Telling the truth is greatly overrated, especially to people who don't want to hear it. Ask anyone in the prime minister's caucus. Or your children.

"Well, Pierre, you seem to know what you are about. I'll relieve you of the damage deposit and first month's rent, since you seem to have come prepared with cash."

We shook hands, and the deal was done. I had my new tenant in August without waiting for the school year to begin. One down, two to go. The previous year's crop of tenants had cleared out in the spring, after their exam period. Summer had been a bit sparse as far as rental income went.

Just after Pierre made his exit, Captain went into a pointer pose, what I call his Mary Alice alert. Captain has excellent hearing, even though he has no visible ears. They consist of a hole on each side of his head, covered discreetly by feathers. My parrot guardian can hear Mary Alice's side door open. At that sound he lowers his head and raises his long tail, so his emerald parrot physique is one long pointer aimed at our front porch door. This is a sure sign that Mary Alice is heading our way. Batten down the hatches and put the kettle on for tea. There is no escaping a surprise visit from Mary Alice Macdonald.

Fortunately, a ninety-two-year-old woman who is challenged by height and gravity doesn't move as fast as she once did. Her track speed may have deteriorated, but her squinting grey eyes could still decipher the tiniest label in the discount bin at Lucky Foods. Given that level of acuity, she didn't miss who came and went from Shady Shingles. We had no need for a security system; we had Mary Alice.

I knew Mary Alice's mission before she entered the door. I had quite likely rented a room and violated the time-honoured protocol whereby she would orchestrate the selection process. In this suspicion, she was correct. Occasionally, I take life-altering risks without thinking through the matter. Mountain climbing in a thunderstorm, daring to skateboard at age fifty, and buying stock in Nortel all fall into that category. Now I could add failing to consult with Mary Alice when I was interviewing a potential renter. It was too late to turn off the lights and pretend I wasn't home. Better to play innocent and hope she couldn't stay long. Other parts of the realm might need her oversight and intervention. I could only hope.

Mary Alice mounted the front steps and let herself in. The door was obviously unlocked, so she didn't need to check the secret hiding place for the key. The creak of the porch floor and her wheezing announced her imminent and laboured presence. One could say that Mary Alice was a person of bulk, which explained why the porch floor creaked for her but not for most others who trod on it. Moving that much weight took a certain amount of aerobic energy.

She entered the living room and paid homage to Captain by giving him a Red Flame seedless grape, produced magically from her apron pocket. I presume they were on sale that week at her favourite store. Usually, she just presented him with a lonely sunflower seed, always amused at how deftly he shelled it before making it disappear.

Captain used his rosy beak to take the grape gingerly from between her thumb and index finger. He held the treasure in his left foot and began eating it like an apple. The world is a good place when the intruder brings grapes, even if the intruder is Mary Alice the Terrible.

Captain eyed Mary Alice sideways. *The chubby lady has her good points.*

The Dowager Empress continued her trek into the kitchen. "Stanley, isn't that tea ready yet?" Her bark was worse than her bite, mostly. I could be entrusted to boil the water, but the kettle plug had to be pulled at the nanosecond that the water hit the boiling point. Some of the water was used to "prime the pot." Mary Alice took over at that point because I might only do half a swish and miss some part of the teapot's interior. Apparently, it's all in the wrist action. Who would have thought a gay man wouldn't know how to swish properly?

Allegedly, it is also the case that I don't know how to dress, but that wasn't the focus of her mission on that visit. Mary Alice is not patient with amateurs. She reached up to the second shelf of the cupboard and retrieved a canister of the "good tea," not the stuff I got in the discount cart at Lucky Foods. That was reserved for tenants and criminals.

While Mary Alice usually approved of bargain purchases, she had no truck with counterfeit tea. The loose tea leaves went in the bottom of the teapot, and the perfectly heated water was poured over them. Tea bags were verboten. This is, after all, Victoria, and tea culture is almost as important as curling or complaining about the ferry service.

After the tea steeped and we both sat down at the kitchen table to sip it, Mary Alice launched in. "Stanley, my boy, you've been up to something."

Her low-pitched voice resonated with ominous gravitas. The charge from the prosecution was now on record—I was up to something that I shouldn't have been. When Mary Alice is on the bench, the options are to flee or confess. She knows where I live, so it seemed most prudent to confess rather than feign innocence.

"I've just rented one of the upstairs bedrooms to a nice young business chap," I replied, sounding as casual and as confident as possible.

"Oh, indeed. That's nice. What kind of business is he in?"

Mary Alice has a way of homing in on the weakest part of an ill-considered defence. Her tone implied that I had allowed the inner gates to be breached by the Cosa Nostra.

Since I didn't know precisely what Pierre did, other than have a fistful of cash, I fidgeted. "He works as a salesman at an auto dealership." That sounded plausible and respectable to me. Not to Madam Prosecution.

"You mean you rented a room to a used-car salesman?" Mary Alice drew out the words and glared through her imaginary reading glasses at the accused. Put in those terms, it wasn't really a question. I felt the need to defend the honour of used-car salesmen everywhere but thought better of it.

"He paid in cash," I said, sensing the possible collapse of my argument. "I've got the first month's rent and the damage deposit. See here!"

Mary Alice has an eye for money, and she could tell how much was there without even handling the bills. It was apparent from her downcast glance that this bit of evidence tipped the scales of justice a little bit but not enough to win her approval or my reprieve.

Captain had finished his grape and was tilting his head to one side. *You're in trouble, bozo.*

She sighed. "Vi and I would have looked inside his head a bit and then told him that she would get back to him within a day or two. Maybe he's legit, and maybe he isn't. I guess you'll know soon enough."

With that pronouncement, Mary Alice shook her head and then took her leave. The verdict was inconclusive, but I had staked my ground. It's just that it turned out to be shaky ground. Victoria is situated in an earthquake zone, so people there accept shaky ground as normal. At least that's how I have explained the outcome of some of my entrepreneurial adventures.

Now I was a shaky landlord running a rooming house called Shady Shingles. Maybe "running" is one of those strong, definite words again. I was the caretaker and nominal owner of a heritage property managed by a salty matriarch and a testy parrot. What could go wrong?

4

One Down, Two to Go

I GENERALLY DON'T need to imagine how trouble will come knocking; it finds me on its own.

The phone rang. It was Jerome Fairchild, the loans manager at the bank. I face a great ethical dilemma whenever he calls. I can pretend not to be home and let him leave a message on my answering machine. Liam says answering machines are from ancient times, but it doesn't charge me a fee every month. With any luck I would accidentally erase the message before I listened to it, and life could continue on pleasantly . . . for a time.

Experience would indicate that my communication strategy is not 100 percent effective. Jerome calls back. That leads to the second part of my ethical dilemma—I can actually talk to him, and then I have to fabricate contrition on the spot. The possibility that Jerome would be bearing good news is not within the constellation of possibilities. Banks should have promotions, like giving away bundles of stale money before they let it go to waste by shredding it. Then people would be glad to answer their calls.

One of my inventions, which still needs perfecting, is a telephone signal that lets people know before they answer if the person on the other end has something to say that the recipient of the call wants to hear. Somebody sideswiped me with caller recognition, but knowing who is calling is only half the issue. They should have to register the content of their call before they make it. Like I said, I'm still at the perfecting stage.

Since I had just weathered a visit from Mary Alice, I decided I might need further reserves of energy before dealing with Jerome. Bravery is greatly overrated. I opted to let the answering machine get the call. Jerome's nasal voice records annoyingly well.

"Good afternoon, Stanley. I hope you are well. Please call me soon. I have the result of your most recent loan application. Over and out."

I think Jerome is an aspiring taxi dispatcher, because he always ends his calls that way. The carrot of knowing about the fate of my application to get a loan for fixing the roof is one way of getting me to call back. Probably his real motive was to get me in his office and put on the squeeze about my ever so slightly exceeded line of credit. What advice would Dad have offered in this situation? "Never do today what you can postpone until tomorrow." Or maybe it was the other way around. I get a lot of things backwards, according to Mary Alice.

Since the day was largely gone, it seemed sensible to retire to the living room and meditate. Some people meditate with breathing exercises, assuming a lotus position, lighting incense, kneeling toward California, or whatever. I meditate with sherry. I am eternally grateful that apartheid in South Africa was overthrown because then we could end the boycott of South African sherry. There are more profound reasons why one might be concerned about the political system in that country, but none affects me so immediately as sherry. I could not have faced a lifetime of Canadian sherry.

One should not drink alone, so I always invite Captain to share. Strangely, he has trouble holding onto the sherry glass, and I have to hover mine under his beak. He enjoys this ritual but never actually sips the sherry. Pity. How did I end up with a Presbyterian parrot? I'm assuming that Presbyterians don't drink, but I have several Scottish friends who purport to be devout Presbyterians, and they drink like fish. Maybe there are dry Presbyterians and wet Presbyterians, and I only know the wet ones.

Captain is of the teetotaller ilk. He sniffs the sherry, shakes his head, and poops. This is not necessarily a sign of disapproval, although it isn't exactly an endorsement. Birds in general have short digestive tracts, so they poop forty times a day. For this reason, large geese do not make ideal house pets or even acceptable lawn ornaments. It doesn't take long for anything to go through them. I've always had the same problem with French irregular verbs failing to linger in my mental digestive system. I digress.

After I invite Captain to step up on my hand, I just have to utter the magic word, "Poop." I ask him to poop before carrying him wherever we are going in the house. There really isn't a more elegant way of going about it. Better to do the niceties while I am holding him over the newsprint that lines the bottom of his cage than the alternative. Three times out of four he has a prolific response. Parrots are made of parrot poop and feathers; therefore, they nearly always have a reserve of potential geranium fertilizer at the ready. Having performed this initial ritual, Captain can safely be transferred to a free-standing perch near the couch. Then we can meditate together while I sip my sherry and stare out the window at the neighbour's house across the street. It has an immaculate lawn, landscaped flower beds, and a freshly painted exterior. In short, it's quite depressing, so I need another glass of sherry. Captain agrees, I'm sure.

Lay off the booze chubby. You need to stay awake and clean my cage and your cage too.

The rest of the day was uneventful. I put Captain to bed at 7:30 p.m. and covered him with a sheet. He believes that going to bed at 7:30 and being covered is his constitutional right. He emits a loud squawk if this bedtime ritual does not happen on schedule. I imagine that a parrot day is easier to handle if it is only twelve hours long. I, on the other hand, am a nighthawk. Don't mention the word "hawk" to Captain though. Parrots and hawks are generally not on good terms in the wild. All relationships need a few secrets.

Alas, there is no one to cover me with a sheet at night and put me to bed. Being a thoroughly self-reliant individual, I always manage to stagger to bed on my own. The decision to actually go to bed is the more vexing issue. I always believe I'll miss out on something important if I go to bed too early. It's not that I think an important telephone call will come; rather, another device is the culprit: the TV. There's the late-night news, followed by a few minutes of one of the talk shows. Then just one more guest on the talk show, and I'll actually turn off the TV.

If I dawdle too long, Captain uses his beak to bang the steel mirror on the side of his cage. This means he has had enough Letterman or Fallon, and the light from the TV is annoying him through the sheet. Supposedly, he has been asleep, but he wakes up now and then to check on me. Either that or he has insomnia. I prefer to think he is motivated by deep concern for his longsuffering master. Like I said, it's good to have some secrets in a relationship.

Secrets can be innocuous enough. I don't really want to know everything another person is thinking or everything they've ever done. And many such secrets don't matter much anyway. Of course, if money is involved, the issue of secrets can become dicey. Revenue Canada is not known for overlooking secrets that mask undeclared money. Even riskier is trying to keep a secret from Mary Alice. Captain probably knows my deepest secrets, but if he does, he doesn't let on to Mary Alice or to anyone else. Trappist parrots make good soul mates that way. They listen and nod, and they tell no one.

Captain sat with his head seemingly sinking into his chest. He blinked. *I know more than you think.*

Even more difficult than the decision to go to bed is the reality of getting up in the morning. In that department, there are two kinds of people in the world—morning people and those who are not. I wake up in installments. Usually, the first thing I hear is a robin chirping at thunderous volume in the yard below. I think it's the same one every morning, staking out his worm turf and warning interlopers to take a hike. Apparently, this message has to be repeated for a good half hour because other robins are either slow learners or hard of hearing.

I am not usually prone to violence, but I would be willing to duke it out with Rob and persuade him to move to another lawn. While I take great satisfaction in imagining this encounter, I realize the SPCA has spies everywhere, and the real event would result in my being incarcerated. Just when Rob wears himself out, a flock of delinquent sparrows comes to life. They create a great cacophony of cheeping that forms the basis of choral concert number two. None of them chirps in key.

It's probably the same thing as what happens during Question Period in the House of Commons, except the sparrows don't get analyzed by TV reporters. The shred of hope in all this is that the bird mafia terrorizes the neighbourhood for only a few months in summer. When the days shorten again, the plague lifts, and all non-morning people know peace and tranquility once again.

The next day, I was still on the alert for potential tenants. Victoria has a plethora of educational institutions and, therefore, a rotating crop of students. Most of them are not keen to take up residence on a park bench, so there is a potential clientele for landlords like me.

In midafternoon, a civilized time, the phone rang. I heard the voice of a live person, as opposed to reading a text message. He was in town and wanted to come over right away, if the room was still available. He arrived within the hour, and I met him in the porch.

Brian was a history major returning for his second year of university. His parents had divorced, and his father lived in the city with his new wife and her children from a previous relationship. His mother had moved back to Saskatchewan. Brian couldn't very well live at home and go to school. He had a summer job at a mill on Vancouver Island but was close enough to come and look at the room in person.

My seemingly polite applicant was only in his early twenties, but he came across as mature and unlikely to be at the stage of just leaving home and seeking a party experience. Interviewing an introvert is a bit of a challenge because they don't say much until long after I want to know their answer.

I did my best Johnny Carson imitation. Fortunately, Brian was far too young to know who Johnny Carson was. Patience is sometimes rewarded. I learned that, the previous year, he had lived with two other guys, but there were disagreements about noise, sharing expenses, and cleanup. This time around he wanted his own room and to be in a quiet place. I took his first two questions as a good sign. "Who else is going to be living here? Is the house quiet?"

I gave the boy five gold stars. I explained I had one new tenant who indicated that he worked at night, so he wouldn't be around. I also said there would be a third tenant, who I had not chosen yet, but he or she would certainly receive the third degree about the noise code.

Brian smiled awkwardly. Then came that poignant silence where I hadn't offered him the room, and he hadn't said he would like to take it. When both interlocuters are introverts, no one wants to risk going first. Finally, I broke the silence. "You haven't actually seen the room, so I'll invite you now to go upstairs and have a look at the second room on the left. I'd go with you, but I'm not doing stairs as much lately."

"No problem. I can check it out and be right back." Brian strode up the stairs, two steps at a time. I could hardly remember the last time that I was able to accomplish that feat. He returned a couple of minutes later, and I continued on to stage two of the interview.

"There is one more occupant of the house whom you should meet. Just come this way."

We walked into the rustic living room, where I'm sure Captain was eavesdropping. I recognized his body language—leaning slightly forward on his perch, as if about to launch into flight. Brian walked cautiously over to the cage and spoke calmly to him. "How are you doing, buddy?"

Captain hesitated a little and then came over to the side of the cage closest to Brian, clucking softly. Then Captain did his happy dance. This consists of stepping rapidly from side to side while swinging his head vigorously in a figure eight. Parrots can do this manoeuvre because they have thirteen bones in their neck, versus our seven. Like so many who would follow him, Brian began trying to do the same head swing. On a parrot, it looks cool. On a human, it's painful to watch someone give themselves a neck injury while doing a courting dance for a bird. In any case, this was clearly Captain's belated stamp of approval, even if the Dowager Empress was not there to give imperial assent. Brian didn't ask if Captain could talk; he just admired his colourful plumage.

"Cool bird. I love that he has that long yellow tail."

"You aren't allergic to feather dust, are you?"

"No, no. That wouldn't bother me at all."

I invited him to be seated, now that we had covered the basics. Brian looked around the living room rather wistfully. "I like the hardwood floors and the character house, and I like the room very much. I'd like to take it, but the rent is a bit more than I can do on my own."

He looked decidedly embarrassed to admit his limited finances. I resisted the temptation to rescue him. Rescuing ducklings does not stave off bank foreclosures. And a bigger duckling rescuing a smaller duckling is scarcely a path to security for either one.

"Could you hold the room for a couple days, and I'll ask my dad to help? He's an engineer here in town."

I had not received a flood of applicants, and I would still likely be able to rent the room later. "I'll hold the room for a couple days, but you need to come back with the rent and damage deposit if you're serious about taking it."

For someone with no parenting experience, I can fake a pretty good dad voice. Besides, when renting rooms, I don't generally get flush renters. If they had money, they would be renting an apartment or a suite, not a room in somebody's house. While university students with rent money seem to be an ever-scarcer species, a university student with an engineer for a father probably knew how to tap the parental ATM. In my mind, this cash umbilical is another reason not to have children. I had empathy for Brian's father but hoped he would cave.

While having children is not exclusively a heterosexual enterprise, and I could have been an Elton John who found a partner and adopted, I think retirement is a bit late in the game to do the offspring thing. Retirement is a bit late to do the rooming house thing too, but the need for shelter and food is a marvelous motivator to stay the course in one's twilight years.

I escorted Brian to the door. "If you get your dad's backing and still want the room, you can come back for tea, and we'll settle on a deal."

Brian looked slightly puzzled about being invited to tea, but he would learn soon enough what that innocuous phrase really meant. The pronoun "we" can be conveniently ambiguous. I made no mention of Mary Alice, but I did say "we." That could mean Captain and me or Mary Alice and me or even Brian and me. Ambiguity is a great thing. No doubt it has saved many a marriage.

I received no serious inquiries over the next couple of days, and then I got a text from Brian. Nobody's perfect. "Can we have T? I have rent."

People don't write essays in text messages, but I took the T reference to be positive. Just to be on the safe side, I called Mary Alice and invited her to tea at 4:00. Given Mary Alice's unannounced visits, I thought Brian may as well meet her now and not be startled by her turning up in the kitchen someday. Learning to recognize a tornado dropping down from the sky may not make a person any safer but at least they'll know what hit them. As well, the prospect for peace at Shady Shingles was much greater if I did not take Mary Alice's benign reign for granted.

At 3:55 p.m., Captain did his Mary Alice alert. If she ever has her creaky porch floorboard repaired, he's going to be one surprised parrot. She came a few minutes early to make sure the tea would be made properly. Her ladyship generously delegated me to answer the door when Brian rang. I invited him to come through to the kitchen, prepping him a bit on the way.

"You're going to meet my longtime neighbour, Mary Alice, who has also come for tea. She's kind of like family here." I suppose Genghis Khan was kind of like family to somebody. Better to understate than overstate.

"Good afternoon, young man," Mary Alice intoned in her most matronly manner.

"Pleased to meet you, ma'am," he replied. I didn't know that anyone but the lieutenant- governor was called ma'am anymore, but Mary Alice seemed pleased. When a woman is ninety-two, she can give up on being called Miss, even if she is one. Brian's presumption of "Madam Mary Alice" was a good call.

Brian looked a little unsure though. "Is this a good time, or should I come back later?"

I explained that Mary Alice looked after the house when I was gone and was very familiar with any of my dealings with renters. It might have been more accurate to say she also organized the house when I was there, but he would find that out soon enough. Better to ease him in gently.

"My dad thinks I'm making a good choice about where to stay this year. So, he didn't mind too much when I asked him to help with the rent." I heard relief in his tone. Brian presented me with cash extricated from his father, and everything appeared to be in order. I wrote out a receipt and got him to sign my homemade rental agreement. Mary Alice raised her eyebrows, and I took my cue.

"Because you are renting a room and sharing a common kitchen and bathroom, this is considered to be shared accommodation rather than something governed by the Landlord and Tenant Act," I said. "Legal suites are covered by the Act, but shared accommodation is not."

Brian looked slightly overwhelmed at the clarification of his peasant status.

Captain clamped his feet on the side of the cage closest to us, leaning into the conversation. *Pigeon plucked.*

"What are you going to be when you graduate?" Mary Alice prodded.

Brian hesitated. "I know I won't get a job with a major in history, but maybe I can go on to become a teacher or a lawyer."

He probably thought that made him sound responsible. Mary Alice had not liked lawyers since she got sued for verbally defaming one of the candidates in the last civic election. Her eyes narrowed, and I saw her colour changing. Danger alert. I decided it was time for a quick intervention. "I'm sure Brian would make a fine teacher, and now he needs to go do his volunteer work for the Red Cross."

Brian looked decidedly surprised at the news of his hitherto unannounced volunteer interest. I grabbed the cash, stuffed the receipt in his hand, and steered him toward the front door. The tea party needed to end, even if it was short by Victoria standards.

"It was good to meet you, Brian. You can move your things in during the last week of August, and I'll give you the keys then."

No need to sully his mind with too much information too soon. It turned out that the same thought was likely on Pierre's mind when he gave me the cash for his rent. Landlords and used-car salesmen have a lot in common, and students generally know a thing or two about what to tell or not tell a new landlord.

Tricky business, this landlord and tenant dance. One step forward and two steps sideways. The Shady Shingles waltz is not a dance for the faint of heart. But if I never risk the dance, I never get the rent. Even when the rent is secure, other issues emerge and a new dance step is required.

5
When Three Is Not a Crowd

THINGS ARE NEVER so bad that they can't get worse. The corollary is that if things are looking good, look a little deeper, and you'll see they probably aren't. I had come to this conclusion long before getting into the room-renting business, and Shady Shingles did not require me to alter my mantra.

Initially, it seemed like I was off to a good start. Pierre paid his rent in cash, and Brian got backing from his father. Within a week, Mary Alice and I had interviewed three more prospective renters. Of those candidates, one actually made the grade and accepted the room. The other two were scared off when they discovered the owner lived in the house, and the lady next door was bonkers. I'm not sure which was the bigger tipping factor.

Certainly, if someone had visions of moving into party central, Shady Shingles did not fill the bill. That was the impression that we wanted to convey. That being said, our screening strategy has not been foolproof. Trenchant insight is usually only achieved with hindsight.

Katrina was a purposeful young woman in her mid-twenties. She came to Canada on a student exchange from Germany. That much I gleaned from her first phone call. "Are you Herr Landlord? I call now to scrutinize room. Have you rented room?"

I wondered what "scrutinizing" might look like. "No, I have just listed the room. I meet prospective tenants in person before committing to renting."

"I am not prospector. I am physical therapy student. Yesterday I am coming from Germany. I need place to live before class starts next week."

Clearly Katrina was not big on social niceties. Then again, she had called rather than text. I sensed potential. "If you can come at fourteen hundred hours today, you can see the room, and we can discuss renting over tea." Since Katrina seemed to come at things with military precision, I thought giving her the time in military terms would create a good impression.

"Are you English old lady? Am I talking to tea house or pension house?" Her tone would have easily suited a sergeant-major on the parade square. I feared I had fallen down the rabbit hole and was somehow meeting Mary Alice in her youth.

"Uh, well, no," I stuttered.

At first I thought that by "pension house" she meant some kind of house for elderly pensioners. Then I remembered seeing the "Pension" sign when I travelled to Germany. In German, "Pension" means guesthouse or B&B. Clearly, Katrina didn't know what to call Shady Shingles in English. Admittedly, some of my neighbours probably echo her confusion.

"My house is like a Pension in your country , but I don't give breakfast. You prepare your own food."

"This must be Canadian custom. I like custom, if room is cheaper than Pension. "We seemed to have established a lingua franca around how much things should cost. "I come at fourteen hundred today. How many kilometres is it to walk to non-pension house from University of Victoria?"

It had never occurred to me that somebody would need to know the precise walking distance. Then again, a lot of essential things have never occurred to me. Mary Alice reminds me of this shortcoming on a regular basis. I started to explain the bus connections, but Katrina cut me short.

"That will not be necessary. I shall walk. How far?" You'll have to imagine the distinct Prussian accent on your own.

"I think about eight or nine kilometres. People usually ride a bike or take a twenty-minute bus ride."

"For such short distance, this is wasteful. I walk now. I have map. I will be there at fourteen hundred hours. We end now."

There seemed little room for doubt in her plan, so I resolved that I had better round up Mary Alice for an audience at the stated hour. Except for Mary Alice, it would be advisable that she come a little before 2:00 p.m.

When I looked over at Captain, he was doing his frenetic drunken sailor dance, swaying his head from side to side in a figure eight. It was puzzling behaviour, because nobody was offering him a treat or praising his avian beauty—the usual catalysts for such a routine. *This is gonna be good. Batten down the hatches!*

Lest I forget, I telephoned Mary Alice. After six rings and no answer, I began to contemplate what a tea interview would be like without the Dowager Empress. She answered on the seventh ring, panting somewhat. "Hello. Who's there?"

"It's Stanley, my dear. Were you out jogging? You sound out of breath."

"Don't be impudent. You know ninety-two-year-old ladies do not jog. I was in the basement, and I had to come upstairs just to answer *your* call." I detected a distinct lack of frivolity in her tone.

"Sorry if I'm calling at an inconvenient time. Maybe you're too busy to come by for tea this afternoon? I have a young woman coming to inquire about the room. She's a university student from Germany."

Mary Alice was still panting as she answered. "Well, you don't give a person much notice, do you? I have my own affairs to look after, you know. I suppose I can manage to get there. This appointment is for two o'clock precisely, I presume. And is this one who will really be there?"

"She's German, Mary Alice. Unlike some of our no-shows, she will definitely be there. Even as we speak, she is walking from the university." An empress has a busy court life, and one must assure her that her valuable time will not be wasted.

"Does the poor girl have no money? Why would she walk all that way? Don't they ride buses in Germany?" The range of Mary Alice's queries can be daunting sometimes, mainly because they are not queries. They are pronouncements couched as questions, and I, as a loyal subject, need only defer to her once she has pronounced her opinion.

"I should have offered to go and get her, but the university campus is designed like a rat maze. I get lost whenever I drive there because everything is in, on, or beside a circle. What kind of university teaches its students to go in circles?"

Captain bobbed his head. *You're not a very bright rat.*

"Oh, Stanley, what are we to do with you?" Again, Mary Alice did not really expect her lament to be answered. Nor was it clear who was the antecedent of "we." Perhaps it was indicative of a collective guardianship exercised by Mary Alice and Captain. The two are not usually allies, so I think the "we" was simply the "royal we."

"That's why I so need your advice, my dear. I'll see you a little before two. Bye for now."

With a minimum of grovelling, my mission was accomplished.

Following Captain's obligatory alert pose, Mary Alice arrived at 1:55 p.m. Unlike the queen, she was not wearing a pastel hat with matching purse and shoes, but she did appear ready to inspect the troops. Her apron was not the usual gingham but a starched white number with stitched edging. She wore a dark cotton dress with a white paisley pattern, and her manner was unmistakeably matron-in-charge. Clearly, Mary Alice was ready for a German maiden, even one from Prussia.

"The water has just boiled. I put the tea canister on the counter for you." I am remarkably good at stating the obvious. And if there is a safe script to follow, why not just do that?

"Stanley, you look like an unemployed grocery clerk. Couldn't you wear something with a little more gravitas when we're interviewing?"

I hadn't realized that my corduroy home attire was so plebeian. Nor did I imagine that Mary Alice would ever use a word like "gravitas." I never thought Shady Shingles required much gravitas. A sense of the whimsical, maybe, but gravitas? No.

Before the conversation could go further, the doorbell rang. I left Mary Alice to the tea and hurried to the front door. When I opened it, there stood a sturdy young woman with an alarmingly huge backpack over her shoulders. Katrina looked only slightly flushed, given her recent trek through the several neighbourhoods that stretch between Shady Shingles and the university.

"Good day, Herr Landlord. I am here for the room." Katrina had short blond hair and a complexion that radiated vigour and health.

"Do come in. You can set your backpack down in the living room here. Then we'll have some tea. You must be thirsty after your walk."

I didn't offer to help her with her pack, in case I fell over. Then I would really lack gravitas. We proceeded into the living room, where Mary Alice had just poured the tea.

"Katrina, I would like you to meet Mary Alice Macdonald, my longtime neighbour and business colleague."

I wanted to introduce Mary Alice in such a way that it would be clear why she was part of the interview. To accomplish this aim, I probably should have said Field Marshall Macdonald, but Mary Alice sometimes lacks a sense of humour about such things.

"I am pleased to meet you, Fraulein Macdonald. This must be a large Pension house if it requires two officers to manage it."

As was already evident to me, small talk was not Katrina's speciality. Mary Alice looked only slightly irked, speaking more deliberately than usual. "Well, Katrina, we do what we do. Let me pour you some tea. Milk and sugar?"

Katrina looked slightly appalled. "Do you have some Zitrone with the tea?" Mary Alice and I looked puzzled at what this German substance might be. Katrina blushed at her faux pas. "You will excuse my English. I mean, may I have some lemon with the tea?"

I scrounged a plastic lemon from the fridge—the kind with lemon juice that keeps forever. Katrina took it from me the way a lady in waiting might politely receive a dead fish. I guess plastic lemons are not a sign of deep refinement among German tea drinkers. She glanced over to Captain's cage. "Do I also meet little green pigeon bird? He is cute one."

Captain did a courting dance and half opened his wings. *Needs training, but good judge of character.*

Mary Alice decided to seize the agenda. "Katrina, do tell us a bit about where you are from and where you have lived recently."

"I am coming from north Germany, near Berlin. I lived at home with parents and did complete part of course for physical therapy in Berlin. I want to finish course here and also to make better my English." This was quite a speech for Katrina to organize. I had the impression that she would prefer a session of rigorous calisthenics to a session of light conversation in English.

"And what sort of pastimes do you have when not studying?" Usually, I ask this innocuously to find out if a potential tenant likes loud music, coming home late from bars, or practicing the tuba at odd hours. Katrina stayed in character.

"I am finding much pleasure in walking, mountain biking, holistic medicine, and gymnastics. Also, I am learning yoga." At last we seemed to be in a realm that Katrina loved.

Ever the guardian of chastity and propriety, Mary Alice took over. "How about a boyfriend, Katrina? Is there a young man in the picture? Maybe back in Germany?" Clearly, that's where Mary Alice would prefer any young man to be.

"No, I do not wish boyfriend. They are distraction, and I am here short time for study and English."

Katrina's no-nonsense attitude was obviously a big hit with Mary Alice. I wasn't sure that having a second Mary Alice around would be good for my psyche, but at least Katrina had not fled in the manner of the previous two candidates. Aside from rent money, only one area of concern remained.

"Katrina, I would want you to feel comfortable at Shady Shingles," I said. "There will be myself, two male tenants, and Captain. Are you OK with being the only woman in a household of men?"

"This will be no problem. I am older sister in family with three boys. I did train them properly."

Mary Alice nodded, and that was my cue. "If you go upstairs, Katrina, you can see the room before you decide to take it. Your room will be at the back of the house on that floor, across the hall from the bathroom. It's quiet in that location, and it's the only room that I have left."

Katrina did two steps at a time on the way up the stairs. Better her than me. She returned in less than a minute, beating Brian's reconnaissance by a hefty margin.

"The Zimmer is satisfactory. It is only place to sleep. I shall eliminate dust immediately."

I looked at Mary Alice, who glowed at the prospect of having a kindred spirit in her orbit. I wondered if I might be allowing a Trojan horse within the gates, but Mary Alice declared Katrina to be "a fine girl who would be a most welcome addition to this household." It was hard to contradict that assessment when the young lady pulled cash out of her money belt. I looked at Captain for a potential ally. He was blithely doing his happy dance.

Bring on the sauerkraut, princess. This one's a keeper. She thinks I'm cute.

Maybe parrots and German physical therapists have some kind of simpatico rapport? As long as Katrina was not evangelical about her commitment to physical fitness, maybe we could co-exist. And that third bedroom did need filling. So, Katrina was in.

"I shall make order in my room now. Thank you for Zimmer, I mean, room. Gutentag."

With that she picked up her backpack and moved in.

What seemed a routine addition to the household would later prove to be the first part of a transition for me. We never know what ripples will spread from the smallest pebble cast into our little pond. The ducklings bob up and down with the ripples, and even the old birds may have to adjust their course.

Katrina's academic plan would get revised in due course, and I would need to do some adjusting myself.

6
The Inquisition

WITH THE THREE rooms rented, there was no longer any excuse for not returning the call to Jerome at the bank. A direct audience with his eminence would not be possible. First, I had to call in and deal with the automated reception menu. I assured myself that in the fullness of time, I might get to a live person who would assign me an appointment slot.

I thought of those fuzzy, cuddly bank commercials filled with cute penguins and heart-warming testimonials from happy seniors who had already retired at age fifty-five. Maybe the penguins retired at fifty-five too. I could always aspire to be a retired penguin, gorging myself on sardines. For the moment, I would had to remain an obsequious client begging for mercy from the owner of my soul. Mary Alice says I get too melodramatic about such things. Personally, I think melodrama enhances the begging. Jerome expected it. What other gratification could there be for a bank loans officer?

Unlike the penguins, Jerome was neither cuddly nor fuzzy. One might infer that in his fifty odd years, he had rarely ventured forth into sunshine, given his pale demeanour and squinting eyes. He could stand in for Ichabod Crane; indeed, his pinstriped suit hung from his gaunt frame like sagging sails on a windless day.

We Victorians think in nautical terms. We know our sagging sails because we see lots of them at the annual Swiftsure International

Yacht Race, held in late May every year. Normally, it's windy in the Strait of Juan de Fuca, especially if you happen to be on a ferry bouncing across the choppy water on the way to Port Angeles or Seattle. Your lunch may or may not arrive with you when you dock on the other side. But if the yacht race is on, sometimes a devastating calm will descend, and all those graceful yachts will just sit dead in the water, with sagging sails.

Senior citizens have empathy for those with sagging sails. I wish I could feel a kindred warmth for Jerome in his sagging suit, but it's asking a bit much for the condemned to have sympathy for the Grim Reaper.

When I got to the bank, they had comfy chairs and a coffee pot in the waiting area. I couldn't decide whether to regard the coffee as a gesture of hospitality or an indicator that I'd need something to keep me awake because I was likely to be cooling my heels for a good long time.

I sat down for a while, rehearsing my grovelling in my head. Then I caught up on the previous year's magazines. Eventually, the receptionist suggested that I might want to help myself to a second cup of coffee. That is never a good sign for anyone sitting on Death Row, fiscally speaking.

Already it felt like my innards were beginning to dissolve, so I declined her generous offer. I doubt Juan Valdez was their principal supplier of coffee beans. A more likely candidate for the java juice was the Jiffy Oil Change around the corner. Bank visits bring out the morbidity in me. My existential angst increased when Jerome strode forth from his office with hand extended, greeting me like a long-lost brother. Perhaps I was in more trouble than I thought.

He ushered me into the inner sanctum of sacred usury. As Mary Alice has noted, I can get a bit over the top about these things. But when bankers go out of their way to be warm and hospitable, usually, it means professional kindness before the coup de grace. The latter may present in the slow death of an increased interest rate or the strangulation of terminating one's line of credit. I understand that some people go to visit their banker to hear how much money their investments have made. I go to hear if life support will continue. Jerome likes to keep me guessing until the last moment.

"And how are you this fine day, Mr. McFadden?" he inquired with his gleaming smile. If I'm Mr. McFadden, the prognosis may only be a severe warning. When he starts off with, "Now Stanley . . . ", I know the diagnosis is terminal.

"Oh, I'm still breathing, and I hope you don't have any news that would take my breath away." When jousting with euphemisms, it helps my blood pressure if we can get un-euphemistically to the point.

Jerome uttered a forced chuckle. "Now, now, Mr. McFadden, you know we here at Liberty Bank have only your deepest welfare as our concern." Usually, the bank is concerned about liberating any money from my fleeting grasp. Liberty is a relative thing when one is talking about dollars. The bank's liberty to lend is considerably greater than my freedom to borrow.

After I smiled weakly at Jerome's allusion to my welfare, he went on. "Clearly, we wouldn't want you to get into a situation where you were unable to meet your financial commitments. By that I mean your obligation to meet payments on the loan you took out for those much-needed renovations on Shady Shingles. We approved the loan, but you have already missed the most recent payment—not an auspicious indicator for your credit rating."

After receiving the house in the estate from Violet's will, I discovered that getting a free house is anything but free. There was the little matter of the back taxes, which had to be paid up front. To get insurance, the house had to be inspected by an engineer and an appraiser. The engineer was young and a real keener. He declared that the roof needed replacing, the outside drainage system needed upgrading, and the electrical wiring did not meet code. While the City did not deem the house to be architecturally significant enough to designate it as a heritage building, it was on a list of buildings that were "of historical interest." In practice, that phrase meant they didn't want me to do anything that would change the outer appearance of the building, but I wouldn't get any public money to cover the cost of keeping it that way. Since I am not talented enough to take up counterfeiting, it seemed the lesser of two evils to get a loan from the bank to cover the core renovations. The application required that I produce a business plan for Shady Shingles, proving I could repay the loan. Remember how I said that Mary Alice has an eye for money? When I moaned about this requirement over tea, she whipped off a business plan on the back of a napkin. It looked a little more sophisticated when I transferred the information to a computer document and made a printout for the bank. On paper, the numbers looked plausible. Somehow the lived reality was different from the financial plan. I have had to take out several loans along the way.

The recent loan payment came due before I was able to collect the rent from my tenants. However, by then I was armed with a top-up of cash in my pocket because Katrina had taken the room and paid the day before. I was part way to redemption, but I still needed my begging speech.

"Well, Jerome, I have good news, and I have not-so-good news. The good news is I have cash today to complete my current mortgage payment."

Jerome raised his eyebrows and lowered his gaze to the cash that I had just laid out on the table. Always lead with your strong suit. "And pray tell, what is the not-so-good news?" Jerome does not relish suspense.

"Oh, it's not a big thing, just a little matter of that line of credit that I may have exceeded when I wrote a cheque or two this month," I said in my most casual tone.

"I was about to get around to that subject," Jerome pronounced. "You realize a line of credit means your overdraft will be covered up to a certain limit, but you still have to repay the amount with interest?"

His tone was questioning, but his question was rhetorical. Earnest pleading alone rolled off Jerome's back like water off a duck. We had been down this road before, and he had made me painfully aware of the distinction between a bank and a charity. My best strategy was to have some concrete indicator of new income with which I might pay off the line of credit. I can do a pretty passable imitation of the minister of finance.

"Mr. Fairchild, I would like to impose on your bank's generosity just a little longer, as I am expecting a royalty payment any day now on my latest invention." Judging from Jerome's expression, I might as well have slapped a fresh piece of roadkill on his desk.

"And just what is your invention this time?" he queried, parsing each word.

Being an optimist, I sensed I might soon achieve the upper hand. "It's a snowball launcher. It's like the ball launcher that people use to throw tennis balls for their dog to chase. People get cold hands making snowballs, so this device shapes the snowball, and then people can launch it with the ergonomic handle."

"Stanley, my man, you realize it almost never snows in Victoria. Who's going to buy such a thing, assuming it works?" Jerome is the original Mr. Killjoy, devoid of entrepreneurial imagination. That's why he's a banker and not Steve Jobs' successor.

"Ah, Mr. Fairchild, we live in a country where most people experience six months of winter and six months of bad skiing. The market is far beyond Victoria, just waiting to be conquered."

Admittedly, I have more experience in ignominious defeat than in conquering, but there's no need to underline the obvious when pitching a compelling dream. One inconvenient truth was that it was early September, and only Inuvik and Cambridge Bay would be expecting snow anytime soon. I couldn't guarantee that my snowball launcher would be a hit in either place, especially since my distribution network did not extend quite that far yet. But success would only be a matter of time.

I threatened to tell Jerome all about the engineering dynamics of my project, in great detail. It didn't take too long to wear him down, and he begrudgingly signed a form that spared me from the bailiff for another month. Pride and self-respect are greatly overrated. By sacrificing both, I managed to exit the bank and prop up Shady Shingles until our next crisis. It would also help if it were to snow big time in Calgary in September . . . a not unknown phenomenon, according to prairie refugees who have decided to retire in Victoria. Generally, migrant Albertans are willing to recount their tales of weather woe at the drop of a hat. They have lots of data to document their case.

The suffering of the many can sometimes lead to the prosperity of the few. This has always been the key to population growth in Victoria, as people from other parts of the country migrate here to escape winter. Meanwhile, it can't hurt anything if I profit from a successful invention that will help those who cannot emigrate be happier where they are.

When I returned home, it was midafternoon. I didn't have to imagine what Captain would be up to. All sensible parrots have a midafternoon nap. True to form, Captain was sitting on his sleeping perch, the highest point in his cage. His skirt feathers were draped over his foot. I don't mean to imply he had suddenly become an amputee. He still had his foot, but it was tucked into his feathered breast, and he had shifted his weight, so his body was centred over one foot. Parrots can sleep in this odd position because they have special muscles that lock their feet in the hold position, even while asleep. Meanwhile, his head sinks into his neck, and his peach fuzz eyelids come down over his eyes. Overall, he turns into an avocado cocoon. While Captain may look lifeless while napping, he will awaken at the slightest sound, especially the opening of the refrigerator or the squeak of Mary Alice's porch floorboard. Both sounds imply imminent food. My arrival warranted his opening of one eye to see if I might be carrying items of interest from the grocery store.

I've heard elephants that make less noise walking than you do. Be gone or be quiet.

I wonder if parrots dream. Probably that moment was not the time to ask him. As the busy manager of Shady Shingles, I made the executive decision to settle into my recliner chair and spend some quality parrot time. Since playing chess together isn't exactly an option with Captain, quality time translates into a variation of nap time. Captain already had a head start on the game, but I am a reasonably clever understudy and know how to catch up.

The principal action in the napping game is each opponent watching the other and blinking suggestively. The object is to see who can remain awake the longest and watch the other go to sleep. This is signalled by both eyelids closing and staying that way. Because I have both eyes in the front of my head, it is obvious to Captain when he has won. Conversely, he has an eye on each side of his head, and I can only see one at a time. I blink slowly, and he tries to resist the suggestion, but his eyelids flutter tellingly. Then his eyes open wide again because he knows he can outlast me. Or so he thinks. Those parrot eyelids soon get heavy again. Oh, so heavy. So do mine. Gravity and aging seem difficult to resist for those of us who battle the sirens of midafternoon napping. The main problem with this napping duel between man and feathered beast is that it is never entirely clear who has won because we are both asleep. We need a nap referee who can stay quiet and remain awake. Auditions are pending if I can get Liam to help me post the position online.

A key turned in the front door, and both of us were startled awake. Captain raised his skirt feathers and shifted to stand on two feet again.

I wasn't napping. I was keeping guard the entire time. Someone could be breaking in to steal my Red Flame grapes!

Katrina was returning from an afternoon class. She had the sprightly step of a tap dancer on steroids. "Good afternoon, Herr McFadden. Please excuse my interruption of seniors' meditation class. I get ready to jog now."

She ascended the stairs in a nanosecond and was off to her room. The woman had just walked five kilometres home, and now she was going jogging. Clearly, we shared no genetic material in our ancestry.

I remember walking five kilometers in the summer of 1978. My car broke down in the middle of Saskatchewan. People in Saskatchewan walk five kilometers from the house to the barn.

In my case, the motivation was to get somewhere that had a telephone. In 1978 we didn't have cell phones, so if someone was out in the country, they either waited for another soul to come by or walked to a farmer's home quarter. Ideally, this did not happen in a Saskatchewan winter. Given the vastness of the prairie and the sparseness of the population, the last somebody who came by might have been a stray dinosaur. In the stranded auto situation, patience is not its own reward.

I did find help, because most Saskatchewanites are friendly and neighbourly. Admittedly these are not the fierce gladiators who attend Roughrider football games. That being said, Saskatchewan folk are to be congratulated on succeeding in their mountain eradication program. Based on this geological observation, I decided to settle in BC, where the locals leave things as they are.

The exception to BC's "live and let live" motto is the issue of deer roaming about Oak Bay, which is a quaint colonial outpost that prides itself in not being part of Victoria. Its population is divided between those in favour of deer eradication and those who believe in ungulate protection. Although divided on the deer issue, residents of Oak Bay would vote to leave the mountains where they are—clearly but distantly visible.

We have lots of mountains in BC, mostly located in inconvenient places. Lovely snow-capped mountains are visible from any high hill in Victoria, but we don't have to maintain them. They are called the Olympic Range, and on a clear day, they are visible parked across the Strait of Juan de Fuca in Washington. If one gets tired of seeing the Olympics, they disappear regularly behind a fog bank that frequently shrouds the north coast of the Olympic Peninsula.

It is only a matter of time before Katrina swims the strait and scales Mt. Olympus before dinner. Lest you think she knows a shortcut to Greece, this Mt. Olympus is in the middle of Olympic National Park. She might need to rest en route, because it's a thirty-nine-kilometre swim from Victoria to Port Angeles. And then there are some other mountains in the way before one arrives at Mt. Olympus, Washington. I have this only on hearsay.

I prefer to see mountains below me from a plane rather than climb them. I know Katrina will ask someday, so I am prepared with her potential itinerary. I am prepared for many things, most of which never happen. But now and then I hit the jackpot. Sadly, none of my jackpots has ever involved cash. I guess an unexpected turn of events for the better could be considered a jackpot. Usually, I don't see those coming either. Until then it's good to carry on and harvest a good nap, where possible. The journey ahead may well require some fortitude. I'm sure Captain agrees.

7
Normal Is a Relative Thing

MY POST-NAP MUSINGS were interrupted by Pierre stumbling down the stairs, newly emerged from hibernation. Generally, he comes home early in the morning and heads to bed. His repose lasts a good eight hours or so. Signs of life can be detected in midafternoon. Pierre feeds at that time of day, then exits the house. There are no car plants in Victoria, so his odd work schedule does not arise from working the night shift at General Motors. It also seems implausible that he is actually a salesman at a car dealership that has an all-night showroom. Whatever he does, it results in fistfuls of cash.

"Salut, monsieur. How it goes for you and Corporal?" Pierre asked.

So far, he could not remember my name. The francophone equivalent of "Hi, sir" was a good cover. Demoting a parrot from captain to corporal was less convincing. Good thing Captain is a patient parrot.

Captain eyed Pierre carefully. *Somebody call the cops. The convict is out of his cell!*

Speaking on behalf of someone who cannot speak is always a dicey proposition, but I decided to express curiosity for both of us. "We're managing the empire quite well, thank you. By the way, what kind of auto business are you engaged in? I might need a new car someday, you know." If he were in sales, that would be an irresistible carrot to dangle in front of him.

"Ah, dat is a very interesting topic, monsieur. I don't exactly have new cars to sell. My auto business is, how you say, very spécialisé."

With that Pierre disappeared into the kitchen, and I heard a clatter of pots as he pulled the frying pan from the drawer at the bottom of the stove. Soon the smell of pork chops, fried potatoes, and onions filled the house. Nothing on the menu was of interest to Captain, so he busied himself with preening. This is a more or less endless activity for parrots. I guess if one happens to be wearing thousands of feathers, it pays to keep up with maintenance.

Pierre made his entrance again carrying a plate of hot food and some cutlery. He settled in at the dining room table, testing it for stability before sitting. "I have not seen a table like this one inside a house. Maybe you moved in not long ago, non?"

I assured Pierre that I had lived there for some time but had not yet located a suitable period piece for the room. In the next few minutes, Pierre shoveled in the rest of his meal, and there was no time between mouthfuls to ask me further questions. When he was finished, he was going to exit, leaving his dishes in the sink. After I uttered an emphatic "Ahem," he smiled sheepishly and did a cleanup. The distinction between indulgent landlord and prison warden is sometimes quite fine.

"Bonsoir, Monsieur Stanley." Clever boy. He had read my name on the address label of some mail that I had left on the table. "Maybe a friend from Montreal will come tonight. He is Jean Philippe, and he has a car for me. I go out now to my work, but you can send him there. You know Sam's Garage, t'ree blocks from here, non?"

"I know the place, but don't they close at six o'clock?" I asked cautiously.

"Yes, that is so. But Sam is a friend, and he lets me work on my cars after he closes. Friends bring me cars from Quebec, and I fix them up here before selling them. I am Mr. Recycle!"

Captain had finished his preening session. *Shady carnivore at Shady Shingles. Scam alert!*

Pierre's specialty auto business was now clear. He bought used cars from eastern Canada. They were lower priced because of the rust that occurred from winter salt on their roads. Pierre did body-work on them, so they looked presentable, and then resold them, neglecting to mention their origin. Presumably my cash-laden tenant also did minor mechanical repairs, so the vehicles could pass the safety inspection that was required for cars that come from out of province. Strictly speaking, it was all legal . . . or so I thought.

Pierre made his exit. Captain and I had the house to ourselves, a state of solitude that never lasted long.

The doorbell rang, and I prayed it wasn't a missionary of some kind. Clearly, it wouldn't be Mary Alice because I was sure she didn't know the location of the doorbell. When I let down the drawbridge and opened the gate, so to speak, Liam was on site.

"I'm here," he announced. One could hardly argue with that objective presentation of the facts.

"Why are you here, Liam?" I queried. I realize Liam didn't need a reason, but it was always enlightening to know what was passing through the mind of a future NASA scientist.

"Captain might be lonely," he declared. Apparently, he didn't consider my physical presence as evidence that Captain was not, in fact, lonely.

"Come in, Liam. I'll get you a grape, so you can feed him." I proceeded to the kitchen.

"When you get a grape, bring some jujubes," he yelled, "so Captain doesn't have to eat alone!"

When I returned with sustenance for man and beast, or at least child and bird, Liam gave Captain the grape. Liam was willing to share the jujubes as well, but I reiterated that Captain could only have the grape. Captain had already squeezed the juice from half the grape and was wiping the pulp off his beak while keeping an eye on Liam and his jujubes.

"Have you wrecked your computer yet today?" Liam probed. I detected a slight lack of confidence in my home office skills.

"Well, the Internet connection seems to be gone, and I don't know which do-hicky to push to reset it," I replied.

"That's OK, Mr. M. You just gotta reboot the router." Giving the machine a boot sounded quite appealing, but I wondered how hard I should kick it. Before I could contemplate the physics of the matter any further, Liam ran to my computer station and performed restorative surgery, without any foot action. I was disappointed. Fortunately, Liam has a short attention span. Having exhausted the available supply of excitement at Shady Shingles, he scurried out the door and headed home for supper. I didn't even have time to notify his mother that he had been here.

It seemed like a good idea to hit the kitchen before there was competition from Katrina or Brian. In the midst of making a chef's salad from whatever wasn't moving in the fridge, I heard the front door open, and our resident historian entered. True to character, Brian's first stop was the kitchen. That posed no real problem because usually his chosen technology was the microwave, and mine was the stove.

"I'm too upset to eat," was his opening statement, uttered in a trembling tone. Something major would have to be amiss for Brian not to be interested in eating. The range of possibilities went from a death in his family to girlfriend trouble. It turned out to be neither.

"What happened?" I asked. Once I got that far, I'd crossed the point of no return. I was committed to listening, whether I was interested or not.

Captain picked up the emotion in Brian's voice and looked at me. *Join the club. I have to listen to you all the time.*

"I bombed on a history survey essay that I just got back. It was the one that I was working on for the last three weeks, and the prof gave me a C. I've never gotten a C."

The despair in Brian's voice was palpable. I tried to think of an appropriately comforting cliché that didn't sound obviously like a cliché. No luck. Most of my inventions got the equivalent of a C or less. My life was a C. But I guessed telling a budding scholar that mediocrity was nothing to be ashamed of was not quite what he wanted to hear. I did the most sensible thing in the circumstance. "Brian, would you like a beer?"

If there is one thing that I know about university students, they know how to make beer disappear. For that reason, I usually hide my beer supply where they would never think of looking . . . in the cleaning supply closet. Fortunately, I had moved a couple of bottles to the fridge earlier that day.

As we sipped our beers, Brian talked about school, his girlfriend, and his family. Generally, when the bottom falls out of one area of life, there is still enough left in other areas to keep a person afloat. It's just necessary to have someone to talk to for long enough that either you realize that fact on your own or someone else points it out to you. Of course, if you keep drinking beer, you will remember none of this, and none of it matters. For this reason, and not for any lack of generosity on my part, I limit my largesse to one beer per roomer per lifetime. Brian had just used up his quota.

Cheap, cheap, cheap. It's a travesty of justice that I'm rationed to four grapes a day.

Brian's cell phone rang. It was his girlfriend, Natalie. "I got it back. He only gave me a crappy C. He wrote in red that my presentation 'displayed a lack of original insight.' Right now? Sure, that would be awesome. Be there in ten."

A call from one's girlfriend can have great medicinal value, especially if she is offering supper. Considering the prospect of my now soggy salad, I almost asked if I could come too. In a rare moment of good judgment, I didn't. Brian was out the door at a considerably livelier pace than when he came in.

You can drop ducklings, and they bounce. They look fragile, but unless they get gobbled up by a predator, they soon carry on without Mom or Pop doing very much. Note to self—don't waste good beer on ducklings.

Captain hung over the side of his open cage. This meant he wanted first choice of the salad. I offered him my bowl, and he looked it over as if he were deciding on a complicated chess move. He extricated a snow pea, and I ate the rest.

The ugly duck should put sunflower seeds in his salad.

Not a bad day at Shady Shingles. Normal is indeed a relative thing. I'm not sure if normal applies at Shady Shingles, but we carry on, hoping normal is just around the corner. Or not.

8
Surviving Festive Holidays and Other Inconveniences

IN MY HUMBLE opinion, holidays are a tedious way to punctuate the year. I cherish my mundane routine, and then it all gets thrown askew by dubious holidays, like Labour Day, Thanksgiving, and Christmas.

Shady Shingles is not known for its festive holiday making, at least in my reign. Tenants brag to their peers about the miserly nature of their landlord, and it's the least I can do to give them some objective evidence for their complaints. In particular, I don't offer them a turkey dinner at Thanksgiving or a goose at Christmas. My general excuse for these avian omissions is that serving a roasted fowl would be deeply offensive to Captain and his parrot kindred. We can't have a turkey dinner together because all the parrots of the world would be aggrieved, and Captain is their surrogate spokesman at Shady Shingles. When I offer tofurky instead, the peasants drift away, insisting they have been invited out for the day or are returning home for whatever long weekend is being celebrated. No one has ever called my bluff. I'm not even sure how to slaughter a tofurky, if it's even possible to find one somewhere.

What a crock. I love turkey bones. Who cares about ugly birds that can't even pass for a third cousin once removed? Bring on the turkey and stuffing, you cheapskate!

Labour Day at least has the advantage that no festive meal is associated with it. There is little pretence for the event other than it being the last chance for a summer long weekend. Organized labour proponents in Victoria (i.e., civil servants, teachers, health-care workers) are compelled to attend a Labour Day picnic marking the occasion. In Victoria, this counts as a radical demonstration. Disorganized labourers like me can do as they please. We are liberated from the shackles of duty.

In contrast, Victoria Beer Week lasts for nine days in March, and it purports to "educate Victoria residents about craft beer," according to something called the Victoria Events Calendar. One might infer from this that Victorians are slow learners, in that they need to add two extra days to a week to accomplish what others can accomplish in one. At the Piddling Poodle, my local watering hole, we have gifted learners who can teach people all they need to know about beer in one afternoon. The cab ride home costs extra. I suspect the nine-day crowd isn't really as slow-witted as the length of its festival would suggest. Victorians just like to find an excuse to marinate and then purport that the process is "educational." After a nine-day beer festival, the line between education and stupor is considerably blurred. I digress.

Thanksgiving is slightly more challenging than Labour Day. Mary Alice believes the purpose of the day is to thank God for all the blessings of autumn harvest. And the best way to do that is to eat as much of that harvest as possible at one sitting—preferably after having gone to mass.

My more secular-minded contemporaries see Thanksgiving as our being thankful to no one in particular; it's just a good civic virtue to have a thankful attitude, as opposed to the usual spiteful aura that characterizes civic and provincial politics in British California. West coasters are thankful about living in heaven on earth, but we all have strong views on how heaven should be improved. Usually, this boils down to our own viewpoint becoming the universal one. And clearly, those who offer a different viewpoint are motivated by unspeakable evil and should be vanquished to the Outer Darkness, or at least Edmonton. That is BC politics in a nutshell.

It should be said that not all nuts are in shells, but I leave you to discern that truth on your own. For Thanksgiving in Victoria, you only need to know that it is considered civil to suspend the usual hostilities and adopt a benignly thankful demeanour with a restrained smile. This can hurt, but it only has to last a day. Local free-range turkeys don't smile; then again, it's hard to tell if a turkey ever smiles. We can probably be thankful that we are not turkeys. That is the extent of my prophetic insight into the significance of Thanksgiving as a holiday.

Mary Alice is a bigger fan of holidays than I am; however, such genteel observances generally don't overflow into Shady Shingles. For most occasions she has given up trying to shape me to the contrary, but Christmas is another matter. Even people with no religious inclination whatsoever will gush about how much they love Christmas. Mary Alice is a martyr with a mission about Christmas, and anyone who tries to rain on her parade does so at great peril. In general, I avoid great peril, and, for that matter, even small perils.

Avoiding Mary Alice is not an option, so when she pops in for tea in late November, I always have a box of Christmas decorations sitting on the couch. This manoeuvre creates the impression that I am about to engage in action without actually doing anything that requires much sacrificial effort. In this regard, I have learned from how Canada participates in any UN or NATO venture. Talk a great deal about the importance of the work and then delay involvement for as long as possible. If the principle works for high-level international relations, why not for Shady Shingles?

In a good year, one or two of the tenants will offer to help decorate if I leave the box out long enough. This particular year, the box had been out until the beginning of December. I was seated at my dining room table in the early afternoon with various overdue bills arranged artistically and chronologically on its surface. Sometimes a solution can leap out at me if I just study the battlefield long enough. I heard the key turn in the front door. Brian trekked in, backpack in hand.

"What's up, Mr. McF? You look like you're in a chess game without the chess board."

Clever boy. No doubt he'd make a great unemployed historian. Somehow, McFadden was too much to say, and I had become Mr. McF. Brian was a firm believer in abbreviated politeness.

"Actually, I'm just studying my data to decide how much I need to raise the rent. Any historical perspective to offer, O learned scholar?" The best defence is a good offence. Brian winced noticeably. Landlord 1, tenant 0.

"Hey, Mr. McF, that doesn't sound very much like the Christmas spirit. Surely you're not thinking of raising the rent at Christmas? Nobody does that, not even in Victoria."

"As an historian, you'll appreciate that the Puritans abolished Christmas and somehow people got along just fine. I'll bet Puritans even raised the rent now and then. I have historical precedent on my side."

"You can't be off Christmas that much. I've seen that box of Christmas decorations sitting on the couch for a couple of weeks now. You wouldn't have decorations unless you were into the Christmas thing." His elevated tone was like that of a crown attorney presenting his summary punch to the trial jury. Hmm . . . somebody had taught Brian about evidence-based research. I decided it was time to change tack and try the "sympathy for the elderly senior citizen" approach, a tried and true, albeit overworked, mantra in Victoria.

"Glad that you brought that up. I used to put this garland and a string of lights up because Mary Alice said the house needed to look more Christmas-like. Nowadays I am wobbly on the ladder, and I don't want to take a chance on stringing garlands and lights anymore. Sadly, Captain is no help at all." A wistful tone added to the effect. I had it down pat.

Leave the parrot out of this. You'd be on that ladder in a flash if there was a coupon for the Piddling Poodle nailed to the top.

Brian stepped over to the box and pulled out a tangle of plastic holly garland, looking decidedly skeptical. "You mean all you put up is this plastic stuff? Looks like you got it at a Dollar Store clearance sale." I grimaced at him. "I guess I could do that much," he said. "Where does it go?" Even Boy Scouts think they're comedians these days, so I didn't complain about Brian's unsolicited editorializing regarding my shopping habits.

"There are nails along the top of the porch windows, and you just hang the garland and the lights from them, letting them sag a little between each nail. The stepladder is already in the porch."

"No problem. This stuff is so retro, it's almost cool." Brian carried the box out to the porch and set up the stepladder.

The front door opened, and Katrina made her entrance. "Greetings, Herr McFadden. I see Father Christmas elf is at work for you." I would never have expected Katrina to display such humour. Brian seemed less than amused at being the object of Katrina's Teutonic admiration.

"Even Father Christmas has a hard time getting good help these days," I intoned. There was no sense letting too much praise go to the boy's head. After all, his sudden interest in helping me only came when he thought he could distract me from raising the rent.

Katrina assessed the scene further. "And are you getting also Tannenbaum?" Brian and I looked equally puzzled. "I mean, how you call it, the Christmas hedge?"

"I think you mean Christmas tree," Brian volunteered. He moved the ladder to the next nail and kept working on the garland as he untangled each section.

"Ah, yes, it is Christmas tree. In Germany we make such nice green tree on December twenty-fourth. Do you have that also here?" Her query seemed to be directed at me, since Brian was only a Christmas elf.

"Many people have a tree with decorations, and they put it up around now or a little later in December." I was careful not to imply that I had the intention of doing any such thing.

"In Canada you can choose any day you want for Christmas Eve? In Germany it is not so. We have Christmas Eve on proper day."

Brian chuckled, and I accidentally bumped the ladder. He stopped chuckling when it looked like I might bump the ladder again. History students should be acutely aware of the fragility of life in the present moment if they plan on having any future. By Brian's silence and clutching at the wall, I inferred he took due notice.

"You are correct, of course. Christmas Eve can only be on December twenty-fourth, but most Canadians don't wait until Christmas Eve to put up their Christmas tree. They put it up ahead of time, and it might be artificial or natural. Christmas customs are pretty mixed, because Canadians come from so many backgrounds." In all this cultural bafflegab, I remained careful to omit any commitment about what happens at Shady Shingles at Christmas. It's what the Spanish call "nada."

"I see. So, tree does not come on special day. When does tree come at your house?" Katrina had a certain tenacity that would serve her well in gymnastics but was a trifle irritating in the social realm. It was time to revert to my proven strategy that the best defence is a good offence.

"Usually, there is no one around to bother much with Christmas at Shady Shingles. Are you planning to be here at Christmas, or do you go back to Germany?" You may infer that I was cheering for Germany.

"It is too expensive to go home for Christmas. Friend has invited me to travel to friend's home for Christmas. So, I am in this country but not in Victoria. I hope that is OK."

I tried not to look too relieved. Since we were on the subject, I turned to my reluctant elf. "And what about you, Brian? Are you around for Christmas, or are you heading out somewhere?" It's good to sound as casual as possible when one is devoid of sincerity.

"Well, I have to stay until the end of term, and then I have a Christmas job in Red Deer, where my mum lives. I'll be leaving in a week."

I uttered a silent thanks to his unknown employer in Red Deer. Kudos also for Brian's mother. It was looking like I would not have to think up an excuse for why I was not hosting Christmas dinner for my beloved tenants. "Captain and I will just have to celebrate Christmas without you. Putting up a tree doesn't seem worth the bother when there's no one else here to see it."

"But you will have kindly Mary Alice, and you said she looks favourably on Christmas. Does she come for Christmas meal and presents?" Katrina did not let go of a topic until all sub-categories were exhausted.

"Mary Alice usually gets invited to her daughter's house, and they do the big Christmas thing there. Fear not, she does turn up here on Christmas Eve, and we have sherry instead of tea before she goes to mass."

"What about Captain?" Brian asked. "Does he get a special treat for Christmas?" Since Brian was suspending the last of the garland, he was able to turn his attention to the historic import of parrot welfare.

Three cheers for the monkey guy on the ladder. Remind Stanley about that treat thing!

"I think Captain is a Presbyterian parrot, but maybe he's a Baptist," I replied. "Mary Alice says he's definitely not Catholic. In any case, Captain doesn't drink sherry. He gets an extra grape at Christmas. Given the price of grapes in December, that's a considerable treat. I'd have one too if they weren't so expensive." It never hurts to stress the importance of frugality to the younger generation. Katrina looked slightly puzzled at the denominational affiliation of parrots. She proceeded up to her room while Brian came down the stepladder for the last time.

"All done, Mr. McF. Should I put the stepladder somewhere, or is it alright to leave it here?"

"Just put it in the corner of the porch. It will be handy when it comes time to take down that garland in January. Thanks for the help. I wasn't serious about raising the rent, by the way."

Brian beamed brightly and then headed inside, almost colliding with Pierre, who was on the way out. The two exchanged nods, and Pierre stopped to peruse Brian's handiwork.

"Salut there, Monsieur Stanley. The place, it looks ready now for a big Noel. I see you are going to be a jolly landlord for the holidays, non?" Pierre could be insufferably cheery at times.

"Not exactly. It's the minimum that I can get away with when Mary Alice asks if I have the decorating done yet. I was just chatting with Brian and Katrina about their Christmas plans. They're both going away at Christmas. How about you?" I need not declare to you my reasons for asking.

"For sure I am here in Victoria. And Claudette, she will invite me for the Christmas Eve. I know she misses me even if she says nothing now. She will call me soon, dat's for sure."

When not depressed, Pierre was an incurable optimist. To my knowledge, his beloved Claudette had not expressed even the slightest interest in contacting him since their parting of ways. That never stopped Pierre from regularly assuring me that she would call any day when she was not so busy. Other people might take a hint from the fact that she chose to have an unlisted number, but Pierre was not one to be daunted by overt rejection. His confidence in a rendezvous at Christmas was certainly in character, even if it had no basis in reality. For most people, reality is an overrated thing. And certainly, it is not a good idea to confront people with reality at Christmas.

"I'm sure you're onto something, Pierre. Sounds like you have your Christmas plans in place. Just so you know, nothing is planned here on Christmas Day because everyone goes their own way."

"Dat's all cool, Monsieur Stanley. And what about your Christmas parrot, all dressed in green? Where does he go at Noel?"

"Captain doesn't have a winter coat, so he stays right here in the house. If he behaves for the next while, he gets an extra grape on Christmas morning. For Captain, every day is Christmas."

That's a tall one coming from Mr. Scrooge himself. Every day I'm lucky to survive with the rations I get.

"Does Madame Marie the Alice give you an extra grape too, Monsieur Stanley? You will have to be good, like the parrot!"

"Actually, she makes a mean shortbread. If you behave, I might give you a piece."

Pierre zipped up his coat and headed out the door. It seemed that none of my ducklings would need sheltering at Christmas. I returned to my bill display on the table and decided to pay the most delinquent ones and delay the others until the following month. Never do today what you can put off until tomorrow. This has been a creed at Shady Shingles for generations.

Although long and dark, the days passed quickly. First Brian and then Katrina disappeared on their holiday treks. Pierre kept to his usual routine, assuring me almost daily that Claudette would call "tomorrow." Hope springs eternal.

When I was a child, I thought Christmas Eve would never come. The year dragged by, and in December, the days seemed to go backwards. Somewhere along the way, somebody oiled the clock, and the thing has been spinning in overdrive ever since. This difference in perspective was driven home to me by a recent visit from Liam. It was the last day of school in December when the doorbell rang.

"Hello, Mr. McFadden. I stopped in to see what Captain wants for Christmas. If he doesn't ask for too much, maybe he wouldn't mind if I added some of my things to his Christmas letter."

Liam is not one to waste time on social niceties. Certainly, he has learned the important seasonal message of being sure to get stuff at Christmas. I know his parents try to indoctrinate him otherwise, but kids know the score. "Well, Liam, we can go visit him, but I don't know if Captain is into sharing any more than you are. And by the way, does your mother know you're here?"

"I stopped at home before I came. She knows. She said I shouldn't pester you about Christmas. She didn't say anything about not pestering Captain." Undaunted, Liam planted himself in front of Captain's cage. "Captain has no fingers, just toes. How does he write his letter to Santa? Do you write it for him?"

Being a scribe to an illiterate parrot is probably as high a calling as I could aspire to. "Captain's letter fits on a postcard, so it doesn't take long to write."

"Mr. M, what do you think about the naughty and nice thing? Do I really have to be good before Santa will give me anything for Christmas? How good do I gotta be?"

"I don't know, Liam. You might be borderline. Have you done any good deeds lately? You might need to cancel out some recent behaviours." Raised eyebrows and a hesitant voice helped achieve the desired effect. Although I didn't have a precise inventory of Liam's recent misdemeanours, the mere suggestion that I had such information was effective enough.

"Okay, Mr. M, if I fix your computer for free, will I get on Santa's good side? Maybe Santa's computer needs fixing too. He's old like you, isn't he?"

The fact that the theology of Santa Claus was outside the realm of my expertise was neither here nor there. I sensed an opportunity. "Alas, we are too far from the North Pole to check on Santa's computer, but I'm sure he'd be pleased if you were to help a fellow senior in need. My computer won't open any of the things saved on a disk that I've kept."

Liam left Captain behind and installed himself at my computer desk in the living room. There was a flurry of little hands, and soon he got the same result that I did.

"Got another disk, Mr. M? It doesn't matter what's on it." Liam took out the old disk and put in a new one. Curiously, it worked fine. "Sorry, Mr. M. The other disk got corrupted, and you won't be able to use it anymore."

Senators get accused of corruption, but I didn't realize computers were subject to corruption too. Who had committed this heinous crime? Who went around corrupting innocent computers? The best I could manage was a ponderous "Hmm . . ."

"Don't feel bad, Mr. M. It happens even to people who know what they're doing." Liam's confidence was reassuring. "That old disk is toast. I hope you saved whatever was on it somewhere else."

"Don't worry, Liam. Ya done good. I think Santa will be very pleased, unless you mess up between now and Christmas Eve. Can you be good for an entire week?"

Liam fidgeted. "I'll think about your question and get back to you." The boy was obviously cabinet material. When the present prime minister gives up the ghost, we have Liam in the wings. I wonder how the first jujube scandal will go over in the media.

"I gotta go now. My mom said not to be too long. I'll let her know that you keep in touch with Santa, in case she needs something too. She's good all the time, so she won't have any trouble." My IT specialist sidled up to Captain's cage. "I hope Santa is good to you, Captain. Maybe he'll bring you a better cage. Bye."

You and me both, buddy. Personally, I'm not into old guys with long beards. They don't usually travel with decent grapes.

Liam disappeared out the front door, and peace finally descended on the realm. Alas, it's not good to become too cocky about peace and such. It has a way of oozing out through the bottom of the bag when no one is looking, even at Christmas time. At least that's how it turned out at Shady Shingles.

9

When Christmas Goes South

WHEN THE WORLD unfolds as it should at Shady Shingles, we nod at Christmas and let it pass by. At least this is my idealized imagining of the event. I realize other people look forward all year to this festival of love and indulgence; indeed, there are Martha Stewart-type books to tell you how to do it right. You may conclude that I do not keep one of those on my shelf.

Everything was wonderfully bland and uneventful until Christmas Eve arrived. The evening started well. I had an uninterrupted communing with Madame Sherry and Alister Sim's *A Christmas Carol*, that 1954 black-and-white classic, on TV. Every year I cheer for Scrooge and hope Dickens has changed the plot. And every year I'm disappointed.

Just as the final credits rolled, Captain did his Mary Alice alert. As per established custom, she would make an appearance before she headed off to Midnight Mass, sometimes with visiting family members in tow and sometimes solo. On that night, she opened the door and puffed her way in alone.

"How about a sip of sherry, O Spirit of Christmas Present?" My offer of hospitality caught Mary Alice off guard. There was always a chance that a bit of Christmas cheer might derail her from her annual Christmas homily.

"It would do you good to go to church on Christmas Eve. No one should be alone on Christmas Eve. It's not natural." Her tone can get quite indignant when she has an irrational position to present. Muslims, Jews, Jehovah's Witnesses, and atheists manage to avoid church on Christmas Eve, and presumably, they get along fine. Actually, I can think of several atheists who go to some kind of church service on Christmas Eve, either because of family pressure or because they feel moved by the aesthetics of the Christmas ritual.

"I'm sure you'll enjoy Midnight Mass, but I think I'll do what I've always done. In a bit I'll head out for the late service at St. Mathew's." My reason for going to church on Christmas Eve is more prosaic. I allow Mary Alice to badger me into it, because then she will not insist that I come along with her to mass. Being a generic Protestant comes in handy at such moments. I can insist that I want to go to the church where Grandma Vi attended, and Mary Alice won't challenge my "understandable sentiment."

I don't know if God does an attendance check on Christmas Eve, but Mary Alice does. The penalty for being found wanting can be dire, to the point of not getting Christmas leftovers. And it's actually the case that a candle-lit sanctuary on Christmas Eve does evoke particular memories of Grandma Vi. She was buried from that space. When Mum and I would visit from Saskatoon, the three of us would attend that church on Christmas Eve. We do what we do for mixed motives, not only on Christmas Eve.

Mary Alice checked her watch. "You'd better make yourself presentable and get going right quick if you want to get a seat. I'll check on you and the pigeon tomorrow, if I get a chance." With that oblique blessing, her ladyship brushed out the door, tossing the end of her scarf over her shoulder as she went.

All the above would be moot in light of a new development. The first hint of something out of the ordinary was Pierre not coming downstairs to leave for work at his usual time. That could be explained by the garage being closed for the holiday, but Pierre would still need to be up and around at some other time. Could it be that he had slipped out earlier in the day without my noticing? After Mary Alice left, I had a niggling doubt at the back of my head, and it wouldn't go away, a feeling of something amiss without being able to define exactly what it is.

Part of me reasoned that it would be a waste of energy to trek all the way upstairs to the second floor. As time went on, the stairs got steeper and longer in some perversely magical way. And after all that effort, I would likely find three empty rooms and innumerable orphan dust bunnies. Or not. The only way to resolve the mystery would be to commit to the upward climb. If eighty-year-old seniors run marathons, I guessed I could make it up one flight of stairs. That being said, I do as much as possible to avoid eighty-year-old marathoners.

After a little pause halfway up, I reached the second floor. I could see down the length of the hallway, two bedrooms on the left and a bedroom and bathroom on the right. A somewhat threadbare and faded Oriental carpet ran down the middle of the hall. Another staircase continued up to the third floor, but the rooms up there were not occupied by tenants, except for the odd rodent interloper. If a house is shaded by a chestnut tree, rodent interlopers with bushy tails tend to find their way in.

Pierre's room was closed, so I rapped cautiously on the door. At first there was no sound, and I was about to leave when I heard a muffled moan. Squirrels are not much into muffled moans, so I presumed the source to be human. I knocked again.

"Who is dere?"

Without doubt it was Pierre, although he did not sound very lively. "It's me, Stanley. Are you alright?"

There is always the danger that when you ask someone if they are all right, they will actually go into detail as to why they are not. When passing on the street, there is little danger of real conversation starting. But talking through a bedroom door is definitely a higher-risk scenario because it's hard to make believe you were just passing by. I had crossed the Rubicon, so to speak.

Pierre opened the door, looking bleary eyed and more disheveled than usual. "Ah, Monsieur Stanley, you didn't need to come up here. I am fine. Well, maybe not so fine. Claudette, she should call by now because we always have the dinner on Christmas Eve. And then we go to the Midnight Mass. And after we have Le Réveillon with thirteen desserts. But she no call."

His voice was thick and laboured. The medicine for this Claudette trauma seemed to be rye, judging from Pierre's potent breath and somewhat slurred speech. The half-empty bottle on his nightstand confirmed my astute observation.

"I'm sorry Claudette didn't call. I was concerned when I didn't see you this afternoon or this evening. Maybe you should come downstairs and eat something?" I wasn't really asking a question, but when men have a broken heart, the general remedy is booze or food. Of course, a miraculous reconciliation would also do the trick, but I had long ago realized that Pierre could not count on that option. It would take Pierre longer to catch up to his new reality. At the moment, reality was not looking very good.

"The women, they can be very cruel, non?" His tone was that of a wounded warrior. A downcast expression and stooped shoulders added to the effect. Just as my question wasn't really a question, neither was his. Sometimes I actually pick up on this kind of thing, especially when people philosophize about affairs of the heart.

"Let's head downstairs and see what falls out of the fridge." It seemed wiser to renew my suggestion about getting some food into my morose tenant. Ducklings need feeding.

Down is usually easier than up for yours truly, though I had a swaying Pierre at my side, and I was a tad anxious that we might end up in a crumpled heap at the bottom of the stairs. Despite a couple of close calls, we made it to the bottom. Captain gave a start, half raising his wings to steady his balance.

Call the undertaker. Don't let the deadbeat fall on my cage!

Once we gained the sanctity of the kitchen, Pierre was able to navigate solo to the refrigerator. I find that tenants have an autopilot that can guide them to that destination. I only have to set them in motion, and they home in. Pierre was no exception—a bit wobbly maybe but soon he stood gazing into the abyss of the refrigerator.

The previous night's tuna casserole was in deadly peril, but I had no intention of defending it.

"Hey, Monsieur Stanley, it looks to me like you have big famine in the frigo. Der is only 'dis fishy grey t'ing.'" It's amazing how someone who downs half a bottle of rye can purport to have a discerning palate.

"It's a traditional English meal on Christmas Eve," I assured him. If I was going to lie, I figured I might as well tell a big one. "If you heat it up, it's actually quite good." Big lie number two.

Pierre gingerly carried the casserole to the counter, making sure not to drop his only culinary option. I contemplated whether or not I was morally obliged to stay with him and decided he could survive that phase of the crisis alone.

"Pierre, I am heading off to church. After you've had something to eat, you are welcome to watch TV or head to bed. You're welcome to come with me, but the service at St. Mathew's is Protestant, and we don't do the Réveillon thing afterwards."

Pierre furrowed his brow and tried to absorb all those ideas, but the "fishy t'ing" was in the microwave, and he obviously wasn't thinking that far ahead. "Dat's OK. I stay here. Who knows? Maybe Claudette will call with a few words. Alone is not so bad." His morose voice belied the content of his words.

"I realize this is not how you planned to spend Christmas Eve. Sorry about that. Maybe we can do something on Christmas Day. I don't have time just now. But see you tomorrow, and maybe things will look brighter then. Bye for now."

I made my exit, having tossed out a bit of gratuitous hope. Since Pierre wasn't likely to get any better offers, I didn't feel so bad about being the purveyor of gratuitous hope. Captain could keep Pierre company. Maybe a parrot wasn't much of a substitute for Claudette, but at least he was in a cage and couldn't escape. Society frowns on putting Claudettes in cages, unless they happen to commit a criminal offence. Captain had dealt with stories of jilted lovers before. He just preens, yawns, and then goes to sleep. With any luck, Pierre would fall asleep before the bird did. With a bit more luck, Pierre could wake up late the following day and forget my vague offer of "doing something" on Christmas Day.

My annual Christmas Eve trek to St. Mathew's was satisfying, if not uplifting. As usual, there was no snow to reflect the moonlight. Winter nights in Victoria are especially dark for that reason. Islands of yellow light surround the streetlamps, but the rays go only a short distance before being absorbed into infinite darkness.

The stained-glass windows of St. Mathew's cast a multi-hued glow in the distance. Usually, the church's profile is dark at night, but on Christmas Eve it exudes luminous warmth and vitality. I reached the stone steps and mounted them to the interior. The volunteer greeter was one of my neighbours, Agnes Rourke.

"Evening, Stanley. You're just in time. The place is filling up."

I inferred by her tone that this was an unusual problem. She gave me an order of service, and I found a spot near the back. The candlelight and the carols were reminders of those Christmases long ago, when Grandma Vi and my mother attended as a little troupe. The service itself was both familiar and somehow remote, perhaps because I was more of a visitor than a parishioner.

The service ended with the singing of "Silent Night" as everyone held a lit candle in the darkened church. There is something timeless about candles and gathering people by candlelight. It could be an ancient druidic ritual, or it could be a Christian worship service of today. It would probably look and feel the same. In any case, the primal light and the evocative carol touch something of the heart. There is a good dose of nostalgia in such rituals too. Churches know how to market nostalgia. Christmases of the past seem to resurface naturally in such an atmosphere. The carol ended, and we extinguished the candles.

I exited the church and retraced my steps to Shady Shingles. The house looked dark and even foreboding, except for the string of Christmas lights Brian had put up in the porch. Sometimes a little light in the darkness is all it takes.

I unlocked the front door carefully, so as not to wake Captain. Snoring rumbled forth from the living room. Pierre must have put the cover over Captain's cage before falling asleep on the couch. I decided to creep by the sleeping beauties and gain the sanctuary of my room. Sometimes Captain wakes up when he hears the floorboards creak, but if he had tuned out Pierre's snoring, my stealth would be sufficient.

Indeed, I needn't have worried—neither creature stirred. Once in my room, I could pull up the drawbridge and sojourn until first light. At that time of year, dawn would likely be after 8:00 a.m. I intended to take full advantage of the opportunity, having missed my afternoon repose. No sugarplum fairies danced in my head, but sleep came quickly.

Christmas morning comes early in households with small children. That kind of high- level energy was not the case at Shady Shingles. I think what woke me was the sound of Pierre talking to Captain in the living room. Pierre always assumes that if he talks loudly to Captain, his highness will be more likely to understand him. Actually, Captain has very good hearing, so I don't know that the volume of a human voice much matters to him. It's more a case of discerning what the human is about to give him.

"Joyeux Noel, little corporal. Da Christmas Parrot was here last night, and he left you a grape." It would seem that Pierre had found the fruit crisper in the refrigerator. I could not see or hear Captain's response, but I'm sure his estimation of Pierre had risen, and he was probably eating the grape.

The Furry Face is way too loud, but at least he's trainable. I need to reinforce this new behaviour. Give grapes to the parrot, and don't eat the parrot."

I shuffled into the living room. Stubble-faced, Pierre looked rather bleary eyed and tired. "Dat couch, Monsieur Stanley, she is stuffed wit' rocks and old springs. Maybe I go upstairs now and have a Noel morning sleep. You don't mind?"

"That sounds like an excellent idea, Pierre. You get some rest."

I was relieved that there would be an interlude before Pierre emerged again. I thought perhaps I should think of what Captain and I could round up for a special meal, now that we had company

83

for Christmas dinner. Mac's and Seven Elevens tend not to have a frozen goose or turkey on hand. Most inconsiderate of them. The usual food stores are closed on Christmas Day. They're equally inconsiderate, although even Scrooge let Bob Cratchit off on Christmas Day, so I suppose we can't roll back the clock on that one.

Usually I just make a sandwich on Christmas Day, knowing that bounty will arrive from Mary Alice on Boxing Day. That strategy would not cut it though. I suppose I could have weighed upon the Dowager Empress to invite us both to her family gathering for the festive meal, but that would be pretty crass at the eleventh hour. And I would owe May Alice big time for that faux pas. Better not to ring up a hospitality debt that could take me decades to repay. No, there had to be a simpler and cheaper solution.

When all else fails, make a reconnaissance mission to see what lurks forgotten in the cupboard and the bottom of the freezer. Let us not quibble about minor details, like expiry dates. Desperate times call for desperate measures. Christmas dinner at Shady Shingles requires either a certain creativity or an ample dose of "anything will do."

I kept this creed in mind as I peered into the cupboard beyond the tea cannister. I found some long-forgotten things in there, most of them in Tupperware and recycled yogurt containers. The most promising prospect was an economy-size pickle jar, repurposed to hold macaroni. That seemed a safe bet. One shelf over and two up was a can of spaghetti sauce, in behind some boxes of crackers and bread sticks. The can had a bar code on the label, as opposed to the inked price stamp on a jar of olives. Stores first started using bar codes in 1974. If the olives came from Lucky Foods, which was a bit behind the big chains, the olives might be forty years old. That was a sign that the Mediterranean delicacy should not be on our Christmas dinner menu. I moved the olives to another shelf that I had mentally labelled "Must remember to throw out when I get around to it." That one had become the best-stocked shelf in the cupboard. Further rooting and moving things aside turned up a can of baby peas recommended by the Jolly Green Giant. Peas are green, and spaghetti sauce is red, so I already had the basic Christmas colours covered. Mission almost accomplished.

My bounty thus far would have been adequate to keep body and soul together, but Christmas dinner required a greater demonstration of opulence than macaroni and peas. We live in an age of consumer excess, especially at Christmas. Even I had to yield to the Spirit of the Age and take the big step. Yes, that meant a descent to the basement and a visit to the chest freezer. While the latter was largely full of distressed bread that was on sale, I knew other unidentified treasures lurked under the bread layers. The treasures kept accumulating from year to year, and I just added to them, such as when I didn't know what to do with Mary Alice's annual fruitcake offering. At least the fruitcakes were recognizable, frozen bricks wrapped in aluminum foil.

I descended the basement steps, forgetting that the return trip would not be as easy. Once there, I lifted the freezer lid and dug down to retrieve the oldest of the aluminum ingots. Better to bring it up then, because it would take the rest of the day to thaw. At least dessert would be substantial, but I still needed to find something to expand the first course. I came across a thin rectangular block. After I scraped the ice off the label, it was revealed to be "cod product." I wondered why it couldn't just be "cod." I understand that in some countries, the Christmas meal is built around fish, so perhaps there was precedent for a cod feast. If Pierre were from Poland or Italy or Slovakia, I would have hit the jackpot because cod can't be all that different from carp, which is the fish they use. I read that on one of those coffeeshop news sheets they provide for worldly customers like me.

Pierre would be a tourtière kind of guy. I didn't read that on a café news sheet, but I remembered him pining about his mother's tourtière and how he couldn't find anything like it in Victoria. I tried to convince him that a haggis is just a rolled-up tourtière, and we have butcher shops that sell haggis, but he didn't buy it. Maybe it's because haggis comes wrapped in a sheep intestine rather than lard-based pastry. Somehow that puts people off.

I discerned a roundish object wrapped in several layers of plastic. It had the right profile for a frozen haggis, but closer scrutiny revealed a Celtic relative of a different ilk—a Cornish game hen. It might have been the runt of the clutch, and somehow it arrived solo. No companion fowl was slumbering in cryogenic bliss at the bottom of the freezer. But undeniably, it was a fowl, and it would require considerably less time to thaw than a turkey. The Cornish game hen and the fruitcake could have a race to see which would come to room temperature sooner.

The trip down under was worthwhile, but then I had to face the stairs. I don't remember exactly when stairs became such a challenge. I knew I would have to pause halfway up and have a coughing fit. My dry cough was chronic and intermittent, but I could count on stairs to bring it on. True to form, I had to stop on the fifth step and wheeze a little aria. It passed quickly, and I continued the rest of the way with my largesse. No pain, no gain.

I deposited my retrieved items on the kitchen counter. The Cornish hen somehow got smaller when I unwrapped it and set it in a bowl of cold water. It wasn't going anywhere, so I retired to the living room. Captain was craning his neck in my direction—a cue for me to return to the kitchen and bring back a tiny piece of cheddar cheese. I obliged.

Must I remind you every day of this minimal ration? If I were a poodle, you would have the expense of doggy treats and flea collars. I only require three grams of Old Cheddar once a day.

My reading chair beckoned. It was too early in the day to sip on sherry, although it was within reach when I sat down. Maybe a little therapeutic nap would be in order, now that Christmas dinner was virtually in hand. The sun streamed in, there was no traffic outside, the bird was in nap pose, and all was well in the land.

I awoke with a start. It was early afternoon. I heard the bathroom door close upstairs. That meant Pierre had emerged from hibernation, and I should start to look busy in the kitchen. A little push, and I was mobile. Onward to victory.

The Cornish hen had not learned to swim, and the fruitcake was still solid but not brittle. I put the miniature hen into a casserole dish and popped it into the oven. Along with the items I found earlier, these things would have to constitute our banquet. I hunted around for a tablecloth, then proceeded to make coffee.

"Hey dere, Monsieur Stanley, what is happening? And Joyeux Noel!" Pierre was at the kitchen door, having made a barefoot entrance clad in his pajamas.

"Good afternoon, Pierre. I trust you slept well?"

"For sure, Monsieur Stanley. I had a baby sleep. And you?"

"Well enough, thank you. Captain and I had a little nap this morning. By the way, would you like to join us for Christmas dinner?"

"I t'ought you do not do de Christmas eating t'ing. I don't want to make a big trouble for you."

In such situations, social convention requires that we lie through our teeth. It's expected. "Oh, it's no trouble at all. Captain and I have to eat anyway, so you're welcome to join us for our humble fare."

"Well, I won't say no because I am not hearing from Claudette, and now the Noel is almost past."

"I think you are used to the special meal coming on Christmas Eve, and you open presents then too? Here the Anglo custom is for presents on Christmas morning and the meal on Christmas Day."

"Dat's kind of different, but I guess it doesn't matter as long as everybody is together."

While this a cheery aspect of Christmas for most people, the fact that others are not together with whoever they ideally want to be with is cause for remorse. Clearly, Pierre was not together with his beloved Claudette. He would need a distraction, other than his remaining half bottle of rye. Food is a great distraction. It distracts me all the time—an observation that my doctor makes at regular intervals.

"Captain and I have a rather small-scale Christmas. You can join in and help. Here's a tablecloth, and you'll find some cutlery and dishes in the cupboard there."

Pierre seemed happy enough to be doing something. People visit more meaningfully in the kitchen than they do in any other part of a house. This has its pros and cons.

"Monsieur Stanley, maybe I should not ask, but why is der no Madame Stanley? Maybe the wife, she has died?"

"No, Pierre. There was never a Madame Stanley. I have only ever been attracted to women who are incredibly good judges of character."

Pierre laughed a little and then looked puzzled. "What makes you the bad character, mon ami? Do you rob the banks every Friday?" Pierre seemed unduly pleased with himself, and his eyes twinkled as he laid out this possibility. It was my turn to laugh. I envisioned Jerome with his hands in the air as I robbed the branch where he worked. At my age, the mind wanders.

"Uh, no, actually. I never married because I'm gay, and I didn't want to lead some woman down the garden path."

Pierre looked puzzled as he tried to figure out how my being a gay gardener would explain singlehood. Then the penny dropped, and his face lit up—never a good sign with Pierre. "You don't like gardening, and you don't like the women. Maybe the Marie Alice, she gives you the bad impression of the women, non?"

I had noticed that many of my tenants were imbued with pop psychology, so why should Pierre be any different? It's a generational epidemic, especially in British California. My regard for pop psychology is comparable only to my regard for curling. At least curling is more grounded, and those who practice it sometimes hit the target.

"Actually, Mary Alice and I don't talk about sex very much. She stopped presenting me with eligible women a long time ago. I was always aware of my identity, but I never met a suitable partner. Solitude is an honourable state, especially if the alternatives are not very appealing." If my spiel sounded a bit slick, it's because I had given it a few times before.

"I see, Monsieur Stanley. Dat's no problem by me. My cousin in Rimouski, he is a papillon, and everybody, they like him."

"Papillon?" It was my turn to be puzzled by a metaphor.

"Oh, sorry. A papillon is a butterfly, you know . . ." Pierre flapped both wrists, looking very earnest all the while. This is quite a feat if one is built like a burly linebacker.

"I see." I smiled and flapped my wrists in return. I've known a few butterflies in my time, or at least some flighty people, some of them gay and some of them quite straight. One never knows for sure.

Pierre seemed to have learned more than he intended, and he quickly moved on to a topic of much greater interest. "Somet'ing smell good from de h'oven. What is cooking?" I detected a new note of eagerness in his voice.

"It's a small chicken. I need to get some other things ready before the bird is done, so you can go sing French Christmas carols to Captain. He'll like that."

Pierre took the hint and went off to the living room with plates and utensils while I boiled water for the macaroni. I didn't want Pierre there when I opened the can of peas—just in case. After hunting for a can opener, I unsealed the treasure, and the contents still resembled canned peas. The tin of tomato sauce was more questionable, as bad tomato sauce probably looks much the same as good tomato sauce. My sense of smell went on sabbatical some years ago; therefore, a visit to my food tester was in order.

I brought the can out to the living room and held it under Captain's beak as he hung over the side of the cage. He examined the contents and didn't shake his head violently. I have always taken this to be a sign of approval, since he thinks I am going to feed him whatever is being tested. If food fails the test, he picks out a piece and flings it against the wall. Parrots are not subtle.

Looks like blood to me, but I don't smell anything strange. Where does he get this stuff? Probably roadkill. Not very interesting.

"Da bird, he eats tomato sauce? I t'ought they eat the crackers and the yellow flower seeds." Pierre was showing off his avian knowledge.

"Actually, he does like tomato sauce on cooked pasta. I just wanted to be sure he would like *this* tomato sauce." Better not to be too specific as to what might or might not make the tomato sauce special. The key to a good bluff, be it in the kitchen or elsewhere, is to sound confident and not to give out too much information. It has been a time-honoured pillar of Canadian parliamentary democracy, so I figured it should work for a mere landlord as well.

I returned to the kitchen. Meanwhile, Pierre laid out the table. At the right moment, I asked him to bring out the two plates. On each one I deposited half a Cornish game hen, macaroni with tomato sauce, and half a can of heated peas. Probably the menu would not have met with Grandma Vi's approval, but something is better than nothing. This is the same logic that the government applies when dispensing my old-age pension.

"Monsieur Stanley, what happened to the chicken? Maybe dey don't feed the chickens in BC? She is very petite, dis one."

I imagined explaining that we were going to eat a Cornish game hen that was not from Cornwall. In the same instant, I decided not to. "It got smaller in the oven. The quality of chickens is not very high these days. We'll just have to make do."

We returned to the living room, which was also the location of my improvised dining table. It looked quite elegant with the white cloth draped over it. One just had to be careful not to kick the crates propping it up. Must attend to that some day.

"Me, I'm a little nervous to eat the little chicken in front of Corporal Parrot. Maybe he will be sad to see this t'ing?"

Pierre was attributing an empathy to my omnivorous parrot that was misplaced. Captain was leaning over the side of his cage, casting his gaze upon both the chicken and the pasta. I gave him a macaroni noodle, and he gobbled it up. What he was really waiting for was a drumstick bone. Given how fast Pierre ate, one was soon available. I asked if I could have it, then brought it over to Captain. He snatched it most un-daintily.

I've had to wait all year for this. Don't expect any of it back. Gotta love that marrow. Captain cracked open the bone and proceeded to eat the marrow. No one has to teach this trick to parrots. They just know what to do.

"Mon Dieu. The corporal, he eats the relatives. I never see dat before." Pierre would think twice about offering his finger through the bars to Captain.

"Have some sherry. I just happen to have some open." I presumed that sherry could only lubricate the meal a bit. Maybe it could even help a rye hangover. Or not.

"Me, I never had da English Christmas dinner before. T'ank you for the invitation. And da sherry, she is not so bad ei'der."

"Leave some room, Pierre. The best is yet to come. We're having some marinated fruitcake for dessert. It was specially made." Of course, I needn't mention that it was specially made fourteen years earlier, according to the label that Mary Alice had attached. I poured a little sherry on the fruitcake before serving it on a saucer. I thought of flaming the sherry for dramatic effect but then recalled that brandy is the liquor of choice, and I didn't keep anything as expensive as brandy.

"Very good cake, Monsieur Stanley." Pierre pronounced his approval as he made the fruitcake disappear. After I saw that it was apparently safe, I had some too. Sherry does wonders for cake. It also adds a certain civility to Christmas, even the Christmas that went South.

Amen and amen.

10
Year's End Is Not Life's End

WHEN I STUMBLED downstairs to the kitchen on Boxing Day morning, I was greeted by an angelic visitor who had passed magically through the locked front door. No, it wasn't one of the heavenly hosts that got lost while flying home from a Nativity pageant. This angelic messenger of hope and goodwill was Mary Alice. She gets that way once a year, as she showers the needy and the destitute with leftovers from her family's Christmas dinner. Actually, she feels overwhelmed with guilt about this Yuletide feast and atones for her hedonism by bringing succulent leftovers to Captain and me.

"I brought you and the pigeon some treats for Christmas, even though you don't deserve any!" our Angel of Mercy declared.

Mary Alice will never be accused of nurturing anyone's delusions of grandeur or goodness. Although appearing tough, this angel was tainted by Catholic guilt. I hope some new pope doesn't get carried away in absolving the faithful of guilt. Otherwise, waifs like me will have to start cooking for themselves at Christmas. Some of us need to uphold our position as parasites, or the do-gooders of the world will have no outlet for their charitable compulsions. Even homeless shelters get inundated at Christmas, so I don't feel too bad about taking advantage of Mary Alice's misguided sense of charity.

"The Captain and I are most appreciative of your Yuletide generosity, and we extend to you our humble thanks for this bounty bestowed upon us." I intoned this platitude with regal solemnity. The Book of Common Prayer must contain a line like that. If it doesn't, it should. Captain looked annoyed that I wasn't around to see his Mary Alice alert. She had already removed his cover, and he was scrutinizing us both.

What a crock, McFadden. She knows you're a leech. Just dole out the goodies, and be quick about it.

"Here, have some shortbread. Agnes doesn't make hers as good as mine, but it's passable." Mary Alice's culinary reputation trumped any maternal pride for her daughter that would otherwise bolster her matronly persona.

Actually, shortbread and coffee are not a bad way to start the day. I broke off a piece, and Captain took it daintily, knowing it was probably his total treat ration for the morning. In such scenarios, shortbread is a good first course. If I ate it slowly, I would have an excuse not to cut into the inevitable fruitcake, which had the heft of granite. Eventually, Mary Alice would leave, and I could, with effort, re-locate that year's fruitcake to a more permanent resting place. Perhaps an unmarked grave somewhere in Victoria needed a headstone. Alternatively, some ocean-going container ship might require ballast. One must be creative in considering the options for gifted fruitcake; otherwise, it migrates to the bottom of the freezer for another year, and I already had thirteen others stowed away. I needed to think of something to say before she asked me to sample that year's offering.

"How did things go at your daughter's place yesterday?" Such a polite enquiry was tempting the fates, because the politics of family gatherings in Mary Alice's world can be more involved than any sane outsider would want to hear. Since I knew she was dying to tell me, it made sense to feign interest and get it over with. Married couples who want to stay that way pursue the same communication strategy.

"Well, I don't want to tell tales out of school, but my son-in-law is a piece of work. Albert watched TV before dinner, and he slouched there afterwards. Didn't bother to visit with me or the cousins. Just sipped his barley sandwiches the entire time." Mary Alice's laboured tone and disdainful expression indicated she was not amused. The wrinkles on her forehead don't turn into furrows unless the transgression is major. Albert may have been living on borrowed time if Mary Alice had any sway with the Creator.

I sensed a kindred spirit in the son-in-law but thought it wise not share this insight with my visiting angel of mercy. Angels of mercy can be a vengeful lot when riled up. "I'm sure that must have been disappointing, but at least you got to spend some time with your daughter and the grandchildren," I said. Cowardice is an underrated virtue.

Captain eyed the shortbread tin and leaned in our direction. *Now that we've had the blarney, how about some more of that shortbread? It's Christmas, you know.*

I chose to ignore the pantomimed hint. I won't have some vet chastise me for allowing my parrot to overdose on shortbread. Mary Alice didn't look much assuaged by my feeble attempt at empathy. Her considered reply was melodramatic. "At least we could all be together at Christmas. It's better than them all getting together at my funeral."

She sniffled. That was a new twist on Christmas and not one that would have come readily to my mind. I hadn't heard Mary Alice allude to the prospect of her funeral before. That she would bring up the idea at Christmas seemed bizarre. Then I remembered that Grandma had died just after Christmas, when Mary Alice was in her sixties. That was twenty-five years earlier, and suddenly I realized the ageless Mary Alice was in fact ninety-two. This angel of mercy could, in fact, be mortal. Despite past associations, all I could visualize was Mary Alice in a casket trimmed with holly and garish twinkling lights. I am prone to such brain burps. A gaudy Christmas casket wasn't an image that I could share in the moment, so I looked in desperation to Captain. He had picked up on her tone of voice and was looking very pensive, his head tilted to one side. Captain was either empathetic or waiting for more shortbread. Parrots are inscrutable that way.

"I think there will be a few more Christmases yet before we need to contemplate your funeral," I said. "Anyway, who would plan it if you weren't here?"

Mary Alice smiled, and the twinkle returned to her eyes. "Indeed, they'd have to put Captain in charge because my daughter couldn't organize her sock drawer, and you would make a mess of it too!"

Captain snorted and raised his wings a notch. *She should be so lucky.*

With that, Mary Alice made her exit, but not before putting away the various food treasures and making sure the kitchen was organized properly. She was off to the Boxing Day sales, stocking up on wrapping paper and Christmas cards for the following year. I took it as a sign of hope, even if her morbid musing seemed to indicate otherwise. Only if Mary Alice ever expressed indifference about the sales flyer from Lucky Foods would I need to call 911.

I settled into my comfy chair in the living room. Captain preened and groomed himself in preparation for his after-breakfast nap. I've never been quite sure why attention to such fastidious detail matters is necessary before napping, but I suppose there is always the chance that he might meet an impressionable female parrot in his dreams. He hasn't let on about his love life.

I savoured my second cup of coffee and stared out at the leafless chestnut tree, which stood guard over the house, as it had since my grandparents' arrival on Orkney Street. It was strangely naked at that time of year, yielding no hint of its dark-green canopy, which would surely burst forth come spring. Such a patriarch had to be the custodian of many secrets.

Mary Alice's cryptic remark got me thinking, not about the prospect of her funeral but about our shared past. In my mind, she had always lived next door, when not actually at Violet's side, like an attentive younger sister. As a child, I thought of the two women as old beyond belief, so it didn't occur to me that one day the two would become one, and not in the matrimonial way. They were the Martha and Mary of the neighbourhood. Mary Alice was the Martha, making sure all the practical details got looked after. Tenant references were vetted, and rental agreements were signed under her watchful eye. Grandma was the Mary, engaging strangers and newcomers in conversation, prodding them to stretch their wings and become what they were destined to be. It's the helping-the-duckling-across-the-tracks gene that seems to run in the McFadden clan. Or at least the gene turns up every now and then, usually at inconvenient moments.

"Captain, do you ever think you should help a duckling?"

I can't say I was expecting an articulate answer, but he was the only one available to hear my existential query. Captain ruffled his feathers and began shifting into his pre-nap position, one foot tucked up into his breast feathers and the other centred under him, balancing his body on the perch.

The world has lots of ducklings. Some of them make it, and some of them don't. That's why ducks lay so many eggs. Parrots help by taking a good nap when landlords ask pointless questions.

Initially, it had not occurred to me that I would end up at Shady Shingles, following in Grandma's footsteps. After high school, I had gone to university and completed a couple of years of English and psychology. I was entertaining the idea of becoming a teacher and raising the level of civilization among Saskatchewan's youth. It gripped me as a noble mission, until I heard there was a glut of teachers on the market. The Baby Boomers had not yet started to retire, and teachers were holding on to their jobs like winter hangs on to the last March snowbank in Saskatoon.

Studying to become an unemployed teacher seemed to be an inglorious fate. I moved on to saving the earth, if I couldn't save civilization. More specifically, I started to work for a farmer whose niche was market gardening. The more I got into market garden-ing in the next couple of years, the more it felt like high-stakes gambling. All our labours might pay off, but it was equally pos-sible that all might be for naught because of hail, frost, drought, or grasshoppers. Public sentiment was just beginning to shift toward organic produce, and I could see the writing on the wall for our style of operating.

Next on my quest for a viable livelihood was night auditor at a hotel. My prime qualification for this leap into the world of higher commerce was that I was willing to start work at 11:00 p.m. and end at 7:00 a.m. It may have helped that my employer's expectations were rather low. Anton was a Greek immigrant who had worked his way up to hotel manager. None of his five offspring wanted to be night auditor. When he heard I had gone to university, he assumed I must be capable and could adapt to any job necessary. This goes to show that either Greek immigrants have an excessive faith in human nature or Anton was a desperate capitalist in search of a proletarian to exploit. Fortunately, I had a friend who had actually graduated in commerce and could coach me on the rudiments of night auditing.

While the numbers added up, my social life did not. It seemed that I was always going when other people were coming. I probably should have cultivated a mentoring relationship with a raccoon, so I could learn to sleep by day and gain sustenance by night. I suppose burglars have perfected that technique, but like raccoons, their skill set is not appreciated by the general population. On the other hand, having a steady income was an incentive to hang on to an uninteresting job when the alternative was the Great Unknown. All proletarians have learned this lesson.

Years have a way of flitting by, especially as one becomes older. My earlier life was filled with various jobs. After a few years of night auditing, I went on to become a waiter, a hardware store clerk, a delivery van driver, a real estate agent, and finally, a home renovations helper. The latter often involved gutting old houses and rebuilding them to meet modern code. Saskatoon had no shortage of old houses, but people with cash to fund renovations were harder to come by. Better simply to work for someone who had already lined up well-heeled house owners seeking to actualize their dream. The dream sometimes turned into a nightmare, but at least in the beginning, renovators wanted owners to believe in their dreams. That was where I specialized.

Angus McGregor of Right Renos hired me to accompany him on his initial visit to prospective new clients. Angus was a self-made man with a Belfast-made accent that was unintelligible to the average Canadian. He and his wife had immigrated to Canada after the Second World War. Prior to enlisting, he had been a carpenter, so he readily found employment in his adopted home. It may have helped that the boss at his first job was Seamus Fitzpatrick, a fellow Irishman from Dublin. Seamus could provide a simultaneous translation when needed and feign ignorance when Angus uttered things that shouldn't be translated to folks who had led sheltered lives. This benevolent relationship was all the more surprising, considering Angus was actually Scots Protestant and Seamus was Irish Catholic. Despite these confessional differences they were united in the common bond that neither of them went to church, but they faithfully attended the same pub.

Angus did precision work, but fellow tradesmen and customers only pretended to understand what he was saying. Somehow his Ulster Scots accent become more pronounced rather than more diluted with the passing years. When he said, "The job is going to cost more than you estimated," it came out something like, "Th' job is gonnae cost mair than ye haste mated," which looks more recognizable in print than it sounded in his lilting brogue. My ability as a translator came from having had an Ulster-born Scout leader who smacked me every time I asked him to repeat himself. It was another era. Pain is a marvellous motivator in linguistic studies. My preparation for becoming Angus's spokesperson was an accidental learning from my youth. Think of being forced to take piano lessons as a child and only in adulthood appreciating that music is a language that makes a difference.

After some years of working for someone else, Angus struck out on his own. His carpentry and design skills were many, but he didn't particularly like people. Angus would have preferred to skip the initial contract discussions and get right into the work, with as little said as possible. My own job interview with him lasted all of twenty seconds.

"Dae ye want tae wark ur dae ye nae?" In case you missed it, "Do you want to work or do you not?" I said yes, and that was that. Whether it was a blessing or a curse, Angus was the sort of person who formed a judgment about people very quickly.

On my first day on the job, I turned up at the potential site just before Angus did. If you are not highly competent, at least you can be early. I thought I would be pulling nails and knocking down walls right away, but my debut was of another order. I introduced myself to the homeowners and indicated that my boss would arrive shortly. Fortunately, Angus did not make a liar of me. He arrived in a few minutes with a sheaf of sketches and some cost estimates. I stood slightly behind him, out of deference to his being the boss. Angus laid the papers in front of the couple and then stood back, offering only a curt question. "Haur it is. Whit dae ye thank?"

I noted that the couple looked somewhat bewildered, and Angus grew impatient. I stepped forward and piped up, as if I were some-body in authority. "Here it is. What do you think?" The pleasant couple was expecting a bit more of a sales pitch. They hadn't even been aware of what it was that Angus was asking, although it must surely have to do with their dream home. Angus sat stone faced and was obviously not intending to say anything more, because to him the proposal was self-evident for any intelligent, breathing person. And if someone didn't fit into that category, they should not be wasting his time. Remembering my Scouting days, I knew better than to ask Angus for further elaboration. Instead I improvised a bit of realtor babble-speak and assured the couple that previous clients were very satisfied with Right Renos. This is called applied psychology. People pay to be told what they want to hear. No used car would ever sell unless this were true.

The couple seemed relieved, and they trustingly signed off on the contract notes that Angus had brought with him. Even my short realty career was put to good use, in that all realtors learn the art of selling the dream, not the house. Realtors also use applied psychology. I suspect the only people who don't use applied psychology are professional psychologists.

Angus was impressed, although he said nothing aloud. In the future, Angus brought me along to all his initial interviews. The estimates and the concept drawings were his, but the sales pitch was mine. Lest this minor role go to my head, he made sure that the rest of my time was spent learning "real work," which included destruction as well as construction. Sometimes these efforts involved removing old insulation, pounding down lath plaster, reconfiguring attic spaces, and so on. In hindsight, we should have worn masks against the various kinds of dust. Although the work was uncomfortable at times, it was satisfying. In particular, I could be part of a project that took a ramshackle house from virtual ruin to upscale character home.

My relationship with Angus was also a bonus, perhaps because he became like the father that I didn't have. Angus was never chatty or effusive, but he was always fair and respectful. It would have pleased him if I would have been able to learn the craft so well that I was able to take over from him someday. It was our unspoken covenant. Fate would cut that agenda short.

It was while I was still working for Angus that I received word of Violet's death. The telephone rang before I left for work one dark winter morning. Most people knew I didn't believe in mornings, so I was prepared to be annoyed. "Hello, Stanley here," I said in as even a tone as possible.

"Stanley, it's Mary Alice."

I knew she was calling from Victoria and that she would not be making a long-distance call to Saskatoon unless Violet was unable. The only question in my mind was how unable Grandma might be. The quavering in Mary Alice's voice was both unmistakable and ominous. "I have some bad news, Stanley. There's no easy way to tell you this. Vi died of a heart attack in her sleep last night. The doctor said it was very quick, and she didn't suffer. She just went."

Mary Alice sounded as if she had used up her last breath. Even before she uttered the words, I knew the world had changed. For ninety years the world was a stable place because Violet was in it, and Shady Shingles was her realm for a good part of that time. Given that I was forty-nine, it should have been obvious that Grandma would not be there to my own end, if I lived as long as most McFaddens. Now there would be no more phone calls, and I was the last McFadden. That's the selfish side of grief.

Like most people, I accepted the principle of death but not the event when it actually happened to someone I knew and loved. I was glad that Mary Alice had not tried to sugar-coat the reality by saying Grandma had "passed away." Worse yet, if she died today, she would simply "pass." Grandma came from a world where people actually died, and there was no need for a euphemism to deny something natural and final.

Despite the onset of a deepening numbness, I replied to Mary Alice. "Thank you for calling me right away. I know this must be hard for you. I'm not quite sure what to do."

"I don't want to interfere, Stanley, but your grandma did leave some notes and a will. At our ages, we thought each other should know these things . . . just in case. You know already that she named you as her executor. I have the envelope that she kept aside for you." Mary Alice was calm and composed. It would be what Vi would expect and want of her. She took a breath before continuing. "The coroner has been here, and the funeral home that your grandma chose is ready to move her body. Should I tell them to go ahead?"

My usual mode of decision-making is to procrastinate, but the reality of death is not easily put off. Even if I could book a flight immediately, it would be late in the day before I could get to Victoria. Mary Alice's question was actually rhetorical, but I needed to answer. "Yes, go ahead. I want my last memory of Grandma in the house to be one of her celebrating Christmas, not one of her lifeless and gone."

Mary Alice couldn't suppress a sob. She quickly regained herself. "I think that's better too. Let me know when you're coming, and I'll meet the plane. We'll manage, we will."

I wasn't sure if she said that for my benefit or hers. "We" had always meant Mary Alice and Violet, and it would be hard to think otherwise. Then it occurred to me that for Mary Alice, the last memory she would have of her friend would, in fact, be "lifeless and gone" in the house that was Mary Alice's second home. I immediately regretted my choice of words. Later, Mary Alice assured me that she didn't experience what I had said as uncaring or callous. I had simply said aloud what she felt, and for her there was a closure in seeing Vi at final rest. This hopeful matter-of-factness was something that I envied and could only grow into with time. Perhaps it was reflective of her common-sense upbringing in Cape Breton.

I did end up getting to Victoria that day. All the decision-making with Mary Alice is a bit of a blur now. There was a funeral and a reception, with the old-timers of Orkney Street turning out in force to pay their respects—at least those who were still mobile. In time I formally inherited Shady Shingles, with Mary Alice managing things until I moved permanently. It took a couple of months to finish up in Saskatoon. Angus was disappointed that I gave my notice, but I left with his blessing, "Be gaene with ye and com' bak when you cum to y'r senses."

I think he was misty eyed, but it could have been just the piercing cold of a prairie wind in March. I had always intended to go back, but a couple years after his retirement, he died of a virulent lung cancer. Like many men of his generation, Angus didn't work for a living—he lived for his work. If retirement meant not being able to work anymore, his incentive for living was considerably lessened, and the decades' accumulation of various kinds of construction dust in his respiratory system did the rest. Some people make a seamless transition to retirement, and others find it an alien experience. Angus belonged to the latter group, and perhaps the illness simply ended his exile. If we live life at many levels, then it follows that we die at many levels too. Part of our fate is chosen, and part of it just is.

A car door slamming outside woke me from my musing about Christmas past, Grandma and Mary Alice and Angus, and the frailty of living. My remaining coffee had gone cold, and the noonday sun was streaming into Captain's cage. He stirred from his nap and stretched first one wing and then the other. This was a prelude not to flying somewhere but warming up for some serious lunch.

If you don't move from that chair, they are going to come and compost you. Is any of that shortbread left? How about some turkey bone?

Other life forms began to stir. Pierre emerged from his lair, also in search of lunch. "Salut, Monsieur Stanley. I see in the frigo that you have leftover Christmas dinner, and dat's a miracle because yesterday der was no Christmas dinner left after we finished."

The point of Pierre's culinary observation was not lost on me. "Go ahead, Pierre. Mary Alice was here with some Christmas leftovers. Just leave some turkey bones for Captain."

"You mean the parrot, he can also break da big turkey bones? I guess da turkey is not like real family for him."

Captain had heard the words "turkey bones," and he began dancing excitedly on his perch. The moral dilemma of eating poultry bones does not weigh heavily on Captain. Like most birds, he's an omnivore. And the marrow inside the bones is definitely worth extricating if one has a lower mandible shaped like a scoop. I warmed a turkey bone in the microwave and surrendered it to Captain, who could barely contain himself. The shortbread seemed to be forgotten as his nibs crunched the turkey bone and scraped clean the nutritious marrow. It's actually a little creepy to realize I own a parrot who could be Dracula's understudy.

Humans throw away the best part of whatever this was. Their loss is my gain. Is there any more where that came from?

Pierre found enough leftovers to keep body and soul together. Then he headed off to the garage to work on another automotive project. I too raided the leftovers from the meal that never existed, at least at Shady Shingles. My central creed about the holiday season had been confirmed once more, i.e., the best thing about Christmas is leftovers. Usually, I could stretch them out to New Year's Eve, but Pierre and Captain were eating into my reserves. I resolved to take a harder line on unauthorized mooching.

The notion of unrealized resolutions sparked something in my memory. We were coming up on New Year's, and the previous New Year's I had resolved to walk vigorously, three times a week. Somehow that resolve had slipped downward a notch to three times a year. And I hadn't done the third walk yet. I bundled up and headed out.

Unlike in most of Canada, walking outside in Victoria is not a life-threatening activity in December. Bundling up consists of donning a light jacket or sweater and carrying an umbrella. Serious rain is a rarity in Victoria, but the bouts of falling mist can convince you it's cold. Winter storms are mostly wind, and umbrellas get mangled quickly, so it's wise to leave your good one at home. I have had a good umbrella standing by the door for the past twenty-five years.

Like many Victorians on Boxing Day, I made it to the Dallas Road Waterfront Trail. The paved trail beside Dallas Road seems innocuous, although power walkers are a bit much as they speed by mere mortals like me. They are not to be outdone by the Nordic walkers, who swing their ski poles deftly and threaten to skewer any slowpokes who get in their way.

It was a bit of a surprise that Dallas Road should be so populated on Boxing Day. Decent folk should have been deluging the malls, returning awful Christmas sweaters and buying up left-over holiday kitsch. Perhaps the import of the day had become diluted once Boxing Day sales morphed into Boxing Week sales. On the other hand, jogging along Dallas Road in pursuit of one's greyhound could be peremptory training for a later assault on the mall. Victorians' unquenchable commitment to outdoor exercise must have some goal other than pure fitness. After an entire day in close proximity to one's immediate relatives, an exodus to the Great Outdoors is quite understandable, if not essential. For the same reason, pubs do a roaring business on Boxing Day. We love our families . . . in limited doses.

All seemed to be going tolerably well until I had to stop for a bit of a coughing fit. As a prairie boy, I was sure the damp sea air rubbed me the wrong way. Or maybe one had to engage in this walking foolishness more than three times a year to get into shape. That being said, a similar thing was beginning to happen when I was at home listening to the TV news. There I attributed it to listening to the prime minister's latest pronouncement on public policy. But mainly the coughing arose when I was climbing stairs. This aging thing is a bit of a nuisance at times. The prime minister should do something about it. For my part, I resolve to age less next year. As with fervent election promises, you can take that resolution with a grain of salt. Actually, I only think of aging when we get to the dark remnants of December.

Year's end is not life's end but a hiatus to put things in perspective for the year to come. At least that's how it is in the world of Shady Shingles, where nothing really changes. I like a world where nothing really changes. Perhaps Grandma Vi thought that too. But such a world is not really an option. What is permanent is only permanent until it's not. That realization would come soon enough in the new year.

11
Seeking Spiritual Solace

HOLIDAYS END, AND reality returns. It's a fact of life. With the passing of New Year's, two of my three tenants remained. Pierre, of course, was not bound by the rhythm of the school year, and perhaps even less so by the bounds of consumer laws. More on that shortly. Brian had his second term to get through and didn't have enough money to move elsewhere unless he took on a substantial part-time job. Roomers aspire to be able to rent an apartment, so I did not begrudge the lad his unfulfilled fantasy. The one who flew the coop was Katrina. She returned on the afternoon following New Year's Day. She had discovered true love over the Christmas break and decided to move in with a jock from the university hockey team. Sometimes the logical ones are not so logical, especially when hormones are involved. I am, of course, speaking of other people.

"Dimitry has biceps like iron tree, and his grandmother was born in East Prussia," was her cryptic summary of his credentials. I have lived long enough to realize I can't refute such logic when someone has succumbed to primal instinct. And Dimitry sounded pretty primal. Lest I think it was some frivolous whim, Katrina elaborated with trembling passion. "My heart beats for him, and we are moving to Moose Jaw when this term is over. We live with his family, and we do summer job there. It is settled."

Smart move that he didn't invite her home for Christmas. I suspect the geographic location of Moose Jaw was not one of the romantic details shared by the allegedly gallant Dimitry. Introducing her to that part of the world in December might put a chill on a heated romance, if you get my drift. Moose Jaw in July would be enough of a shock. Since I had been down that road before with tenants, it did not shock me that Katrina was chucking common sense and heading off with her imagined Prince Charming. It was a corollary of, "The bigger they are, the harder they fall." And falling in love can as unpredictable a fall as any other.

Purely out of concern for Katrina's welfare, with only a passing thought to the loss of January's rent, I offered one last bon mot. "Katrina, my dear, you are, of course, free to do as your heart demands. I would only ask as one last courtesy that you say goodbye properly to Mary Alice. She will certainly want you to come for tea."

Captain cocked his head and stared intently at Katrina. *You have just been lured into the spider's web, my German princess. Beware the terrible tyrant who dwells so near. Your heart is about to be crushed.*

"Of course. It is polite thing to thank the kind Mary Alice for hospitality to me. I shall do it now." Katrina marched purposefully out the front door, suitably oblivious to what awaited her.

While I couldn't be sure that Mary Alice would change her mind, Katrina would at the very least have the benefit of Mary Alice's matronly experience in matters of love. If anyone can shatter's one illusions about romance, Mary Alice is the one to administer the coup de grace. I marvelled that her daughter ever got married, given Mary Alice's dark assessment of potential suitors. This attitude probably arose when her husband died. No one else could come close to replacing him. Apparently, the widow Macdonald, alias the Dowager Empress, had ardent suitors, but all of them failed the grade miserably. I was never quite bold enough to ask Mary Alice the particulars. The urge for self-preservation sometimes makes one discreet. I can only infer that Mary Alice was a woman of the world. Therefore, I have not questioned her credentials when she offers bits of sage advice on the subject of romance. I could certainly predict the tone of the conversation that Mary

Alice would have with Katrina. Better that such advice came from a forceful matron than a bumbling gay bachelor. Some situations call for stormtroopers rather than Walmart greeters.

After Katrina trekked next door, I bided my time. I wasn't privy to the visit, but after half an hour, Katrina returned. By her determined stride, I knew her mind had not been changed.

"The farewell has happened. Mary Alice is kind grandmother, but she does not know about true love." Her voice trembled audibly, and I could see the tea visit had made an impact. In short order, Katrina had packed her things. She hadn't actually given proper notice about her rent, but as a student, I knew she had a limited budget. In any case, she would likely know enough hardship in this new venture, so I wouldn't add to her burdens. We left it that I would only demand the month's rent if I couldn't find an immediate replacement.

A horn blasted from the street. It was Dimitry in his Ford Bronco, announcing the cavalry's arrival. Katrina exited with her rolling suitcase, lifting it down the steps rather than bouncing it. There is something to be said for athletic tenants who are polite. The relationship must have been serious, because she allowed Dimitry to hoist her portable home into the back of the truck. And off they went to Camelot—or at least someplace where they could afford to rent an apartment together. I braced myself for round two.

Captain went into his Mary Alice alert pose. Even I could hear her porch board creak as she came out of her house and crossed over to our front steps. Captain looked fully awake. *This is going to be good. Stanley is in for it now. Batten down the hatches.*

Mary Alice looked a little more flushed than usual. She put her hands on her hips and stood directly in front of me with a steely expression that exceeded even her ordinary demeanor. That is saying something. "Well, Stanley. What have you got to say for yourself? Did you just let her leave?"

"Ah, Mary Alice, my sweet. She is smitten with what's-his-name, and once smitten, how do you make a lovebird come down to earth?"

"That's drivel, Stanley, and you know it!" Mary Alice had built up a head of steam. The veins in her neck were distended, and her brow was deeply furrowed.

"That may be true, but I'm her landlord, not her father. And I suspect a father has even less clout than a landlord in such things. I sent her over to you in the hope that you could exert some motherly concern." I emphasized the "you." The best defence is a good offence.

Captain appeared to be choking as he staggered to his water dish. One would almost think the notion of Mary Alice and motherly concern in the same sentence was too much for him. Of course, parrots don't understand English, so I'm sure his apparent drama was purely coincidental. Probably a millet seed went down the wrong way. He has always been a bit of a drama queen as well as a fast eater.

Mary Alice predicted imminent disaster, and she cautioned me accordingly. "Do not advertise the room yet. Katrina will soon be back. The girl has simply fallen in lust. She will come to her senses soon, and then she'll need her old room again."

I couldn't disagree with the predicted trajectory of the relationship, but I would be minus the rent for the immediate future. Jerome Fairchild at the bank only knew the immediate present, never mind the immediate future. My prayers about a September snow in Calgary had been answered, and I did indeed get enough sales from my snowball launcher to pacify Jerome. But my present-day solvency depended on finding a new tenant immediately. And maybe a good snowfall in Miami.

"She seemed pretty definite, Mary Alice. I can't count on her falling out of love with the hockey player before tomorrow. I'll list the room, and if she does turn up later, there's still an unused bedroom or two on the third floor."

"Well, you might be right. You're not often right, but you can't strike out all the time. Do as you please, but I think you should wait." Mary Alice had shared her wisdom, in her usual objective manner. If I really did end up having to rent a third-floor room, I would have to move some of my projects out. It wouldn't be necessary to consider that drastic measure unless the unlikely became certain. Squirrels and other uninvited rodents had also been known to visit the third floor, and rent-paying tenants might not appreciate sharing with fuzzy-tailed rats—and the other kind. We do have some standards at Shady Shingles, albeit not many. Mary Alice made her way out as abruptly as she had arrived, and I was left to my own devices.

Survived another one. You got off lightly. Now go somewhere and let the parrot nap. Awk. Captain settled on to his nap perch, keeping one eye open just in case a stray peanut might come his way.

The more pressing matter at hand was my need to go through the tedious process of finding a new tenant. I recalled Liam's lecture on the obsolescence of putting an ad in the classifieds section of the paper, not to mention the cost. Probably my best bet would be the online services of Used Victoria or Kijiji. The local universities and colleges also had a room and suite listing service for their students, but prospective landlords who wanted to list had to pay the institutions a fee. These hotbeds of socialist revolution certainly revert to capitalist exploitation when it comes to the bottom line. One must pay for the privilege of rescuing student waifs from a state of imminent homelessness.

The decision of which rental strategy to pursue seemed too daunting. It was time for a religious pilgrimage, so that I could clear my head. The two potential sites were the labyrinth at the Anglican cathedral or my usual seat at the Piddling Poodle, known more commonly by locals as the Piddler. Said establishment is only a couple of blocks from Shady Shingles, whereas the cathedral is at the summit of a hill half a mile away. Since my need for spiritual clarity was immediate, I chose the closer shrine.

Much wisdom can be gleaned at the Piddler. And the more one gleans, the greater the desire to piddle. Mary Alice disapproved of my treks there, which, of course, made it an even more coveted spiritual haven. The Piddler's dark wood decor is something between an English pub and a sports bar. The main draw of the establishment, aside from its location, is the fact it has happy hour in the late afternoon. Various craft beers are offered, each with its own loyal following. I am loyal to whichever draft is today's special. This strategy rarely disappoints.

Many prayers are actually said in the sanctuary of the Piddler, especially for those watching the Canucks lose on the large screen mounted above the bar. My personal theory is that more prayers are said in pubs than in churches. Whether more prayers uttered in pubs get listened to by Someone is open to conjecture. Certainly, the bartender gets to hear more confessions than the Rev. Cromdale at St. Mathew's. I know this because the vicar is a Piddler regular.

I want it known that I don't actually own the third stool from the left at the bar. It's just that other locals know the third stool is the McFadden stool, and no one else sits there. If a stranger mistakenly parks on it during my usual hour of oblation, they are politely told, "That's Stanley's spot. He'll be here shortly." Traditions are not voted on; they just happen and then get enshrined.

In Victoria, one of the last bastions of the British Empire, people take their traditions seriously. Ask anyone in the local chapter of the Monarchist League of Canada. Alternatively, check out the white-clad senior athletes in the Pacific Lawn Bowling Club of Victoria. The tweedy folks at the Union Club can be assumed to be champions of tradition as well. The Empress Hotel also peddles tradition; in particular, high tea is an afternoon offering that will set you back $63 to $93, depending on how much you want to splurge in the high season. No one said tradition was cheap. Not quite in the same league of tradition is the McFadden stool at the Piddler. For the price of a brew or two, I have my tradition reserved. No dress code is required but the management is partial to cash. BC means "bring cash," so it's a provincial expectation, if not an obligation, that one tips suitably, in cash. Just saying. Piddler staff like people to follow the provincial standard in this regard. They tend to be an educated lot who are doing what they are doing because no one will pay them to do what they have studied to do. Anthropologists, Anglo-Saxon ornithologists, and deconstructionist philosophy majors abound. Scholars in a consumer society get used to humiliation and abject poverty. Actors who are moonlighting in order to eat also don the Piddler apron. Said accessory sports a large sign with a poodle in pose, if you get my drift. Both the aprons and those who wear them are unmistakable features at the Piddler.

Conrad is also one of the fixed features of our local shrine to the barley sandwich. He arrives at 3:42 p.m. each afternoon, give or take a nanosecond. His punctuality arises more from his mode of transport than personal discipline. Conrad catches a transit bus that wends its way through our neighbourhood and deposits him a half block from the Piddler's front door. On good days he eventually finds his way back to the front door and stands on the opposite side of the street to catch the last bus home before that route ceases for the day. On more fluid days, the front door is beyond his navigation skills, and Rudy, the bartender, calls Conrad's beloved wife, Cora, to come and get him. This sometimes requires considerable persuasion, but that's how bartenders and suicide intervention counsellors earn their keep.

If you happen to be a passenger on the mid-afternoon run of the #8 bus, you might not suspect that Conrad is a veteran of the North African campaign bound for a new field of battle at the Piddler. Usually, he never gets around to mentioning which side he was on, although his Yorkshire accent is a bit of a giveaway. Conrad is somewhere north of ninety, and he walks with a limp on his left side. The extra weight around his midsection does nothing to help his balance, so the bus "kneels" for him to get on. Victoria prides itself on its kneeling buses. Only buses and Anglicans kneel in Victoria. Conrad is a lapsed Catholic and is not obliged to kneel, but he still crosses himself when the bus goes by the Church of Truth and Sublime Consciousness. This is only a nominal deference, as his true loyalty is to the Fellowship of the Malt Brew. There are many communicants in this fellowship, who gather most faithfully for service at the Piddling Poodle. Their attendance at the esteemed establishment occurs with considerably greater frequency than their attendance at any of Victoria's churches. I count myself among them.

All of this is by way saying that when I arrived at the Piddler at 3:45 p.m., I knew that Conrad would be in his assigned pew. This is more than a figure of speech, because churches in Victoria seem to be unloading pews like cordwood, and some of them have appropriately ended up in pubs. If a place is going to be a shrine for spiritual oblations, it may as well look like a shrine. Somehow, the pews fit right in. People complain about how uncomfortable pews are at church, but after a few brews at the Piddler, no one complains about anything.

Conrad looked a tad more red-faced than usual, and his disorderly strands of white hair did nothing to conceal his much-receded hairline. His hands are large and calloused from his many years as a stone mason. As he grasped his pint of Rickard's Red, the strength in those hands was still evident. "Stanley, my friend, how goes the war?"

I am never sure if Conrad is making an oblique reference to my relationship with Mary Alice or whether this is intended as a general greeting with no insinuation in particular. Alternatively, he may have forgotten that WWII ended some time ago.

"Well, Conrad, I need some more recruits, and the enemy is planning an invasion. Aside from that, life is passably fair." There is no need to burden people with cheeriness, especially at a pub where people come to enjoy being depressed.

"I see. You probably need to throw some money at that Jerome fellow at the bank, and you haven't filled your quota of tenants yet." For someone who never made field marshal, Conrad can size up a battlefield situation quickly.

"How do I get myself into these situations, Conrad? I should just sell the place and go pick grapes in the Okanagan. Do you ever think of just chucking it all and leaving?" Admittedly, that was less than a fully developed business plan, but it seemed appropriate for what I felt at the moment. It's always compelling to think that life must be less messed up someplace else, and that's where one should be.

Conrad leaned back and slowly brought his nearly full glass up to his lips, looking away pensively as he did. The man knows how to give the appearance of listening, even if he's just blanked out. Men rarely have a knack for this sort of thing. In contrast, women value good listeners and are willing to punish those who are not, particularly if they happen to be married to them. Conrad is a veteran of both strategic warfare and marriage. These are complementary achievements, at least according to my limited understanding of the subject.

"Stanley, you're too hard on yourself. You just need to partake of some spiritual refreshment and avoid all that health food. You are no more mediocre that the rest of the local rabble, and they get along fine. That's the way life is. You just have to get along."

"But Conrad, how am I supposed to get along with Mary Alice Macdonald?" When whining, one may as well go for the top prize.

"Stanley, my boy, I give advice; I don't dispense miracles. Attila the Hen is not one to be trifled with, but she is mortal, and her reign will someday cease." Conrad rewarded himself with an extra-long sip of barley elixir. Perhaps without intending it, my sage companion had hit on an insight that changed my perspective. I had always considered Mary Alice to be immutable. In reality, she would be gone someday, and I would miss her. Having Mary Alice scrutinize a new tenant could be tedious, but in the big picture, she was an anchor in my disorderly world.

"What do you think happens when we die, Conrad? Do we go somewhere, or do we just stop ticking and get thrown out, like one of those expired discount coupons for A&W?"

Conrad set down his glass. His shaggy brows wrinkled, and he turned to face me directly. "How the hell should I know? We're here, and then we're not here. It's complicated enough knowing what to do while we're here without worrying about what happens when we're not. What got you onto this anyway?"

"I'm not sure. It's just that when I get one thing solved, two more things always seem to come up. And there's never any end to it. Sometimes I wonder if it all leads to anything or if there's any purpose to what we do. Does Shady Shingles matter? Does any of it matter?"

Susanne, the server, arrived on the scene, overhearing my soliloquy. "Stanley, are you having one of your bouts of existential angst again?" Susanne is a Jean Paul Sartre major and knows all about existential angst. At least she knows about it if it happens in a book or on the stage of the local community theatre.

"Maybe that's what you call it. Don't you wonder sometimes about life and death and all this stuff in between?" It seemed better to direct my query to her than to Conrad. It also seemed like a good idea to renew my supply of spiritual succour. "And while you think about it, a pint of Porter's, if you please."

"Stanley, I don't get paid enough to wonder about the meaning of life. I just live it. You might consider doing the same. Be right back with your suds." Susanne is pretty concise for an existentialist major. Conrad looked relieved that Susanne had rescued him from the void, at least temporarily. He also believes that the best defence is a good offence.

"And Stanley, my man, what do you think it's all about? Shouldn't you leave some questions to God?"

When in doubt, bring up God. People who believe in God often don't have much tolerance for doubt. And I believe in doubt. "Mary Alice believes that God takes care of everything and that we just have to trust and believe. I guess good Catholics are supposed to be that way. But I have too much doubt to accept that there's a god in charge of everything. Certainly, Shady Shingles has slid off God's radar, if God exists." I can sound remarkably sure about things that I don't even think I have an opinion on. Doubters are good about sounding sure because we don't like other people doubting our doubting.

Conrad had one of his mystical moments and stared off into space. The stance implies either someone deep in thought or someone who is getting a head start on dementia and doing a credible job of attaining it. Susanne arrived with the next round of spiritual medicine, which seemed to jar Conrad back into the land of the living. There's nothing like a full pint to rejuvenate a fatigued philosopher.

"Well, I guess you can't leave the big question with someone who you don't believe exists. That's the beauty of God. You don't want to go getting too religious, but if you leave a place for God, there's always the possibility it makes a difference. And we'd have a tough time dreaming up some new cuss words if we didn't have the Lord's name to take in vain." As an ex-army man, Conrad was rather well-informed about such things.

Not one to give up on a quest too quickly, especially when fortified with a new pint of ale, I decided to go for broke. "What about life after death? Where do we go when we die?" Given Conrad's age, it seemed to me that he may already have given a passing thought to what comes next.

"Stanley, I look forward to meeting St. Peter when the time is right. Seems like heaven might be a good place to go, considering the alternatives. But if it's more fun at the other place, and all my friends are there, then I guess that's where I'd rather be. What about you? Where do you think you're going?"

"I kind of think it would be OK for me just to decay into the earth. We are made with earthy stuff, so going back to be with the earth sounds complete. I think there's only a me when I have a living body, and then when there's no living body, I don't need to be anymore. I just become one with the soil, and that soil nurtures new life in some form or other."

Conrad's pastoral response came quickly. "You sound like you look forward to becoming fertilizer for somebody's geraniums someday. Don't think you'll found a new religion on that one, but different strokes for different blokes. Me, I hope God has a sense of humour and a short memory. That would improve my odds."

I began to realize that perhaps Conrad was not a deep well to plumb on the subject of God, life after death, or the meaning of life. Or maybe he had distilled it all, and his outlook only appeared simplistic. The Piddler is a great scholastic centre for collecting people's views on religion, politics, and what to do with a bumper crop of zucchini. That's good, because in British California, there is no shortage of religions, New Age movements, and quasi-spiritual therapies from which to choose. The range of choice seems to parallel the spectrum of microbreweries that have sprung up. At the Piddler, customers can partake of a broad selection of suds or spiritual enlightenment, as long as they're willing to pay for the one and not be too discerning about the other.

When dialogue hits a dead end, it's always a good strategy to ask someone about their health or their family. You may not be interested in either one, but it's a guaranteed strategy to kick-start a conversation. "Conrad, how goes it with the ever-loving wife and your devoted offspring?" You may infer a certain degree of irony on my part.

"You're a cruel one, Stanley. The missus is still out to reform me, and she has the stamina of a Viking. I'm going home to a supper of organic kale and lentils. We'll probably have to go on a route march after supper. Be thankful, lad. Be thankful you're not married to a demented nutritionist."

People like to believe their suffering is incomparable, and it doesn't do for anyone else to minimize it. "Ah, Conrad, this is your cross to bear, and there must be no one who has ever borne so much." Quite probably that was Cora's lament about her sad matrimonial choice. It's good not to cross-reference these things, especially if you do it aloud in the presence of one of the self-pitying parties. Misery loves company, as long as you don't try to one-up them on misery.

"And do you want to hear more? The worst is yet to come." This was, of course, a rhetorical question. No need to answer. Regardless of how much I was actually open to hearing, I was going to get an earful of aggrieved despair. Porter's goes down well with aggrieved despair, so I took a long therapeutic sip from my fast-diminishing supply.

"My granddaughter has arrived in town with her girlfriend, looking for a place to stay. They're camping on our living-room floor for the moment. With three women in our meagre apartment, I may never see the inside of the bathroom again."

Conrad can tend toward the melodramatic, so sometimes it's necessary to parse his laments if I want to get a picture close to reality. "Are they just here for a visit, or are they actually moving in?" Before I dole out any sympathy, I like to know how much is warranted. I am always careful to leave a sufficient supply for myself, valiantly keeping Shady Shingles afloat with only Mary Alice to dispense sympathy. In other words, I am used to sympathy being in short supply.

"I fear the worst, Stanley. Melody is here to start her first year of medical school, and my granddaughter, Allison, is taking up carpentry at the trades college. They're not passing through, and they don't have enough money to get their own place. Cora says we can't turn them away because they're family." Conrad's tone was one of fatigued resignation. The family card is a hard one to trump; indeed, I could imagine him making longer visits at the Piddler if this living arrangement continued. Then again, one man's misfortune is another man's opportunity. Capitalizing on human misery is a time-honoured occupation for both Revenue Canada and cash-strapped landlords. Since I fit one of those categories, the little wheels in my top storey began to turn.

"Don't get your hopes up, my friend, but I might be able to help you out. It just so happens that my largest rental room just became vacant. I don't usually rent to couples, but for a suitably higher rent, I could perhaps make the room available to Melody and Allison. They would have access to the kitchen. And if they need to save money, Shady Shingles is located midway between the university and the trade school; they would be in biking or bus distance of either one." Of course, I meant it was within walking distance for them, not yours truly. If you throw a drowning person a life preserver when there's no other flotation device in sight, they generally thank you for it. A landlord is someone who asks the victims if they are willing to buy the life preserver before he selflessly throws it. It's good to have clarity around one's vocation. Conrad was all too willing to be an accomplice in my exploitation strategy.

"Would you do that, Stanley? Would you save the sanity of a poor war veteran who needs some peace of mind in his dying years? Thank you, my boy! Thank you! I can't speak for the girls, of course, but I'll put your offer to them as soon as the opportunity presents itself."

"I have just one strategic request, Conrad. Knowing my besieged situation as you do, you might help the situation along if you got Cora to suggest to Mary Alice that the girls are in desperate need of rescuing. You are in desperate need of getting rid of them, but let's not split hairs. Cora could ask Mary Alice if she knows of a place where the girls might go. It wouldn't hurt to mention that your granddaughter is Catholic."

Conrad furrowed his brow as he struggled to follow the battle plan. "But Stanley, I don't know at all if the girl is Catholic. Cora and Mary Alice go to the same parish. Our daughter in Penticton goes occasionally, but I don't know about Allison. She's one of those free-thinker sorts."

"Trust me on this one, Conrad. The girl is Catholic. Mary Alice will be much more likely to help if she thinks she's rescuing an innocent young Catholic girl in distress. And if she's not Catholic, tell her to keep it under her hat. Or her construction helmet. Or whatever. While you're at it, a Catholic girlfriend wouldn't hurt either."

"You've missed your calling, Stanley. You should be a strategist for the prime minister in the next election. But unless I head home soon, I'll be excommunicated and unfed."

I believe my eloquence and my colleague's Rickard's Red were instrumental in turning the tide of despair into profitable hope, more so for me than for Conrad. At the word "home," he seemed to remember it was time to catch the last bus home before supper. "It's getting late. Cora will be waiting."

Seniors in Victoria are rarely arrested in late-night crime waves, because they don't go out after seven o'clock unless something is being offered for free. Conrad remained true to his demographic. He rose unsteadily and set course for the door. Lest you feel too sorry for him, I should point out that he left me stuck with the bill. This is an overhead cost that sometimes arises in exploiting vulnerable seniors. They know how to stick people with the bill in a way that looks innocuous and unintentional. This is an art form in Victoria that I have yet to perfect.

All in all, my pilgrimage to the Piddler was spiritually fulfilling indeed. Little did I realize what momentous events would follow my serendipitous introduction to two young women who came to me by a chance conversation at the pub. Or is this what Providence looks like? In time I would learn that it was perhaps Providence, helped along by a meddlesome parrot.

12
The Long Arm of the Law and Celtic Providence

ALTHOUGH I KICKED myself for being bested for the bill by wily Conrad, I consoled myself with the prospect of levelling the playing field at our next pilgrimage to the Piddler. The more immediate challenge was to ensure my prospective new tenants could pay the rent. There was also the little matter of having them vetted by Mary Alice in such a way that their arrival did not look like a fait accompli. I have not necessarily cited these two considerations in their order of difficulty.

When faced with the potential disapproval of a mighty matriarch, it is always better to choose a circuitous path to victory than a direct and valiant path to defeat. This is an insight that one might think came from Margaret Thatcher's husband. He probably would not have disagreed, but my experience with Mary Alice has been sufficient to drive home the point. In other words, I had no intention of telling her that I had virtually promised the vacant room to strangers who had not run the gauntlet of a Mary Alice tea party. However, if Cora asked Mary Alice to use her influence in finding shelter for her Catholic granddaughter, I would be home free. We could leave the matter of Melody's confessional integrity until later.

Since my mission was at least partially accomplished, I parted with the obligatory shekels and made my way back to Shady Shingles. When I got in, Pierre had already left for his "night shift."

That was a reasonably safe conclusion, as the fridge was minus any leftovers, and the sink had dishes rinsed but not actually washed. Both were Pierre's unmistakable trademarks. At least he remembered to lock the door.

Captain was waiting up for me. He was on his night perch but had not yet lowered his skirt feathers over his feet. This is the parrot equivalent of putting on pajamas. If he thinks I might be bringing back a crust of pizza or some other morsel, he holds off on the final stages of sleep preparation. So as not to disappoint him totally, I padded to the kitchen and got a snippet of millet spray. The tiny seeds clustered along a dried-out stem seem like a minimal reward for a bird as big as a parrot; nevertheless, Captain always displays enthusiasm when he notices me coming with a millet spray. Enthusiasm is not hard to spot as he swings his head vigorously in a figure eight before taking the millet spray from me. Then he nibbles the millet daintily, as if he were eating popcorn. The doctor says I should be eating a high-fibre diet like Captain's. My rationale is that I would be depriving a parrot of his favourite food if I ate all the high fibre in the house. Therefore, I make the supreme sacrifice, eating the red meat and the dairy and leaving the whole-grain foods for Captain. It's the least I can do for him.

I smell beer on your breath, you lush. How about bringing home some of that high-fibre beer for a guy? And when will the pizza drought end? It's been over a week now. This millet crap must set you back ten cents a week. Maybe if I eat it all there won't be any left to shove at me next time.

After covering Captain for the night, I settled down in my recliner chair to catch the early evening news on TV. I wouldn't want to fall behind in the latest inventory of tragedy and disaster in the world.

My chair, although worse for wear, is a great source of comfort. From such a throne I can review the events of the day and dispense my judgments upon the world scene. The prime minister is a frequent but, no doubt, unappreciative recipient of my advice. We have not been on speaking terms for some time. I hope he notices the slight. I have spoken at him through the TV, but I have never had the pleasure of not speaking to him in person. Long may it be so.

Another person whom I don't offer advice to is Mary Alice. Her ladyship would claim to have an open mind for all reasonable and worthy advice. Alas, this is a benevolence that exists more in theory than in practice. Offering advice to Mary Alice is like offering rare steak to a militant vegetarian—you might have a choice morsel to share, but the response will not be one of adoring gratitude. With this insight in mind, I hoped Conrad would remember to suggest to Cora that she use her good graces on Mary Alice regarding the two girls. Cora and Mary Alice have a chin wag at least once a day, so I would soon know if Providence was going to shine on me.

I might have nodded off. The doorbell rang abruptly. Mary Alice never rings the doorbell, so it seemed necessary to get up and see who it was. Before I reached the outer porch door, I saw it was one of Victoria's finest—a uniformed constable. I opened the door and invited him to step in.

"My name is Constable Brewster. Are you Mr. S. McFadden, landlord of one Pierre Lafontaine?" His tone was matter-of-fact, and he certainly couldn't be accused of wasting my time with small talk. They must turn out twentysomethings that way at the police factory.

Captain was watching us through the front window that faced into the porch. *Stanley's going to the slammer. Stanley's going to the slammer. Who's gonna feed the parrot? Awk!*

"Yes to both of your questions. And why would you need to know this?" Either Pierre had come to an unfortunate end, and I was being notified as a first step toward finding his next of kin, or he was being investigated for something, and I was a person of interest. In either case, it seemed like a good idea to be cool, calm, and collected—an art I had perfected in many interviews with Jerome at the bank.

"I would like to speak with Mr. Lafontaine, if he is here now."

"Actually, he works evenings and doesn't usually come back until quite late. He's not here at the moment." Despite my attempts at calmness, it seemed to me that I sounded like an accomplice in a bank robbery. If the constable thought so, he didn't let on.

"How long have you known Mr. Lafontaine? And how does he make his living?" He too could play this matter-of-fact game pretty well, revealing nothing in his rather mechanical voice.

"Pierre became my tenant about five months ago. I believe his work is automotive retail of some kind."

"Of some kind? Could you be a bit more precise, please." His inflected tone went from neutral to slightly annoyed. I could feel an interrogation light bearing down on me while I was strapped into a hard, straight-back chair.

"Uh, well, I never exactly asked him. He has always paid his rent on time and in cash. I believe he mentioned Sam's Garage, three blocks that way." I pointed in the general direction of said establishment.

"I've heard of the place. The owner is someone known to us." The way he said it sounded ominous. If someone is "known" to the police, it doesn't usually mean the person is on their Christmas card list.

"Is something wrong? Should I be concerned about having Pierre in my house as a tenant?" It never hurts to play the vulnerable senior citizen card if there is any possibility of guilt by association.

"I'll be visiting Mr. Lafontaine shortly. We have no reason to believe he is a threat to your safety. However, if he ever appears to be leaving town on short notice, we would appreciate it if you let us know." He gave me his card and bid a perfunctory farewell before returning to his cruiser. I inferred that some of Pierre's customers were unhappy with a purchase that turned out to be less of a bargain than they thought. Pierre has quite the gilded tongue, but I wondered if he would be able to talk his way out of an interrogation by steely Constable Brewster. Oh, to be a fly on the wall.

I would have returned to the evening TV news, but I saw that Captain had adopted his Mary Alice pose. A marked police car in front of the house would hardly have escaped my guardian angel's eagle eye. I only made a few steps toward the kitchen before Mary Alice was through the front door and heading my way.

"Stanley, what have you been up to? Why are the police coming here at this hour? What was that all about?" Mary Alice believes patience is highly overrated.

"I was just on my way to make some tea. Would you like some?" In Victoria, the first step in dealing with any crisis, no matter the magnitude, is to make tea. The big earthquake can come, but as long as we are able to make tea, it will be manageable. Mary Alice is steeped in this culture, if you'll excuse the pun. So, she could hardly refuse my diversion. And it would be double-strength chamomile with a shot of gin, for its calming effect. I recommend it with or without the chamomile.

"You're stalling, Stanley. What was that policeman doing here?" Mary Alice was not easily put off. More than anything, a matriarch does not tolerate unauthorized intrusions into her realm. Neither should the reputation of her realm be besmirched by any appearance of impropriety.

"It was nothing, really. The nice young man just wanted to know where he could find Pierre."

"Just what I thought. You didn't let me have tea with that fellow, and look what you've gotten yourself into. He could be an axe murderer, for all we know." Mary Alice could not be accused of being a Pollyanna; indeed, she is not inclined to overstate people's virtue. I nodded at the appropriate intervals as she listed off her suspicions about Pierre's character. By then the tea had steeped and the soothing gin with it. Grandma McFadden did not leave many of her recipes with me, but she thought it advisable to share this one in her "Stanley Box." Perhaps this was the secret to how she and Mary Alice had forged such a compatible friendship over the eons. Smart lady. I poured the tea and prayed I had used a not-too-discernible amount of gin.

"Here you go, Mary Alice, my sweet. I'm starting to get this boiled water thing down pat. See what you think." Being pitiful works sometimes as a distraction with matriarchs on the rampage.

It's the equivalent of throwing yourself on your sword, if you were a committed coward rather than a fearless warrior. I heartily recommend this survival strategy for others who are squeamish about the sight of their own blood.

"For heaven's sake, Stanley, this tea is a little strange. How long have you had it in the back of the cupboard?"

"I'm not quite sure. Uh . . . I think it was here when I moved in. Should I make something else?"

"No, I'll make do and drink it. A body shouldn't waste what the Good Lord has chosen to provide. Actually, it reminds me a bit of the tea that Vi used to make. Those were good times, they were."

Generally, suffering Catholics are in their element. And Mary Alice had already suffered through a half cup of my medicinal tea as an act of pure Christian charity. Now she was beginning to feel both Christian and medicated. I hoped the god I don't believe in wouldn't mind if I prayed for the efficacy of the medication more than I prayed for Christian virtue.

"A spot more tea, my dear?" I can be shamelessly saccharin if the situation calls for it. If Mary Alice sees through me and gives me a Celtic blast, then I know she has not had enough medication. But if she smiles ever so slightly and asks for more tea, I know she is not in her right mind, and I am almost home free. Drugging senior citizens into medicated conviviality is not politically correct, but it cannot be discounted by the ethically challenged, such as me.

"Why thank you, Stanley. Perhaps there's hope for you yet. I'll have that last wee drop, if you don't mind." I emptied the remainder of the teapot into her cup, since her existing reservoir of medicinal tea seemed to have evaporated remarkably quickly. The rugged features of Mary Alice's face began to relax, and I might have even detected a slight glow of Celtic warmth. I could easily imagine her stoking a peat fire in the centre of a thatch-roofed black house on an Outer Hebrides island in mid-nineteenth-century Scotland. Indeed, her Macdonald ancestors had left that Celtic land during the Highland Clearances and immigrated in the 1850s to Cape Breton.

It's ironic that marginalized crofters from Scotland ended up being part of the displacement of marginalized First Nations people, not only in Nova Scotia but also across the British colonies in North America. Generally, we are concerned to better our individual position without necessarily being aware of what role we play in the larger picture. Mary Alice's ancestors, like mine, were cogs in a much larger machine. Hers landed in Cape Breton, and mine were prairie sodbusters.

The cogs of the colonial machine certainly shaped Victoria, which retains many colonial traces in its present-day identity. We no longer have the actual colonial fort for which Fort Victoria was named, but we have coloured bricks along Government Street marking where the bastion and fort walls used to be. There is a lot of "used to be" in Victoria. Shady Shingles fits into that genre quite well. It used to be a boarding house, and I used to be young.

On the Victoria side of the Rockies, people can get away with a lot because what's on the other side does not matter that much. And inhabitants of Vancouver Island have simply carried this motto one step further in that what is on the other side of the Gulf of Georgia doesn't matter much either. Some might call this insularity because we live on an island, but locals simply know that God declared this piece of real estate to be the centre of the universe. The only injustice in all this is that not enough money from the mainland flows across the waters to fund us in the manner to which we would like to become accustomed. This is Politics 101 for British California, in case you're interested.

Part of the Vancouver Island status quo is complaining vigorously about the ineptitude of the provincial government, just as colonial Scots once protested indignantly about the autocracy of the Hudson's Bay Company. The more things change, the more they stay the same. Although a transplant from the prairies, I have assumed the mantle of aggrieved prophet in critiquing the shortcomings of not only the premier but also the prime minister of Canada and the mayor. One's wisdom should not be narrowly focused. Mary Alice has been the beneficiary of many such political lectures—usually over tea, following an interview with prospective tenants. I have noticed that all three topics have the effect of shortening her visit.

"Stanley, quit daydreaming. You look like you're off on one of your tangents. I need you to come back to earth, because we have a situation." Mary Alice has always had a knack for bursting my bubble. Generally, I do not like situations. They usually morph into scenarios that end up with me being on the losing end of something. Mary Alice's "situations" have the potential for wide-scale collateral damage.

"Pray tell, my dear, what kind of situation did you have in mind?" Feigned innocence is often a good strategic opening in confronting a crisis of unknown dimensions.

"A situation of some import has been brought to my attention by a person for whom I have the greatest respect. Cora has graciously offered a place to stay to her daughter and friend who have arrived in town to attend higher schooling. I know that Cora and her elderly husband, Conrad, do not have room for the poor dears, but they are too kind-hearted to tell the girls to move on. That little apartment is fine for Cora and Conrad, but we need to do something to help them regain their privacy."

"Oh my, that does sound unfortunate. Whatever did you have in mind, Mary Alice?"

Captain gave a muffled cough. *Attila the Hen is about to be plucked. This is too incredible to watch. Stanley has more raven in him than I thought.*

"Well, since you are short a tenant for the big room upstairs, and given that Cora's dear granddaughter is undoubtedly a fine Catholic girl, I'm sure she and her friend would be ideal tenants. They could hardly be worse than what you usually come up with." Mary Alice is not one to waste extravagant praise when evaluating my business acumen, so I ignored her barb. Nevertheless, she would expect me to defend my honour at least a little. I couldn't appear to give in too easily, or her suspicions might get raised. There is an art to true guile.

"This is so sudden, Mary Alice. What do we know about these girls? And it would mean having four tenants in the house, not just three. Think of the extra wear and tear on everything." I did my best to sound dubious.

"They wouldn't cause as much mess as that useless parrot, and you keep him around. Look at him now—the silly thing looks like he's trying to drown himself in his water dish."

Captain was indeed gurgling in his water dish, but he looked up suddenly when Mary Alice mentioned his name. *The old biddy has it in for me. Give her what she wants, and let's get this over with. If you keep talking, you're going to bungle this caper!*

"Well, against my better judgment, I guess we could offer them a place sight unseen. Should we invite them for tea, or have you already done the vetting?"

"Why, Stanley, my boy, you know I wouldn't presume to impose my own preference on you without consulting. But given how well we know Cora, it probably isn't necessary, and we should just offer the room." Mary Alice beamed triumphantly. The cause of decency and justice had triumphed once again. And humble servant that I am, who was I to question the wisdom of a Celtic matriarch on a crusade of mercy?

Mary Alice rose somewhat unsteadily to her feet, a sure sign that the royal audience was over. "It's getting late, and I must be more tired than I thought. I'll ring Cora first thing tomorrow and have her send the girls over to look at the room. You might give the place a vacuum, if you can spare a few moments between daydreams."

Mary Alice proceeded a little more carefully than usual toward the door, but I knew better than to offer my arm. It would never do for her to admit that she might need a helping hand. I followed her at a respectful distance until I was sure she made it through her side door. In that moment, I knew how Prince Phillip felt.

Sometimes the gods smile upon Shady Shingles, and sometimes it's better to manipulate fate a little because the gods are busy. I covered Captain and went to bed. Mission accomplished.

13
The Damsels Arrive

DAWN HAPPENED THE next day, as it is wont to do. I have proclaimed mornings to commence no earlier than 8:00 a.m. This decree is particularly sensible in January when nature itself does not provide any light before then. Even at the beginning of summer, when sunrise is out of sync with my world, I abide by 8:00 a.m. as the official start of morning. Mary Alice, of course, lives in a different world, and she would have already had her conference with Cora by 7:00 a.m. One must pass the time somehow while waiting for one's porridge to cook.

A daughter of Cape Breton descended from transplanted Scots is a purist when it comes to porridge. None of that instant stuff in multi-flavoured envelopes. Mary Alice has a proper spurtle—a porridge stick—and she knows how to use it. I think of it as her sceptre, or maybe a shillelagh, although I guess that kind of black-thorn walking stick is more Irish than Scottish. The similarity is that both the shillelagh and the spurtle can be used as a cudgel, in addition to their intended purposes. Impudent family members and erring landlords like me beware. Captain has also been known to sit up and take notice if Mary Alice appears with her spurtle. Sometimes it's just in her apron pocket, but other times she has it in hand and waves it for emphasis, like a celebrity guest conductor at the Victoria Symphony.

I upped the pace of my usual morning routine, lest Mary Alice invite Melody and Allison and have them on my doorstep at thirty seconds after 8:00 a.m. It would be prudent to show evidence of having vacuumed the vacant room, so I retrieved the vacuum cleaner and hauled it upstairs—again with a coughing interlude—to Katrina's former room. When I checked inside, it showed no evidence that it had ever been inhabited. There is something to be said for German efficiency in cleaning. I left the vacuum cleaner outside the door as proof that I had been there. If the new tenants were the ones to carry it downstairs and put it back in its closet, so much the better.

The descent was easier, especially without the vacuum cleaner. I decided to reward myself with breakfast. After uncovering Captain's cage and organizing his food and water, we had a shared breakfast menu. I toast a mean bagel. Along with coffee and a banana, sustenance was achieved. Captain bit the top off a peeled banana I offered to him, and I got the rest. This seems a fair distribution of potassium in that he can't hold an entire banana, and I have to do the honours, while he has first dibs. He never wants any more than one bite. If my doctor had his way, I would be following Captain's example when it came to any of my favourite foods, like bagels. The one exception my doctor is willing to allow is celery. I ignore him.

The phone rang, and I answered reluctantly. My telephone fan club has a limited membership, and one of its most active members is the loans manager at the bank. I was actually relieved that it turned out to be Mary Alice. "Good morning, Stanley. I hope you realize that it's morning, and you haven't been frittering your day away in bed."

"Ah, yes, I am well aware of the time of day. You will be pleased to know that I have already been up to Katrina's room with the vacuum cleaner." One should not lie to Mary Alice, but it is permissible, and often advisable, to leave out certain details. She can infer what she needs to.

"My goodness! Maybe you've finally reformed, at least a little." Her tone was more doubtful than complimentary.

"Mary Alice, I think you must have hung out with Maryon Pearson during her marriage to Lester Pearson. Wasn't she the one who said, 'Behind every successful man, there stands a surprised woman,' or something like that?" It's always good to let Mary Alice know I have, at one time or another, read a book, one of which must have been a biography of Lester Pearson. Even back in the 1960s, prime ministers didn't much heed my valuable advice. I doubt Maryon Pearson would have followed my advice either.

"Although Maryon Pearson was married to that Liberal prime minister fellow, she may have gotten one thing right!" This was a pretty generous assessment from a baptized Tory like Mary Alice. I suppose matriarch types stick together, except when they do battle with another matriarch who disagrees with them.

"Well, what's the update on Cora and the damsels? Are they coming around today?" I thought it was better to steer us on a business course, since I knew that's why her ladyship was calling so early.

"Well, I just happened to be chatting with Cora, and she was pleased that you have a room available. She's sending the girls over just before noon. I trust you'll be home to welcome them?" This was more in the order of a directive than a query. I would welcome the girls indeed. In particular, I would welcome the damage deposit and the rent.

"Not to be crass, my dear, but did you happen to mention that we should settle the business side of things when they first arrive?"

"I'm sure they know how to go about renting a place. And Cora would certainly remind them if they needed reminding." Conrad could no doubt verify that Cora was on a par with Mary Alice as far as being able to remind people about their responsibilities. Conrad is a very reminded person, by all accounts.

Captain overheard the conversation. *They better pay up, or the warrior lady will be here with that lethal porridge stick thing. How come we see the stick but never the porridge?*

"No doubt you are right, O Trusting One. I just wanted to avoid any awkward moments." Like any true Victorian, I prefer to come across as considerate rather than crass. We do "considerate" quite well in Victoria, except for driving and hockey games. Both are combat sports, after all. The crass part is that these two unrelated endeavours are both costly, and it's difficult to see them unless one has money to part with, hence my interest in the rent.

"Well, some of us have work to do, Stanley. I must be off. Remember, the girls are coming with their things at noon. I'll come by later to see how they have settled in. Ta for now."

The phone went silent. Such small blessings are to be savoured. I would also have liked to savour my bagel, but by then it was cold. My microwave is one of those early models that tends to incinerate things, regardless of the setting. So, I munched my petrified bagel and contemplated the imminent arrival of my latest tenants. In particular, I thought of what to do regarding the one queen-size bed in the room. Depending on the nature of their relationship, the cozy sleeping arrangement would be a plus or a minus. I decided to handle the situation by doing what I do well—play dumb. If they looked at the room and didn't request a second bed, we would just carry on. If they asked, "Where's the second bed?", I'd send them up to the third floor to swap two twins for the queen. It went without saying that I could stress my senior years and how nice it would be if they could move the beds for me, frail as I was. Young people can be very compassionate, especially if they aren't given an alternative.

Since I had a bit of time on my hands, I thought I should check my email. Usually, not much comes my way, but sometimes I receive an unexpected treasure—a sale at Value Village or a friend who is going to be passing through town. If nothing else, I thought I should become aware of what might be going wrong with my computer. Then I could report on my digital health to Liam when he turned up next.

Eventually, the black screen gave way to a window and my inbox. "Hi Stanley. Sorry not to be in touch sooner. Bob and I have

a two-week booking at a beach unit in Cuba, and we're heading
there in two days. Bob's brother was supposed to come with us,
but he's come down with the flu and doesn't want to travel. The
second bedroom will be empty for two weeks. It's already paid for,
so you can have it for free. You just have to get there. Let me know
asap if interested."

Andy and I were roommates back in our university days. Such
friendships formed at that time of life seem to last. He and his
partner lived in Winnipeg. Therefore, our paths didn't cross very
often. But when we got together, the conversation would pick up
where we left off. His offer was tantalizing. While winter in Victoria
is hardly bracing by prairie standards, Victorians still like to go
south for the sunshine—and the mojitos. Usually, I only hear sec-
ond-hand accounts of how much other people have enjoyed their
Caribbean break. This time I might be one of those annoying travel-
lers regaling my friends at the Piddler with my tropical travels. But
there was the little matter of getting there, and the money involved.

It was time to rifle through the junk drawer in search of the air
rewards plan that I had registered for so long ago. Every house
has a junk drawer. Shady Shingles is no exception. Mine is conveniently located in the top of my dresser. It might indeed hold a
record of my rewards plan number. Whether or not there would be
enough points to get me as far as Cuba would be another matter. I
had made many short-haul flights over the years, mostly between
Victoria and Saskatoon. Some had been to Toronto. I had always
assumed that such domestic hops didn't amount to much in terms
of points. But nothing ventured, nothing gained.

I made my way to the drawer and dove into the accumulation of
papers, watches that no longer worked, old ticket stubs from long-
ago folk festivals, dead batteries, and other odds and ends. Near
the back at the bottom, I felt a plastic card. When I retrieved it, the
right colours were on it. It was my rewards card. Should I dare call
the 800 number or go online to their website, without the presence
of my IT consultant, Liam? That could be Plan B. Urgency required
that I take the plunge immediately.

Plunges generally last a few seconds. Phone calls to access to the innards of Air Cheapo is a mission fraught with multiple transfers and much waiting, assuaged by interminable interludes of elevator music. Finally, I got to the last recording in the sequence of categories available. A disembodied female voice greeted me.

"Thank you for your patience in contacting Air Cheapo Awards Plan. We are presently experiencing a higher volume of calls than usual. Please leave your name and number after the tone. Or you may choose to visit our website, where all your information needs can be accessed with ease. You may find us at www.AirCheapo. com."

Desperate times call for desperate measures. I ventured solo to my computer, hoping I would never need to involve Liam in this tawdry business. To my delight and surprise, I got to the website. When I scrolled down to the part where the points statement was listed, I entered the long number on the plastic card. Then they wanted a four-digit PIN. Allegedly, I would have created such a thing years ago and committed it to memory for life. What I committed to memory last week is rarely available to me, so I cogitated over what I might have chosen as a cue back then. It couldn't have been my largest bank balance ever, because I wouldn't have been able to fill four digits. Maybe the year of my birth? No, too obvious. Maybe the year that I took over Shady Shingles? Bingo! That got me in.

Things were actually getting exciting. All without having to grovel before the nerdy Liam. The number 31,212 popped up. On its own that didn't let me know if I could be flying to Varadero or swimming the last 2,000 miles. Back to another menu and a place labeled Reward Chart. Indeed, the magic number to get to a Caribbean destination was 30,000 reward miles. My decades of accumulating points would now turn into something. That is, if I chose to go. The fine print mentioned that airport taxes, fuel surcharge, security fee, and extra baggage charges were not included. I wondered if there would be an extra charge if I chose to request a seat inside the cabin.

At least in theory, I could say yes to Andy's generous gift. And if I were really intending to go, I should answer quickly before he offered the place to someone else. Would Mary Alice agree to being left in charge? What if the roof sprang a leak? What if one of the tenants didn't coddle the ancient wiring, and Shady Shingles had a fire? What if the plane crashed? When in doubt, there is only one thing to do.

"Captain, should I fly to Cuba, or should I stay home and look after the house? I need your most considered opinion!" A tone of earnestness has been known to capture a parrot's attention. That and a juicy grape. For the moment, I had to rely on earnestness.

Suddenly you value my *opinion? In case you haven't noticed, I'm the one who can fly. You can barely gain enough altitude for the first step on the stairs. If you go wherever Cuba is, just don't leave me with the Dragon Lady and her porridge stick.*

Captain hunched his wings and gave himself a shake. There should be a manual for parrot sign language. At least he was looking in my direction. Maybe he was telling me to go, or maybe he just had a bad case of feather dust. It looked like he was getting ready to take flight. That probably meant I should go. Some people seek answers to life's deepest dilemmas by praying. I ask Captain. It probably amounts to the same thing. I can infer whatever I want from my earnest request, and no one is likely to contradict me.

Decision made, I emailed Andy, given his tight time frame for an answer. "Delighted to accept your kind offer. Will book with travel points when I know your flight details." I had crossed the Rubicon. I might have also crossed Mary Alice, which was a much riskier border. The Rubicon has the advantage that it is far away in Italy. Mary Alice is only across the fence. Better to act boldly and seek forgiveness later than to ask permission before. That little manoeuvre would have to wait, because it was getting close to noon. If the damsels were punctual, they would soon arrive. This responsible landlord thing at times interfered with the important stuff of life.

"Bon matin, Mr. Stanley! You are starting the new year hard at work, I see. Me, I have no time for breakfast. I have some paperwork business before going to de garage." Pierre had indeed stirred early, compared to his usual routine.

"Before you get too far, I should let you know that you had a visitor yesterday. A Constable Brewster." I tried not to sound too ominous or too curious, but I was both.

"Oh, dat guy. Yeah, he came also to the garage, and we talked. Everyt'ing, she is good. Just he wanted to know some questions about my special cars."

"Glad he found you. And something else—Katrina has moved out, and two college girls will likely be taking her room. You may see them later today sometime."

"OK. Dat was fast, no? I promise not to scare de ladies. But I have to go now. Bye." It was a hasty exit, but at least he wasn't carrying a suitcase. And I don't know how glad he really was to be found by the charming Constable Brewster.

No sooner had I reached the kitchen with my breakfast dishes than the doorbell rang. I deposited my things in the sink and hastened back to the front room. Unlike Mary Alice, the young ladies were at the outer porch door, waiting to be let in. They looked a bit apprehensive, probably wondering what kind of ogre dwelt within. I unlocked the door and waved them inside.

"Hello. You must be Melody and Allison. Come right in." Fake enthusiasm has its place. They followed me through the porch into the living room. I didn't know who was who, but they quickly set me straight. Allison was the redhead with a slender build in her early twenties. The denim overall outfit was perhaps indicative of her interest in carpentry. Melody looked to be slightly older, a little more filled out, clad in the requisite jeans and blouse of a student. Under her canvas cap, she was a brunette. Her facial features seemed vaguely familiar, but I couldn't place who she reminded me of.

"And here we have Captain, my trusty parrot." Not everyone has a parrot in their living room, so it seemed timely to do an immediate introduction for the newcomers.

"Hello." Captain was right off the mark. He doesn't say hello to many people. In fact, I thought he had forgotten how to say it. Finicky bird.

"Well, hello there, Pretty Boy. Aren't you the cutie!" Melody said in an animated voice, and Captain danced his little figure-eight dance. Shameless heterosexual flirting for a parrot. He was wasting his time, because I doubted his new adoring fan was going to elope with him to some luscious tropical island, where Red Flames hung from every vine.

"I think he's hilarious. Did you teach him to dance that way? He's way cool." Allison climbed on the bandwagon too, and Captain was clearly in his element. While it was touching that Captain seemed to approve of the new tenants, the real issue was what Mary Alice thought. Fortunately, their arrival had pre-clearance in that department.

"No, Captain has never required dancing lessons from me. He's just showing off for you, in hopes that you're going to give him a treat. He will likely give you further training later." The girls looked slightly puzzled. They probably operated under the mistaken assumption that people train parrots, extrapolating from the similar myth that parents train their children. Teachers know this to be a fallacy. This inside information comes courtesy of former tenants who were student teachers.

"Perhaps you would like to see the room before we settle up for the first month's rent and damage deposit? You probably have Cora's recommendation, but you should see the place for yourselves. Just head upstairs to the second floor, and the room is the second on the left, right across from the bathroom. There are two other tenant rooms up there, and we all share the kitchen on this floor." I suppose a gracious host would lead the way and explain the finer features of the proffered room, but I had been upstairs once already that day, and I had no desire for a second ascent. They didn't seem to mind going up on their own. It also gave me a chance to dig out my receipt book and find a pen, assuming a rental was imminent. I barely had time to accomplish that mission when I heard their steps descending the stairs. Allison seemed to be the business manager of the duo.

"Actually, the room is quite charming, and it's bigger than we thought. It'll be awesome to have a room in a character place like this."

"We noticed that the room comes furnished," Melody added. "That's good, because we just have our clothes and a few things. Could we have a second desk, since the two of us will be sharing the room?"

I took it that the request for a second desk rather than a second bed was indicative that they were indeed a couple. "Ah, yes. I think that's possible. There's a surplus office desk in one of the rooms on the third floor. You're welcome to use it while you're here."

I conveniently omitted how it might get from the third floor to their bedroom. I had never given anyone access to the third-floor rooms, since that would involve them seeing my project work areas. Alas, I had neglected many of my projects for some time, so the issue would be more the clutter and the dust than the top-secret nature of the work. A bigger concern was how much rent I should charge for two people sharing a room. Clearly, it should be more than for one person, especially since tenants compare notes on such things. And there would be a greater use of hot water, laundry facilities, space in the refrigerator, and so on. I thought there should also be a nod to Jerome, the loans manager, in whose honour my rental income was dedicated.

"I can show you the kitchen and direct you to the laundry room in the basement." We made our way past my easy chair and the dining table to the kitchen. Allison was clearly the more domestically inclined side of the team.

"For a house with so many people, the fridge seems to have quite a bit of free space. That's good. The stove is a bit dated, but presumably everything works?"

I nodded.

"I love the retro microwave! Where did you get it?" Melody elbowed her, but it was too late.

"It came that way when I bought it new at Eaton's in 1968," I replied in my most patient voice.

"That's impressive. We'll be careful with it." Allison's face displayed astonishment more than admiration, and she chose her words carefully. Melody nodded in agreement, but given her medical acumen, I understood "being careful" to mean "standing well back when using it." I sent them down to the laundry room for their own reconnaissance. After a few minutes, they came back upstairs.

"So, ladies, would you like to stay here, now that you've seen the place? I should mention that parking is on the street. Everyone cleans up after themselves, and no loud music after eleven at night. That's about it." They had likely discussed that issue while they were downstairs, so I thought it was time to move things along to the more interesting part of the visit. As expected, Allison took the lead.

"It all looks quite delightful. I'm glad that Grandma Cora could connect us this way. How much is the rent?" She sounded confident up until the part about the rent.

"Well, I haven't allowed a room-share before, but how about the single rate plus thirty percent? The damage deposit is half a month's rent. That's pretty standard around here." My calculation had more to do with what would satisfy Jerome than it did with any cost-benefit analysis.

"We'll take it," Melody said. "Thank you so much."

It seemed that her eagerness overruled any negotiating strategy that Allison might have been considering. Allison was taken a little off guard, judging from the way she furrowed her eyebrows. After we calculated the actual dollar amount, she nodded. "Yes, that would be fine."

They produced the cash, and I wrote out the appropriate receipt. Captain had stopped dancing and was in his midday nap pose. I gave them keys for their room and for the front door. The girls had their things outside in the car, so I indicated they could move in right away.

"Oh, the birdie is sleeping. We'll bring in our stuff quietly." Melody seemed to have an unusual concern for Captain's repose. With time she might be able to recognize when he was only pretending.

I'm not sleeping. I'm just resting my eyes. I'm actually delighted that these thumbies show potential for training. Yes, be quiet when the birdie looks like he's napping.

"Melody, you seem to have hit it off with Captain. Would you be willing to look after him while I'm away? It's a pretty simple routine. He gets mixed seed, fruit salad, water, and part of a boiled egg now and then. The yucky part is changing the newsprint on his cage bottom every couple of days. If you have any questions, Mary Alice from next door can answer them. She has looked after him in the past, but she's getting older now, so I don't like to ask her."

Ban the biddy! Ban the biddy! Give me Melody! Captain's eyelids flickered.

"Well, if you think it's alright. I haven't looked after a parrot before, but in Saskatoon, my mum had chickens in the backyard. A parrot is a lot smaller." Melody sounded tentative but positive. Allison looked decidedly skeptical.

"There you go. Just think of Captain as an undersized chicken with a bigger beak. You'll get along fine." Getting people to babysit a pet is like selling a house. Sell people on the dream, and let them find out the flaws on their own after you're gone.

"He's adorable. And it sounds like I could manage, especially with your neighbour so close. Maybe we could settle in now?"

Melody was reeled in. I'm thankful we have progressed beyond the age of chivalry. The girls had no expectation that I should help them lug their things up the stairs. I didn't volunteer. They had a couple of large duffle bags and several boxes, so the move-in didn't take long. They busied themselves upstairs. Asking Melody about babysitting Captain was perhaps a hasty decision, but I can tell an animal lover pretty readily, and Captain seemed to have taken a liking to her right away. There was the additional safeguard that Mary Alice would be in the picture. She would be relieved not to have to bother with Captain, but at the same time, she would make sure that "the creature" came to no harm.

Perhaps I had nodded off in my recliner chair, since Captain's midday napping is a contagious thing. Suddenly, I heard a female voice.

"Ahem. About the extra desk, Mr. McFadden. Could we organize that now?" Allison was on task and standing in front of my chair.

"Actually, I have a few pressing things to do. But if you just go up to the third floor and open the first door on the right, you'll see the office desk that I referred to. It might have a few things on top, but just set them aside. Here's the key for the room. Usually, I keep it locked."

"No problem. You just carry on. We'll be fine." Allison certainly seemed capable.

"And I forgot to mention. The other two tenants are Brian and Pierre. They each have a room down the hall from you. Brian is a university student, and Pierre is some kind of car salesman." I could also have mentioned that Mary Alice was more than a neighbour and would appear on the scene at regular intervals. I chose to assume that Cora had advised them of that certainty. No sense in burdening them with too much reality.

Melody and Allison's arrival seemed fairly routine. In fact, their entry to Shady Shingles was the first step in a turn of events that was far from routine. They may have started off as damsels in distress, but they soon turned into duckling managers in their own right.

14
Going, Going, Gone

IT WAS JANUARY 3, so the bank would be open. It seemed prudent that I march down there and render a donation to that month's mortgage payment. Jerome would no doubt be pleased. The only negative was that the walk downtown is uphill both ways. I have only come to notice this annoying geographic anomaly in the last ten years. It is a relief to me that my peers at the Piddler have confirmed this observation; therefore, I am not just imagining things.

The sky was overcast, but that's pretty well how it looks for six months of the year in Victoria. One can interpret this heavenly observation to be a sure sign that it has just rained, it is raining, or it is about to rain. Better to bring along a telescoping brolly as I set out. I congratulated myself that I have always made it both ways without anyone having to call 911. One ambulance did pass by with its siren wailing, but it wasn't for me. Such a brush with mortality is considered cause for a Hail Mary among people like Mary Alice. In my own perspective, it was a sign to reward myself with an extra pint the next time that I made my pilgrimage to the Piddler.

In the here and now, I simply arrived at the bank and made my mortgage payment. The sensation of holding so much cash in my hand was both intoxicating and short-lived. The insouciant young teller soon dismissed me with a perfunctory, "Have a nice day." She probably wouldn't have been interested to know that I had made other plans. I believe my restraint in such social settings is admirable, albeit unnoticed.

On the way back, the grey skies above turned black and began to release the liquid sunshine that helps Victoria's mossy lawns stay so green, at least in winter. My good umbrella was, of course, at home by the front door, where it was safe from winter gales. I unfolded the handier rain technology that I had brought with me. Only one strut was bent, which meant I was still a cut above most of the younger pedestrians. None of them would be caught dead using an umbrella; they just pulled up their hoodies and got wet. Ducklings can be obtuse.

Eventually, I got home, glad to be somewhere dry. I had just taken my coat off when Captain did his pointer pose. I headed for the kitchen to put on the kettle, knowing that a tea tribunal was imminent.

"Stanley, what are doing out in the rain? You'll catch your death!" Mary Alice has always had a morbid perspective on the elements. Her voice tended to arrive before she did.

"I was off to the bank. They required my assistance, you know."

Undoing her navy woollen coat, Mary Alice made her way to the kitchen table. "I know indeed what they require, and you would do well to keep up those payments." Her ladyship didn't miss a beat when it came to managing money.

"Actually, it was a productive visit, because I had the rent money from Allison and Melody as well as what Brian and Pierre paid me previously. I think the girls went out, but they were here at noon, and they paid in cash before moving in."

"Well, isn't that nice. Cora will be so pleased. What did you think of them?" It's always a bit dicey when Mary Alice asks my opinion. The prudent thing is either to give her an opinion that she concurs with or to profess complete ignorance.

"They seemed very well-mannered. I hope they stay awhile."

Mary Alice nodded. "Yes, I think that would be a good thing, all things considered." No doubt this was intended to be an understatement. I ignored the boldness of her subtlety.

"On a different note, Mary Alice, I was wondering how busy you might be this month."

"I'm always busy, Stanley. Idle hands are the work of the devil, my dear mother always said." No doubt the devil works overtime in Cape Breton, so I'm sure Mary Alice's mother gave well-considered advice.

"Actually, I have the chance to go to Cuba with some friends from university days. They have an extra spot at a resort, and I can fly there on reward points. It would mean being gone from Shady Shingles for only a couple of weeks."

Captain cocked his head. *You do know you're not talking to Mrs. Santa Claus, don't you?*

Mary Alice had a look of utter astonishment. "Maybe you better pour that tea now. We don't want it to get bitter, do we?" It occurred to me too late that perhaps I should have made Grandma Vi's special tea for the occasion.

Mary Alice sipped her tea thoughtfully. "Well, I suppose if you're not spending the mortgage money, and there's no extra cost, it would be an opportunity that doesn't come every day. Maybe you should go while you can, because there will come a day soon enough when you won't be able to go. We know about that, we do." The royal "we" was completely in character, but her tone was actually a bit melancholic.

"It would be good if you could look in on things. Melody seemed to take to Captain, and he danced for her. She's willing to look after him if I show her what to do. Otherwise, the rents have been collected, and the tenants just come and go on their own." I thought it prudent not to mention that there might be a return visit by the good Constable Brewster, if not a posse, in pursuit of Pierre.

"Oh, I know well enough what has to be done. You forget that I was the one who taught you how to run this place. If Melody is too busy, I can give the creature enough food and water to keep him alive until you come back. He's not royalty, you know."

Captain half-raised his wings and swayed. *I pray to the parrot god that I don't end up in the care of the Dragon Lady! Please, please, let it be that nice Melody thumbie!*

"That would certainly take a load off my mind. And it would be a wonderful treat to visit somewhere that I have never been before. Thank you for indulging me." It never hurts to grovel strategically, if I want Mary Alice on side.

"And when does all this happen?"

"Actually, I need to book flights with my reward points and leave the day after tomorrow."

Mary Alice gulped her tea and rose to leave. "You better get to it then. Time's a wasting." Her ladyship did up her coat and made her exit without any further fuss. And that ended our most successful tea party ever. It all seemed too easy. I'm sure the mother duck thought the same—until she got to the railway tracks with her little brood. Lest I get too caught up in the existential angst of mother ducks, I turned my thoughts to the work at hand.

Over the years, I have made a high art form of procrastinating, but this new reality called for urgency. It never hurts to add a new word to one's vocabulary. However, knowing something in the abstract and actually practicing it are two different things. Ask any of those thousands of anglophone millennials who have gone through five years of French immersion and never speak a word of the language. To be fair, I have a theoretical understanding of how to lose weight—eat less and exercise more—but I don't do any better at applying the knowledge than the bilingually educated millennials do at speaking their theoretical French. Applying this urgency thing could be daunting.

I urgently needed Liam's assistance if I was going to take on the website of Air Cheapo. Their advertising said they were committed to ease of access and convenience for their loyal customers. I hoped my lack of loyalty would not be matched by their sketchy commitment to an accessible website. Like many seniors of my ilk, I know that companies and government offices have conspired to deprive us of the help of anything resembling a live person who knows something. Instead, they have constructed a digital version of Hadrian's Wall, holding the barbarians at bay. This is highly discriminatory, because smart barbarians can get over the wall, but innocent Luddites like yours truly are punished. Clearly, I have to add another issue to the prime minister's to-do list. Must send list someday. I put off corresponding with the prime minister in favour of sitting down at my computer keyboard.

With the help of Mr. Google, I brought up Air Cheapo's colourful website. It had more tabs than a pigeon has feathers. I definitely felt like a pigeon confronted by a maze, wondering which path might lead to the reward of plump sunflower seeds at the centre. In my case, the goal was a booked flight with as few add-on expenses as possible. At least a pigeon can fly off on its own, if it wants to. I would have to rely on Air Cheapo. While I had previously found the tab that led to the tab that referred me to my points statement, there was no lifeline after that. There was no obvious tab that would get me to a place where I could apply the points to a particular flight. This might call for a glass of sherry in order to clear my mind for the complex battle ahead. A key turned in the front door, and Captain lurched. He didn't do his Mary Alice alert, so I knew it was an unclassified intruder.

"Hi, Mr. McFadden. Checking up on the productivity of your oil wells, are you?" It was Brian, who had presumably survived his Christmas in Red Deer. He leaned forward under the burden of a substantial backpack.

"As you know, Brian, the only oil on this property is the cooking oil in the kitchen. You Albertans are the ones with the oil wells. How did things go in the motherland, anyway?" I am always of the opinion that feeble wit should be rewarded in kind.

"It was cold, *really* cold, and I had to shovel snow for my mum. She says hi, and she sent some perogies for you. Is Captain a perogy fan?"

I don't know which was more absurd, the idea that Captain would know what perogies are or that I would share them with him. "I'm guessing that parrots like sunflower perogies, but in case your mother didn't send that kind, I'll eat his share."

Captain leaned into the conversation. *No you don't, you perogy snatcher you! Let the kid bring out whatever those perogy thingies are. I want one!*

"I'll bring them down after I unpack. I think they may have thawed during the flight. They should probably go in the freezer again." Perogy nurturing is one of the life skills that people learn if they grow up in Alberta or Saskatchewan. Clearly, his mama taught him well.

"Sounds like a plan. Thank your mother for me. And after you deal with the perogies, might you have a moment to aid a fragile senior citizen in navigating the Internet jungle?" I tried to sound as plaintive as possible, which is pretty much my normal timbre.

"No problem. Should I go visit Mrs. Macdonald, or do you have someone else in mind?" Brian had a devious streak that I had to admire. He could sound obliging while at the same time, would make me beg more explicitly for help. The boy had potential, another Jerome in the making. If the banks didn't snap him up, the realtors would. "It's the same frail senior who needed help in putting up the Christmas lights and that garland. But my more immediate need is booking a flight on Air Cheapo and using my reward points to pay for it. Can you handle that, or do I have to bring in Liam?"

Brian had seen Liam in action, so I knew he wouldn't want to be outclassed by a ten-year-old. "Just hang in there a bit, and I'll see what I can do."

Brian headed upstairs, and I debated whether or not I should start on the sherry. It wasn't long before he came back down and delivered his perogy cargo to the freezer in the refrigerator. By the time he got to the living room, I had poured two sherries. "In the spirit of the season, I set out a sherry for you. Sip it gently—there's only one coming."

"Awesome. I've always wondered what this stuff tastes like. Usually, my friends only offer beer. But let me get started on your tickets first, in case I book you to the wrong country!"

"Very considerate of you. I should also mention, by the way, that you won't be running into Katrina upstairs. She moved out yesterday to live with a hockey player named Dimitry. Now your new neighbours are Allison and Melody."

"Wow. This is a tsunami at Shady Shingles. Are you renting two more rooms now?" Brian's expression was quizzical.

"Actually, no. They will be sharing the same room." Brian's eyebrows raised. "And yes, they are a couple. They're out grocery shopping just now, but you'll meet them later. It all happened fairly quickly as a favour to Mary Alice, who knows Allison's grand-mother." Better to give him the press release version of events.

"You and Mrs. M. don't waste any time. I thought nothing ever happened here!"

If you only knew, perogy boy. Captain shifted his weight to stand on one leg.

Brian settled into my serious office chair at the computer desk. At least in 1973 the chair was serious. Like its usual occupant, it had begun to sag a little. "This is way retro, Mr. McFadden. You even have an old person's mouse. Cool."

Brian was annoyingly speedy as his fingers flew over the keys. Various screens appeared and disappeared as he clicked his way to Air Cheapo's booking page. "We won't know if you can use your points until we put in dates and see if there's space available. When exactly do you want to go again?"

"Uh, leaving tomorrow and returning in two weeks." I hoped the travel gods would smile on me. Failing that I would take a boost from whatever of their underlings were on duty in early January. A flurry of keyboard clicking followed, and then silence.

"We gotta wait a few seconds while the system lines everything up. Given the age of this machine, maybe you have to open it up and feed the gerbil running on its little treadwheel."

I grimaced. Brian took a sip of the sherry, and his expression was similar to what I looked like when I first tried Buckley's cough syrup. Something that tastes that awful must be good for you. I haven't acquired a taste for Buckley's, but I have warmed considerably to the sherry. I inferred that Brian was not going far down the same road anytime soon. My sherry supply would be safe. A progress bar crept slowly across the screen, and Brian beamed.

"We're in. I mean, it accepted your points, and you got your booking. Hasta la vista!"

"Good work! I didn't think it would really happen. Have another sherry!" Sometimes I get wildly generous when something actually goes right.

"I'll pass, thanks. Maybe a rain cheque for a beer, after you get back. By the way, what happens to Captain when you're gone? Does he get sent to a bird kennel?"

Captain leaned forward and bobbed his head emphatically. *I would love to be sent to the Birdy Bordello. Nobody ever asks the bird where he wants to go. I could still end up with Atilla the Hen as my keeper. Save me, perogy boy!*

"Captain doesn't travel well, so he will stay home and oversee the house, with the able help of Melody. She seemed to hit it off with Captain, so she has the honours. And if she changes her mind, there's always Mary Alice. She tolerates him, and he won't go hungry." Captain pooped. It was pure coincidence that he had to go at the nanosecond that I mentioned possibly leaving him in the care of Mary Alice.

"Sounds like you've done this before. Can I give him anything while you're gone?" Brian seemed more concerned for Captain than I would have imagined. Perhaps ducklings sense kindred spirits.

"Well, I think we can assume that backrubs are out. But if you spritz him now and again with the water in that recycled window-washer bottle, he will likely dance madly as you do it. You can spray him through the bars, or you can spray him when he's standing on top of the cage. I guess he thinks of it like a rainforest shower. Then he'll groom himself for the next hour, whether you hang around or not."

My years of patient teaching have finally paid off. The thumbies are trainable.

"Awesome. I'll try and remember. I'm sure we'll have a good time."

I hoped his cheerfulness was solely because of caring for Captain and not because the prospect of my being gone from the house would open the door to more adventurous social events. Before I had time to raise that topic aloud, the front door opened. Melody and Allison made their entrance, laden with bags of groceries. They had obviously discovered Lucky Foods. Melody had the lead position.

"Sorry to interrupt, but we just got back from stocking up."

"No problem. After you put those things away, come back, and I'll introduce you to Brian." I don't know if young people shake hands anymore, but it certainly wasn't going to happen when two out of three of them were straining to hold on to grocery bags. The girls began heading toward the kitchen.

"They may be a couple of minutes, Brian. Per chance would you be willing to take down the garland and Christmas lights in the porch? The stepladder is still out there."

"Aye, aye. I put the perogies in the freezer and I'll take down the lights and tacky garland." I wasn't sure if the nautical reference was for my benefit or Captain's.

After several minutes, Brian returned with a bag of decorations, and Allison and Melody emerged from the kitchen. The living room was beginning to feel like a bus station. I had stowed the sherry, since I had no intention of depleting my supply further.

"I think you've all met Captain but not each other. Brian, this is Melody and Allison. Girls, this is Brian, who has a room on the same floor. There's also Pierre, but he went out earlier. Usually, he doesn't come in until quite late."

"Hey," followed by a fist bump, was their greeting of choice. Captain sometimes does a beak bump but only after he knows someone well. He doesn't beak bump with Mary Alice. I doubt Mary Alice beak bumps with anyone no matter how long she has known them.

"While I have your attention, I should remind you that I'm departing tomorrow for a two-week trip to Cuba. Cora's friend, Mary Alice, lives next door, and she will be looking in from time to time while I'm gone. If anything comes up, she'll be able to handle it."

"Cuba sounds so exciting," Allison said. "Are you going with someone?"

"I'm flying there alone but then meeting friends from school days, who are vacationing there. The opportunity came up just yesterday, and I still have to pack. So, if you'll excuse me."

I left the young people to chat, if they were so inclined. They could compare notes on their eccentric landlord and the weird lady next door. For my part, I retired to my bedroom, in hopes of having enough clean things to stuff a suitcase, including whatever one needed to take to Cuba in January—passport, ticket confirmation, cash, sunscreen, some summer clothes, a Spanish phrase book? Captain was no help, because parrots don't pack suitcases. Clearly, this was an oversight in his earlier education. After a couple of hours, I had put together what I could, and the suitcase managed to close, albeit with a bulge on one side.

The next decision was to go to bed immediately and get up at 3:00 a.m. to catch the airporter bus. On the other hand, I could sleep a shade later if I were to ask someone to drive me. One's vast circle of friends soon shrinks to a deplorable few when asked about providing a 3:30 a.m. ride to the airport. Mary Alice used to perform the role of airport chauffeur, but that was several years ago. The last time we went, we entered the Three Traffic Circles of Purgatory en route to the airport and ended up heading back toward Victoria. That was only after I heard some new words in Cape Breton Gaelic, which Mary Alice assured me were simply a traditional Macdonald blessing. Somehow her tone suggested a non-blessing, but I kept that bit of speculation to myself. To be fair, I have heard others offer words of blessing upon whoever designed the Three Traffic Circles of Purgatory, and their tone wasn't very blessed either. When in the midst of the connecting circles, it would be over the top to say one had entered hell. But a person can develop an appreciation for purgatory, even if he or she is not Catholic. Supposedly, this unique Victoria configuration of roadway represents a great improvement on the simple controlled intersection that was there previously. Mere mortals should not cast doubt on the marvel of engineering that replaced the previous setup. One simply prays that anyone who arrives in Victoria via the airport for the first time does so sober and in broad daylight. Otherwise, the slalom course from the airport to downtown Victoria, supplemented by a profusion of helpful signs, might prove a tad daunting, and a person could end up in Brentwood Bay, which is a reasonable improvement on purgatory but not a place where I want to spend eternity.

I decided to splurge and rely on the little airporter bus. That meant a trip back to the computer keyboard to reserve a pickup. To my surprise, the process was simple. Once completed, I only had to wonder if such a thing was really reliable. Or would I end up standing outside the local convenience store, minus a ride, looking forlorn? Never mind, I had a lot of practice looking forlorn. I decided the best travel strategy was to set my alarm, go to bed early, and get a few hours of sleep before hitting the road. The day had certainly been full of activity, and I had earned my fatigue. The problem was that when I have to be intentional about going to sleep, sleep doesn't come readily. This reality is commonplace for seniors. After a considerable period of fruitless tossing and turning, I drifted off. Recalling the prime minister's last speech was very helpful in that regard. I must thank him when I send his to-do list.

There is something to be said for loud alarm clocks. When mine went off at 3:00 a.m., I bolted upright and prepared to abandon ship. Then I realized that Shady Shingles was not sinking, at least not literally. I hurried about and got ready.

It was dark when I wheeled my suitcase through the living room. Captain barely opened one eye and gave a little yawn. So much for man's second-best friend. He resumed his position as I exited the door.

Indeed, the airporter picked me up on time, I aged a bit more while going through security at the airport, and Air Cheapo actually provided a seat inside the plane. I uttered a little prayer of thanks to I am not sure whom. Granted, a few loose ends remained back at Shady Shingles. Would Constable Brewster make a return visit? Would Pierre leave as suddenly as Katrina? Would the roof suddenly give up the ghost?

As the plane took off, I had that marvellous feeling of letting go. After all, life is about loose ends, ducklings, and letting go. The hope is that we can carry on after we let go. And we do.

15
Connecting the Dots

FINALLY, THE PARROT is back at the helm. I vaguely recall Stanley stumbling toward the front door that morning while it was still dark, towing a suitcase. That would seem to indicate he had abandoned ship. Clearly, I am now the one to tell the story as it should be told, at least when the narrator lets me. Can't stop him from butting in. I don't know what the thumbies do when they leave the house, but I certainly hear everything and see most things while they're here. I could improve their lives, if only they would listen to me. They seem to have a comprehension problem, so I'll simply tell you what went on in Stanley's absence, and you can connect the dots, if you are a connecting kind of thumbie.

Mary Alice was coming. I heard the side door open and knew the porch board was going to creak. Stanley probably thinks I'm clairvoyant, but I just listen. I pretended to be asleep, in case she'd come to give me a lecture.

"Stanley, have you gone yet? Should you be going to the airport now?"

Mary Alice's resonant voice certainly carried to the back bedroom, and even upstairs to the second floor, according to Stanley.

"I guess he's gone already. It doesn't look like anybody has fed the bird, judging by yesterday's mess at the bottom of his cage. You can open your eyes, Captain, I know you're awake!"

I heard rapid steps on the stairs, and Melody hurriedly arrived at the bottom. "Good morning, Mrs. Macdonald. Mr. McFadden said you would be looking in. How nice to meet you. I'm Melody." She offered her hand, and Mary Alice took it.

"Cora has spoken highly of you, being such a good friend of Allison and all. And where is Allison, if I might ask?"

"Oh, she's not really a morning person. Usually, my day starts before hers, if I have an early lab. I had promised to look after Captain, so maybe you can show me where his things are?"

"Ah yes, Captain." Mary Alice's voice dropped, and she cast a disdainful glance in my direction. "His things are in the kitchen, and he's probably used to waiting until Stanley gets up. We should get his dishes from the cage and head to the kitchen. Just follow me, and I'll show you the routine."

Mary Alice did not seem to be putting much enthusiasm into this important task. She showed Melody how to remove the clamped dishes from my cage, and they disappeared into the kitchen. I could hear them talking. They returned with clean water, my seed mixture, and some cut-up fruit. The kitchen is a magical place that has an infinite supply of these things. At least it is when Stanley is home. Now that he was gone, I wasn't so sure.

Melody snapped the dishes back into place, under Mary Alice's supervision. "Look, he's already climbed down to the fruit dish and picked out a grape. He must have been hungry!"

"More likely he's in the first stages of becoming an alcoholic. I have my suspicions that Stanley has been giving him sherry. I think that beak is redder than it should be. Those expensive Red Flame grapes are just the start."

If Mary Alice had her way, I'd be the founding president of Parrots Anonymous. Melody, on the other hand, seemed a soft touch. I knew early on that she had potential.

"It looks like his papers need changing. What do we do with them?" Melody looked around for someplace to put them, there being nothing obvious in sight.

"You can roll them up, keeping all the muck inside, and put the entire thing in the compost bin in the garden. Half of what we give him ends up on the cage floor and even the living room floor. That's why there's so much paper scattered on the floor under his cage. Parrots are messy creatures. At least this one is."

Mary Alice's indictment of my character is unrelenting. No one gets to see her eat, so I could have a thing or two to say about that if I had a chance. Stanley once got her a T-shirt that said Oatmeal Savage, but I haven't seen her wear it.

"When you put your hands in to get the papers, does he bite? He looks like he has a strong beak."

"Well, I suppose he can, but I haven't seen him bite. He's too busy filling his face. Stanley can pet him, but maybe you shouldn't try anything like that until he knows you better. You never know what a juvenile delinquent is going to do."

Mary Alice made a sour face in my direction. I think it becomes her.

"I don't mind. If it weren't for the fact that I'm going to be a doctor, I think I would have chosen to be a vet. I like animals."

"I like my cat, but I don't see what the attraction is in birds. Each to his own, I suppose."

Melody glanced at her watch. "Sorry, but I need to go soon. I have to get to my lab. By the way, Mr. McFadden mentioned a Pierre, and we haven't seen him yet."

"Count your blessings my child. He's a glib talker and a used-car salesman, and I'm not sure what else. Probably he's still asleep at this indecent hour. He comes in late, and he gets up even later than Stanley."

It would seem that not only parrots come under her ladyship's scrutiny. Mind you, I also keep my distance from finger-wagging Pierre. Furry faces are usually carnivores.

"Well, I guess our paths will cross later. We met Brian yesterday. Allison usually skips breakfast, so probably you won't see her before you go."

Melody grabbed her backpack and headed for the door. Mary Alice followed, locking it as she left. Sensible parrots have an after-breakfast nap. I include myself in that number, especially when the thumbies are gone, and the house is finally quiet. This state of solitude never lasts for long, so it's good to take advantage of "intermission" at Shady Shingles.

After a short interlude, I heard a horse clattering down the stairs. It was Brian, galloping off to something called "class," presumably where a herd of thumbies learned something from another thumbie. In any case, he made a pass through the kitchen. I heard the fridge door open and then close. Then Brian trotted through the living room with a feedbag slung over one shoulder. Except he called it a backpack, which all the younger humanoids seem to be equipped with.

"Hi, Captain. No time to spritz you this morning. Catch you later."

And he was gone. I'm never sure why I need to be caught later. I already live in a cage. How could I be more "caught"? In any case, the top hatch of my cage is always open, and I can come out anytime I want. I just don't go anywhere, because every other place in the house is a danger zone, and there is nothing there that I want. Well, maybe the fridge would be interesting, but the door is too heavy to open. They keep all the treasure in there. I have to rely on trained thumbies to bring me things from the refrigerator. The only valuable things not locked up are the bananas, and I usually get a piece when Stanley asks me to bite off the top of his. I think Stanley is afraid that bananas are poisonous, and I have to bite the top off to show him they're safe. Silly humans.

Since nap attempt number one was unsuccessful, I thought I would make a second attempt. When you have a mission, you shouldn't get distracted from it. After a touch-up preening, I assumed the position. It's very comforting to be able to turn my head around and rest it on my back, between my wings. My eyelids grew heavier and heavier . . .

Then a door slammed, followed by the sound of pattering feet. Allison made her entrance down the stairs wearing a toolbelt that clattered. Unlike the other thumbies, she didn't make a side trip to the kitchen. She seemed to be in even more of a hurry than Brian.

"Hi, parrot. Sorry, I don't have anything for you. Take care."

Whatever it is that these creatures do, they obviously wait until the last minute to get there. Fortunately, I was already where I was supposed to be. And I was also supposed to be napping, without much success. I figured I may as well stay awake, because Pierre was still to emerge. He makes more noise than all of them. He bangs that frying pan thing around and sometimes sings while he cooks. Parrot singing is much nicer, but it's wasted on my local audience.

I waited a while for Pierre to come down, but he didn't. Maybe furry-faced used-car salesmen hibernate at a certain stage of winter. But nothing in Victoria hibernates. The squirrels keep running around, trying to find where they buried things the previous fall. Dogs take their humans out for a walk. The deer continue to munch their way through the neighbourhood. I could see them all through my window, and they were busy by that time of day.

But no Pierre. Not that I missed him. It was just that I couldn't have a proper nap if he was going to appear who knew when. I had trained Stanley to nap on cue, if he was at home. The other thumbies come and go too often to train properly. They bob their heads and try to imitate my figure-eight head swing, but they are too slow to learn the really important stuff—how to nap in sync with me, how to spritz under my wings when I raise them, how to scratch my neck in just the right place, how to trim my nails when they get too long.

After a while, the letter carrier came. His arrival doesn't really count as a visit, because he just shoves useless paper through the mail slot and then hurries on to the next house. The paper is the wrong size for the bottom of my cage, so I don't know why he bothers to deliver it. Stanley just puts it in a blue box thing and then takes it outside somewhere now and then. The useful paper is something called the *Times Colonist*. Sometimes it has pictures of the prime minister in it. Stanley puts those pages on the bottom of my cage. Maybe the prime minister will come and visit someday, and he can see where Stanley has given his picture a place of honour.

I missed Stanley. The house felt empty. Maybe I should have taken that nap after all. It was very tiring thinking about an empty house. Maybe when I woke up again, somebody would be there. *"Must preen,"* I thought." *Must stand on one leg and shift body weight over leg. Must rest head on my back. Must . . ."*

I woke up to the sound of chattering. At first I thought it was those noisy squirrels who run along the window ledge and peek in at my peanut supply. Then I heard the lock turn and the front door open. It was Allison and Melody making human chatter. The sun was already very low, and the shadows were long.

"I don't know about this new lab instructor. She expects us to do experiments way too fast. I hope I can learn to keep up."

Melody seemed to be a wound-up young lady, judging by her tone. I noticed that her pitch went up a couple of notches when she was excited.

"You worry too much. You said the same thing at the beginning of last term, and it all turned out fine. Just chill."

Allison's words of reassurance made her seem more like a doctor than the first-year medical student that Melody was. Maybe journeyman carpenters don't have labs. Or maybe they get excited about other things. In any case, the girls made it into the living room.

"Oh, look. Captain is all alone and has nobody to talk to."

"Melody, he doesn't talk anyway. Even Mr. McFadden said he doesn't talk to him, so he's not likely to talk to strangers."

"Still, he looks like he's ready to say something. I'll bet he knows lots about this crazy old house. I'd love to be able to ask him things."

Right on, sister. I know lots, but Stanley makes it worth my while to stay quiet. He's the guy who brings in the mixed seed and grapes and peanuts for me.

"What's so crazy about the house? It's an old rooming house with broken-down furniture, and the rent is reasonable, if not cheap. End of story." Allison laid things out matter-of-factly.

"Well, for one thing, you forgot to mention that Mary Alice Macdonald lady next door. Your mum said she and Mr. McFadden run this house, but she doesn't live here, and I think the house is actually his. So, where does she fit in? She let herself in this morning, and apparently she comes and goes on her own all the time."

"Kinky but not weird. Kinky is when you use a feather and weird is when you use the whole chicken. I think their relationship is just kinky, if you get my drift."

"Allison! I didn't mean it that way, but still, their setup is a little odd. Then there's that bizarre third floor where nobody lives, but the rooms are kept locked. What could be in them?"

"So, he's kind of reclusive. And he doesn't have very good taste in furniture. He's an elderly bachelor, not Mr. Cool."

"When we went into that one room to get the desk, did you notice the stack of papers and photos on the old couch? There were some albums too, but they are hidden away up there rather than in the bookcase down here. Most people have their family albums close by to look at. Why would his be banished to an unused room?"

"You make too much out of too little. We don't know anything about Mr. McFadden, other than he's sort of a friend of my grandparents. They've mentioned him, but my Grandma Cora is closer to the Macdonald lady. They talk to each other every day. My grandfather is the one who goes to the same pub as Mr. McFadden, but I just know that he's one of the regulars. Grandpa Conrad doesn't go into details, and I've never had reason to ask."

"Maybe so, but I think we should pay more attention to where we're living. We've been told that a Pierre lives here, and Mrs. Macdonald seemed to imply that he was sketchy. His room is on the same floor as ours, and we haven't seen him yet. Who is this character?"

"Well, we've only been here for a day, and maybe he's out of town for some reason. Or maybe he just keeps odd hours. It's too early to get tied up in a knot."

"Then there's Brian, the history student. He seems rather nice. I thought he said he had to put Christmas lights on Mr. McFadden's perogies. Did I get that right?"

Allison laughed. "No. He said the perogies in the freezer were Mr. McFadden's and that he was going downstairs to put away the Christmas garland and lights. No wonder you can't keep your lab instructions straight!"

"Allison, you have a mean streak! Mr. McFadden just said it all so fast, and I was trying to listen to him explain about his leaving. Who rents a room to strangers and then leaves the next day?"

"I guess if you're Stanley McFadden, and there's a Mary Alice Macdonald next door who virtually runs the place, then there's not much risk of an uprising. I have the distinct impression that we are under her watchful eye. No doubt she will report our every move to my grandma."

"And there's poor Captain here. He's been left out of the conversation, and we haven't given him anything. I'll get him a fresh grape."

Finally, the chatter ceased, and something worthwhile was going to happen.

"He's still got food in his dish, so I don't think he's been starving. How do you know he wants a grape?"

Melody reached the kitchen and found the grape supply in the fridge. "Because there was a note on the fridge when I came down this morning. It gives a list of treats that Captain can have. Apparently, he likes peanuts in the shell, a tiny piece of cheese, grapes, or celery. And we're never to give him avocado. The note says it's toxic to birds."

"I thought parrots ate crackers. But if the parrot is anything like Mr. McFadden, I suppose his tastes are odd."

"Don't be silly. Birds shouldn't have processed food, and neither should we, for that matter."

Melody returned to the living room and presented the grape through the bars. I took it daintily to show her that I am a well-behaved parrot and deserve more treats, anytime she remembered to bring them. It's part of the teaching regime for new thumbies. This one was coming along just fine.

"He holds it in one foot and eats it like we would eat an apple. I guess he did want one. Or maybe he just eats whatever you shove in front of him." Allison sounded intrigued but not overly enthused about my eating protocol.

"Well, I'm glad he's not a finicky eater. We need to make sure that nothing happens to him on our watch. I feel so responsible when it's someone else's pet."

"Mum says that Mr. McFadden has had Captain for a while. I suppose he's quite attached to him. Personally, I don't know if I could get that attached to a bird. If we ever get to someplace permanent of our own, I'd like to have a cat."

Allison had just dropped a couple notches in my estimation. Cat people are not to be trusted. Dog people are only one notch above cat people. Clearly, I needed to focus my efforts on Melody, unless it turned out that she loved dogs. Better to shape her before that mistake happened. Too bad she was beginning to look restless.

"I think we've done our due diligence for now. He's squeezed the juice out of the grape and dropped most of the rest on the floor. We can probably leave him. I'd be curious to go up to the third floor and visit that room where we got the extra desk. There might also be an extra desk lamp."

"I'm sure that's the only reason you want to go there. We shouldn't be snooping. Mrs. Macdonald could pop in at any time. And she doesn't strike me as the type who tolerates idle curiosity being given free reign."

"She wouldn't come upstairs, given her difficulty with walking. She would just call out. We need another light, and if we happen to see something interesting along the way, so be it. But I don't want to go up there alone."

"Oh, you're probably just afraid of running into the mysterious Pierre. Maybe he's secretly an axe murderer who only pretends to work on cars." Allison mimed a lumberjack swinging an axe.

"Very funny. But you're coming with me."

Melody set a course for the stairs. Allison shrugged and tagged along half-heartedly behind the intrepid explorer.

"I think this is a bad idea, but I know you're not going to let it rest. So, on with it." They disappeared from view. I could only hear their voices, because I'm a keen-eared parrot, so from here on out, I'll turn things back over to the narrator.

"You just lack a spirit of adventure, Allison. We haven't even gone into the other rooms on the third floor. Mr. McFadden only gave us the key for the one that we got the desk from. Who knows what's locked up behind the other doors?"

"And that's the way it should stay. We don't need to know."

They had reached the mysterious third floor. Melody still had the key to the room. The door opened easily.

"Being up here somehow feels like going back in time. There might be things from when the house was first built."

"For sure—the dust for one thing. The place is probably held together with square nails."

Allison sounded like she was more interested in the structure than the contents. The windows were the old style with putty and glass in wood frames. Certainly, the weathered lace curtains and the yellowed roll-up blinds showed signs of coming from early in the previous century. There were a couple of twin beds, one on each side of the room, against the walls. Each had a knitted afghan on it. Perhaps it had been a place for children to sleep.

In the middle of the room was a crude table that was more of a workbench than an actual table. On it were some objects that looked like they might be broken toys. If they were, they looked homemade, and it wasn't clear what they were supposed to do. Half-finished drawings also lay on the table, sketched designs of the odd toys. A bare light bulb hanging from the ceiling was the only source of light. In one corner was a substantial wingback chair with faded green fabric. On it was a stack of boxes containing table games and jigsaw puzzles. Some of the containers looked like old chocolate boxes.

"Well, if we ever get storm stayed, it looks like we can raid this place for games to play." Melody stood to one side of the table, looking around at the panorama of stored treasures from another era. "Have you spotted a table lamp in any of this stuff?"

"You would think it should be on the work table, if there was one. But I don't see anything other than that overhead bulb. It's awfully stark." Allison didn't sound impressed with Stanley's workplace.

"Maybe Mr. McFadden is near-sighted, and he needs bright light to do whatever it is that he does here. Ow!" Melody stubbed her toe on something. Bending down she saw that she had banged her foot on the brass base of a banker's lamp stowed under the table. It had a single brass stem that led up to a rectangular green shade. A small chain hung down from the frame, but there was no light bulb in the socket. She lifted it gingerly onto the work table. "Hey, look at this. It's really cool. This is what we need for sure. I claim first dibs."

Allison squinted at Melody's find. "How do you know it even works? There's no light bulb and it was forgotten under the table. It's probably a dud."

"I don't see any light bulbs handy, but we can take it down to our room and try it. A banker's lamp would be so retro." Melody's voice bubbled with animation.

"Well, now that we found what we came for, let's go." Allison sounded like she was losing interest.

"Not so fast. The lamp was a good find, but there's other intriguing stuff here. When we came for the desk, we cleaned it out and put some albums and boxes of papers on the floor. We shouldn't just stack stuff on the floor; we should put it away in a closet or at least put it up on the table."

Allison shook her head and started toward the door. "And since when have you become such a convert to neatness and order? Mr.

McFadden loaned us the desk, so he must have realized we would have to take out whatever was in there. He's probably quite capable of organizing that stuff if he really wants to. Let's just take the lamp and go."

"You make it all sound so sinister. We can at least put the things on the table. He's old enough that it's probably hard for him to bend down. We should do that much."

Melody put the small boxes on the table and then retrieved two tattered albums. The first one had a hard cover, and where the binding should be was a black shoelace that tied the two covers and the pages together. The second album was of more recent vintage, with the cover and binding all in one piece. She put them both on the table beside the boxes.

"You've done your good deed. Now we go." Allison's voice was beginning to display impatience.

"Aren't you the least bit curious? The old album might have pictures that go back to the early days of this house. Maybe we can see who lived here and what they were like! I have a real thing for old pictures and the stories they tell."

"And maybe that's none of our business. Or maybe we won't like what we find. Just leave well enough alone. Old stuff is fragile, and you might even damage it by snooping."

"I'll be careful. If we come across something that seems really private, I promise to close the albums, and we'll go. But now that we're this close, I have to look inside them."

Since Melody's determination seemed unbreakable, Allison relented and stayed with her. In fact, she began looking over Melody's shoulder as she turned the stiff black pages.

"Look at the dark fabric dresses and the serious expressions of the people in them. These are Victorian and early twentieth-century pictures. They all seem to be done in studios. There's hardly any that look natural." Melody sounded disappointed.

Allison flipped a few more pages. "I guess that all goes with the time period. These black-and-white pictures look far too old to be from Mr. McFadden's childhood. If they're family pictures, they must be from his grandparents' era. Grandma said that he got this house from his grandmother. She must be in here somewhere, but I don't know what she looked like."

Melody seemed more engaged now. "We could ask Mrs. Macdonald. She probably would know. Or we could ask your Grandma Cora."

"Are you kidding? That would be an admission that we were snooping. Mrs. Macdonald would likely be livid if she knew we were up here in Mr. McFadden's things!" Allison had already developed a healthy fear of the imperial matriarch who dwelt so nearby.

"I suppose you're right. We can only assume these are old family pictures. Look at this one. Most of them are studio shots, but in this one, the man and the woman are out in front of the house, and he's wearing what looks like a World War One army uniform. At least that's what I've seen in TV documentaries."

"And look at the man's face. He's a young man, but he looks a lot like what Mr. McFadden was probably like when he was young. The eyes are the same, and the shape of his jaw. Maybe it's his grandfather?" Allison was getting drawn into the quest.

"I wonder if the man in this photo came back from the war. There's another picture later in the album, and the same lady looks somewhat older, but she's alone and holding a little girl in front of her."

"Melody, that could be Mr. McFadden's mother. We don't know, but she would be a child in that time period. I remember seeing her once with my grandmother and Mrs. Macdonald, but I was really small, and she was very elderly. I can't tell from this picture if it's the same person."

Allison sounded a bit disappointed that she couldn't remember more. Melody kept turning over more pages. "Some of the pictures look a little newer, even though they're all still black and white. I recognize the gardens in front of the BC Legislature. And there are others that show some kind of industrial buildings around the harbour. The harbour looks way more industrial than it does now. There's another one of that little girl with other children in a church concert. Actually, it looks like a Christmas pageant. There must be an interesting story that connects all these pictures. I wish our family had pictures that went back like this."

Allison furrowed her brow. "We don't know that Mr. McFadden would know all the story either. Maybe his mother explained all this stuff to him, or maybe he just has the album. It's not exactly on prominent display. He had it in an old desk on the third floor of his house. Could be he forgot about it."

Melody closed the fragile album carefully and picked up the newer one, which was bound like a more modern photo album. It wasn't nearly as thick, and the pages were a white card stock rather than the black paper of the older volume. "This one has some colour pictures in the last half, although the colour is pretty faded in most of them. At the beginning is a black-and-white picture of a young man and a woman. The guy is wearing a padded suit with wide lapels. She's holding a baby in a christening gown, and they're standing in front of a church. Cute baby. No way to know who it is."

"I'm not a fashion expert, but I think men wore that kind of thing in the late 1930s and 1940s. Hmm . . . if you look closely, you can see that woman is that little girl from the first album but all grown up. Look at her eyes and that pug nose." Allison seemed aware of not only how houses were built but also how people are built.

"Yes, that makes sense. She's Mr. McFadden's mother, and the man is his father. There's another picture on the next page. They're standing outside the church with three older people—two women and one man. The couple are likely his dad's parents, and the other older woman is . . . his grandmother!"

At that point Captain let out a loud shriek, followed by vociferous squawking. Melody clamped the album shut and quickly put it down on the table. She was first off the mark, dashing toward the stairs. "Something terrible must have happened. The bird must be in trouble."

"I'm right behind you. I hope he's all right. That sounded awful." Allison needed little persuasion to leave. Both girls made it downstairs considerably faster than Stanley ever did.

"Salut, ladies. I am Pierre. Monsieur Stanley, he told me that you are the new ones in the house. Me, I was just saying hello to Corporal here, but he does not like it much when I wave my finger between the bars. He is not such a friendly one, I t'ink. How goes it wit' you?"

Beware the barbarian. He looks too hungry for my liking. Awk!

Captain leaned forward, shaking himself and readjusting his wings. Allison took the lead. "Pleased to meet you, Pierre. This is Melody, and I'm Allison. We share Katrina's old room. I guess we'll bump into you now and then."

"Oh, yes, for sure. But where is Monsieur Stanley? Usually, he is here in the afternoon, sipping his sherry. I need to check with him about a little business t'ing."

"Perhaps he didn't have a chance to tell you. He is gone for two weeks to Cuba. He left early this morning. You didn't hear him go?" Apparently, Melody concluded that Pierre wasn't as dangerous as Captain's shriek had suggested.

"Ah, no. Me, I was not here last night because I got invited to stay with Monsieur Brewster. You know him?"

"No."

"Dat's good, I t'ink. Anyway, all is good, and I make supper now. Don't worry, I leave everyt'ing clean in the cuisine. Dat's de rule here. And Madam Macdonald, she will check on de rule!"

As Stanley would say, ducklings need much supervision. Mary Alice was an experienced duckling supervisor. Allison and Melody were fortunate not to get supervised . . . this time.

16
A Secret Revealed

STANLEY WAS STILL gone. Melody was very attentive to her avian duties, and Mary Alice had not threatened Captain with her porridge stick. She even brought a grape when she thought no one else was looking. Occasionally, she would come in ranting about the teapot, and then she would stop. There was no one to rant to, except Captain.

Sometimes I get the front-row seat to a Mary Alice rant because no one else is here. I try to look like I'm listening. I doubt she can tell when I'm listening and when I'm not. All the same, it would be better if Stanley came back and listened to her. Stanley always comes back. I can't tell how long he'll be away, but I notice the days that he isn't here. And he's not here a little longer each day, because the sun stays up longer.

Perhaps days in January go by so quickly because they are so short. Although the hours of daylight increase after Christmas, it takes a while for the difference to amount to anything. In this sense, increases in winter daylight are like increases in Stanley's Canada Pension benefits—there are measurable increments but not enough to warrant a full-blown party. Stanley has made that observation to the prime minister in past letters. We know the prime minister does not pay very much attention to Stanley.

Melody was conscientious in her attention to parrot basics, but she didn't follow the routine of covering Captain's cage with a dark sheet at night. In the wild, most parrots live in the equatorial latitudes; therefore, they get twelve hours of daylight and twelve hours of darkness, most of the year. Their household cousins in the higher latitudes like to have some artificial help in duplicating that balance of light and darkness. Hence, Stanley resorted to a bedsheet, so Captain's circadian rhythms would not be violated by late-night TV or the widely fluctuating hours of summer and winter daylight. With Stanley being away, there was no bedsheet. This turned out not to be such a problem, because the tenants didn't disturb Captain with late-night TV. They were of a generation that watched their laptops and iPads. They came and went and made the odd meal, but they didn't hang around enough to be either a distraction or a source of company.

Stanley had been gone for ten days, and the household routine was pretty much established. Brian went to classes and would say hi, in passing, to Allison and Melody. Alas, he dipped into Stanley's hoard of frozen perogies when the occasion called for a quick supper. Pierre declared that he was working on his last car project before returning to Quebec in the spring. Mary Alice continued her unannounced visits but made them less frequently as she noted that the household was not descending into chaos. Or at least it wasn't descending any faster than when Stanley was there. And the girls settled into their role as house sitters and tenants.

❊ ❊ ❊

The lock on the front door turned, and Melody entered the porch. She set her open umbrella on the floor to give it an opportunity to dry after the winter shower. Then she opened the inner door to the living room.

"Hi, Captain. Were you napping? You look a bit sleepy. It's a dull, wet day, and I could almost have a nap too."

You only get good at something if you practice. I was practicing my napping.

"How about if I sit with you a while? I'll get you a millet spray, and you can munch while I read my assignment."

Captain hunched his wings and raised some of his back feathers. "Eschew-w-w." His grating cough was something between a resonant sneeze and a gurgle.

"Oh dear. Do parrots catch cold? I hope not."

Melody visited the supply drawer in the kitchen and cut a section of millet spray. She made some tea for herself and brought the mug and the millet spray back to the living room.

"Come get your millet." She pushed the short millet spray through the bars. Captain carefully took it in his beak and transferred it to his right foot. He nibbled each individual seed, holding the stem in his foot.

"There's so little nutrition in those bland little seeds. I wonder why you like them so much."

Captain continued to eat. *Why do you like unbuttered popcorn?*

Melody opened her biochemistry lesson and sipped her tea. Captain again assumed a rumpled pose. "Eschew-w-w." The sound seemed to surge forth from deep in his parrot chest.

"That's a nasty cough. I've heard you make that sound fairly often over these last few days. But you don't look sick. Very peculiar. I wish I knew more about parrots."

You and me both, lady. I'm trying to tell you something.

After several pages, Melody put down her book and shifted restlessly. "I think you have everything you need. I'm going upstairs for a while. I want to go back to that bedroom with the photo albums. Allison says it's wrong to snoop, but something is drawing me to those old pictures." Captain shifted position but didn't make any more sounds.

Melody mounted the stairs and kept on going to the third floor. It didn't seem so forbidding now, just alluring. She used the key to unlock the door. Everything was as she and Allison had left it on their last visit. The two albums were still on the work table. She hesitated and picked up the newer one and flipped past the pages that showed early childhood pictures of Stanley and his parents. The baby pictures were in black and white, but some school and picnic pictures were in faded colour. By the time she got to the ones of high school graduation and university, Stanley was looking very dapper in a velvet bowtie and double-breasted jacket. Sometimes the photos included other young people—perhaps cousins or school friends. Then the young people started to get older, as did Stanley.

Generally, the backgrounds were places in Saskatoon, not Victoria. Melody recognized them because she and her mother had lived there through her own childhood years. She felt a little more connected to Stanley, knowing he had probably walked in some of the same neighbourhoods that she did, albeit in a different era. Initially, he was just a stranger, whom she and Allison had met through Allison's grandmother. But seeing the pictures from Saskatoon made it seem like she had a shared history with him, even though she hadn't known him in that history. The album went as far as his mid-adult years, and most of the pictures were of him with various men. When she reached the last page, she heard footsteps on the stairs, and then the steps were on the same floor, getting louder.

"Melody, are you there?" It was Allison. "I saw your books downstairs, and you weren't in the bedroom when I came up, so I figured you must be up here. Again!"

One picture caught Melody's eye, and she gasped. "Yes, I was snooping, and I found something awesome! Come here and see."

Allison gave a twisted expression. "You really shouldn't be poking around in here."

"Never mind. Just look at this one photo of a couple. Who do you see? Tell me honestly." Melody was excited as she jabbed her finger at a photo on the last page of the album. It alone was worth the snooping.

"Well, I see a young fortysomething guy with his arm around a girl who's probably a little younger, and she's smiling back. So, who are they?"

"Let me show you some other photos of that middle-aged guy. It's Mr. McFadden when he was a lot younger. And some of those pictures show him growing up in Saskatoon."

"So, he met a girl and maybe had a girlfriend then. Or maybe it's a sister or a cousin. Why are you so wired up about a simple picture?"

"Because I recognize the young woman in the photo. He's standing with my mother! I've seen pictures of her when she was that age, and that's her!"

"Are you sure? It would be a weird coincidence if they knew each other. If that's so, then maybe they still have common friends in Saskatoon and don't realize it. You can always ask Mr. McFadden when he comes back."

"You don't understand. This is a picture of my mother before I was born. The way she's standing with Mr. McFadden, they are more than casual friends. I'm twenty-five; my mother had me when she was thirty-one. In this picture, she's thirty or so. She always told me that my father abandoned her just after I was born and that she never heard from him again. She didn't say why he left. It's always been this great mystery. Your grandmother said that Mr. McFadden came to Victoria and took over this house twenty-five years ago. I think he's likely my father and that my mother either didn't know where he went, or she didn't want to reveal what she knew, for my sake. He kept the picture as a reminder of whatever happened back then."

"That's all pretty circumstantial. You might be jumping to conclusions. Just take a deep breath." Allison tried to sound skeptical, but the connections did seem plausible.

"If I ask him about knowing my mother, he'll want to know why. And if I tell him about the photo, he'll know I've been snooping. I can call my mother, but I'm not sure if she wants to hear about him if he abandoned her. She probably doesn't know he kept a picture of them; that could be a good memory for her or a bad one. This is all so complicated."

"Maybe we can ask Mrs. Macdonald. She seems to know a lot about this house and probably about Mr. McFadden. That would be a little more discreet."

"She might or might not have that kind of personal knowledge. She mentioned coming here from Cape Breton fifty years ago.

All these things with my mother happened in Saskatoon, so Mrs. Macdonald wouldn't likely know anything about that part of Mr. McFadden's life. I can't tell if they share personal stuff or whether they just kind of act out their parts. We only saw them together that one time before he left."

"Probably the parrot is the one who knows the real story. And he doesn't talk. So, what are you going to do?" Allison sounded dubious about getting very deep into this mystery.

"I don't think Mrs. Macdonald trusts us enough yet. Talking to her is out. I'll have to wait until Mr. McFadden is back, and then I'll ask him if he would like to see some family pictures that I brought with me. Out of politeness, he'll have to say yes. Then I can watch his reaction when he sees my mother."

Allison shook her head slowly. "Sometimes you're so devious. It scares me!" Both women laughed.

"But of more immediate concern is Captain. He has the most awful cough and wheeze. He looks OK, so I don't understand how he can sound so bad."

"Maybe he's just getting old. I've read that parrots can live quite a long time, but eventually they must decline."

"Well, he's not going to live a long time with that kind of cough. If he were human, I would take him to a respiratory specialist. I suppose we could take him to a vet, but that might be expensive, and he's not our bird. And I don't know if he would even cooperate and let us catch him."

"I have an idea," Allison said. "We don't want to risk catching him or transporting him somewhere in that big cage. Maybe we can just transport his cough!"

"What are you saying?" Melody asked. "How can we possibly do that?"

"Easy. Just record Captain on your cell phone, and bring the recording to the veterinary assistant clinic at my college. The teachers are veterinarians, and one of them can listen to the recording and tell us if this is a life-threatening emergency or if it's just something minor."

Melody's demeanour brightened noticeably. "That's a righteous idea! But I'm not sure if we can get him to cough on cue. He seems to have a mind of his own."

"Well, given his size, it's a very small mind. Just try sitting there with your phone and catch him making the sound."

"It's worth a try. Let's do it." Melody closed the albums and put them back where they came from. She and Allison descended the stairs to the living room. They sat on the couch, and Melody took out her cell phone and held it at the ready.

"He's just methodically eating his way through that little branch of seeds. How often does he cough?" Allison wondered how much time they would have to commit to this project.

"It seems to come and go. He fluffs himself up just before the cough. And then he shakes as he makes that explosion of sound."

"Seems to me you have a good handle on his symptoms, Dr. Melody."

"I'm a long way from being a doctor. But in practicums they do teach us to record symptoms and not prejudge what the symptoms mean."

Melody was calm and methodical. They waited a few minutes. Captain began to fidget, and Melody pushed "record" on her phone. Sure enough, he ruffled his feathers. "Eschew-w-w," followed by a gurgling sound, then another rasping "Eschew-w-w."

"Well, he may not speak, but he sure is an articulate cougher. Did you get that?"

Melody played back the recording. "Fantastic. I got both coughs and that gurgling sound. Thank you, Captain!"

Captain swung his head in a figure eight. *I hope you can do something with that little gadget thing. This coughing is hard on a seasoned pro, even someone like me!*

The rest of the evening was spent with the usual domestic routine of supper and working on assignments. Brian came home and remembered to spritz Captain. That set off a major preening session as Captain groomed himself before going into his sleep pose. It's always good for a parrot to look good; you never know who you are going to meet in your dreams.

In the morning, Melody and Allison went their separate ways; however, they agreed to meet up in the early afternoon at the College of Applied Technology, where Allison was an apprentice carpenter.

For Melody, the morning passed slowly as she sat through lectures and fingered her phone. Finally, her classes were over, and she could take a transit bus to the college. She found the student services centre and waited there until Allison came in.

"I'm kind of excited about this," Melody said. "Let's go before it goes off into cyberspace somewhere. It's been known to happen. The building where they have the veterinary assistant program is about a five-minute walk from here."

In a few minutes, the sleuthing duo arrived at the right building and found what appeared to be the front office.

"We would like to meet with one of the veterinary doctors, if one is available." Melody tried to sound professional, supressing her anxiety.

"We offer a veterinary assistant program, but the doctors don't keep clinical hours for the public. I can give you a list of veterinary practices in the city, if that's helpful." The middle-aged receptionist was efficient but perfunctory.

"Actually, I'm doing a study of parrot pathologies, and I need to consult with a doctor about an unusual condition that I have come across in my research. It's a very specific question, so it would not require much of his time."

Allison tried not to look astonished at Melody's assertive overstatement of the facts. The receptionist sat up a little straighter as she reached for her phone. "I'll try and reach Dr. Schlegel. He's our avian specialist. I can't guarantee he's in though."

She fidgeted, waited, and pushed some more digits. More fidgeting. "Hello, Dr. Schlegel? This is Reception. I have here a researcher who would like to meet with you briefly about an avian pathology question. You can? That's excellent. I'll send her up."

"Dr. Schlegel is between classes just now. He's willing to see you if it doesn't take too long. Go up to room two twenty. If the matter is at all lengthy, you should make an appointment and come back. But he is available for a few minutes."

Melody and Allison exited the reception office and proceeded to the stairs at the end of the hall. Melody waited until they were out of earshot. "Well, she was a cool one."

"And you were a suave one. I'm amazed you came up with that line so quickly. Here I thought I had hooked up with Miss Goody Two Shoes."

"Shows little you know. I've learned from a master." Allison panned a shocked face at the suggestion that she was a master at devious deception.

When they got to room 220, the door was already open. The bearded man inside was wearing a white lab coat and sat at a desk overflowing with papers. He was fiftyish and slightly balding.

"And what can I do for you two ladies? Which one of you is the avian researcher?" Dr. Schlegel believed in getting to the point quickly. He spoke like a man pressed for time—always.

"I'm the one with the avian question. I'm actually in pre-med studies over at the university, and I have recorded a troubling cough that my landlord's parrot has. We're in charge of looking after him while our landlord is away, and I'm afraid the bird is terribly sick. Could you listen to the recording and tell me if we should be doing something?" Melody's tone was more pleading than clinical.

"I see. This is not exactly a major research question." He looked over his glasses at Melody. "In any case, why didn't you just bring the bird with you?"

"Well, he's in a big cage, and I don't know if he has some kind of carrier. We're bird sitting, and we don't have a car to transport him. But I have this recording of the sound he makes."

"Hmm . . . a bit unorthodox. But since you're here, and I happen to know something about parrots, you may as well go ahead. I'm not sure I can help based on just a recording, but play it."

Melody played the recording. The unsettling rasping cough was quite audible. Then the cough and the gurgle and the repeat.

"Play it again, a little louder if you can."

Melody upped the volume to maximum.

"Very interesting. Do you know what kind of parrot it is?"

"Well, he's mostly green, about the size of a crow, but with a burgundy beak. He has yellow on the underside of his feathers, and he has a long thin tail, about the same length as his body. He has little dark eyes and a pink band around his neck."

"Sounds like Psittacula eupatria. It's a kind of Asian parakeet that's domestically bred and relatively available in pet stores. What's the condition of this bird? Does it look well-groomed and lively? Bright eyes or dull eyes? " The doctor seemed at least mildly interested.

"He has clean, well-kept feathers and shiny black eyes. He eats well and seems physically active. His droppings are semi-solid, and he doesn't have diarrhea. There is no discharge from his nose." Melody tried to be thorough but concise; she wanted to be taken seriously.

"Not a bad medical history for someone at your stage of training. Tell me, what would you guess the cough to be, based on your powers of observation?"

Melody became flustered. "I don't know, really. What's normal for a bird? He sounds very distressed, and I'm amazed that such a small creature can produce such a deep, rasping cough. And that gurgling sounds like he's drowning or something."

"There's your clue. This bird couldn't have a body mass of any greater than two hundred and fifty grams, and that cough comes from an animal much larger. Birds do cough if they have fluid on their lungs or if they have ingested a foreign substance. But such an avian vocalization is more like a small sniffle or a puppy dog snort. This recording sounds like a mammal of a hundred kilograms or more. The sound is not a symptom of the bird's condition."

"But I made the recording quite close to him. It really is from the parrot!" Melody was alarmed because it was beginning to sound like the doctor didn't believe her.

"I didn't say I doubted the source of your recording. Let me finish. You have confirmed that the bird looks fine. The bird is imitating a sound that it has heard in its immediate environment. In a sense, your recording is a recording of a recording. This species of parrot, like many parrots, can 'record' a sound that it hears. They can imitate household sounds like dog barks or cat meows or even telephone rings. A parrot imitates whatever sound is a bonding sound with its flock. This bird of yours has bonded with a human who has, or has had, a severe respiratory condition. That's my tentative diagnosis."

"That's really wild. My landlord said his parrot doesn't speak. I never thought he was imitating someone!"

"The bird, in fact, may not imitate human speech. Sometimes they can be taught, and sometimes they don't take to it. Parrots, like other animals, have their own personality, and some are more trainable than others. This bird may not say cute phrases, but it has the innate capacity to imitate. And it has chosen to imitate this sound. I suggest you encourage your landlord to visit his doctor, if, in fact, he is the one to produce the original sound. I'm sorry, but that's all the time that I have today. I wish you well in your 'avian research,' as you put it."

"Thank you very much for seeing us. You've been very helpful. We'll see ourselves out." Allison took the initiative to be mannerly, while Melody tried to process everything they had just heard as they made their way out of the building.

Allison broke the silence. "That was both amazing and scary. I'm relieved that Captain is not on death's door, but now we have a bigger crisis. Why didn't we hear Mr. McFadden coughing like that before he left for Cuba?"

"I need to look into it more, but people with certain types of respiratory conditions don't necessarily cough all the time. We need to connect the dots. Sometimes the coughing only comes on with exertion. Did you notice that Mr. McFadden didn't ever come upstairs with us? And he didn't go down to the basement either. He made it seem like he was too busy, but he was probably hiding his cough. Captain is there all the time, so he's heard him coughing often. Maybe he thinks that's the special sound that bonds him to Mr. McFadden." Melody's head was spinning.

"If Dr. Schlegel is right, Captain has ratted Mr. McFadden out. Maybe the bird is smarter than all of us!" Captain should have been there to confirm Allison's endorsement.

"I don't know if he's smart, but he's certainly revealed a secret, whether or not he knows what a secret is." Melody chose to retain some scientific skepticism about Captain's motives.

"Oh, I hate secrets. And I hate knowing what we are probably not supposed to know. We've stumbled onto two secrets in two days. Shady Shingles is turning out to be a lot shadier than we thought." Allison cupped her hands over her eyes and then peeked out at Melody.

"Well, you can't unlearn a secret. Now that we know, we'll have to do something. Mr. McFadden could be my father, and he could be hiding a serious illness. I could gain a father and lose one all at the same time. They don't teach us what to do with this kind of life challenge in pre-med classes!" Melody was beginning to feel overwhelmed.

"This isn't exactly carpentry either. I learn to build and repair houses, not people. Should we even think of getting more involved, since neither of us has known Mr. McFadden very long?"

"Maybe for you it's not something of urgent importance. But if he is indeed my father, then I don't have the luxury of getting to know him for months before acting. This coughing thing could mean he has something very serious and might not be around if I wait. I'd rather risk getting involved and find out that we have no biological connection than play it safe and lose a parent whom I never had a chance to know."

Both girls had much to think about as they made their way to the bus stop and navigated the public transit home. Long bus rides can be good for the soul.

Ducklings like to follow Mum when there is a crisis, because mother ducks know where to go. Sometimes Mum is out of sight, and the ducklings have to follow their instincts. They learn about carrying on and making decisions about which way to go, sometimes even in the face of danger or the unknown. Indeed, some of them don't make it. In the human world, we believe we are superior to ducklings because we can make conscious decisions about interventions and relationships. But in the end, we have to carry on with all the risks involved in living. And isn't that what ducklings do, paddle among the lily pads and choose their own way to go? Life is a risk worth taking for all sorts of ducklings, both human and feathered.

17
A Confrontation Occurs

ALL GOOD THINGS come to an end, even winter trips to Cuba. To my relief, Air Cheapo did produce a plane for the return journey. It was also somewhat of a victory that I am still on speaking terms with Andy and Bob. I have travelled with friends before, and we were less than friends after the trip. In this case, we did things together, and sometimes we hung out separately—I with my book in the shade and they with their bronzing oil on the beach.

Ever since seeing *Jaws*, I have had an aversion to beaches. The sequels to that movie have done nothing to change my mind. However, a Cuban beach in January has the advantage that it exists under a sky that is not grey and rainy. Also, the bank is not going to call. And Mary Alice is certainly not going to arrive unannounced for tea. They are not big on tea in Cuba. Mary Alice is not big on Cuba. So, all in all, it was an opportunity for a change and a catch-up visit with Andy and Bob. I admired their "couplehood" but not enough that I would be imitating their domestic bliss anytime soon. I would only be open to marriage if the other party were very old, very frail, and very rich. Therefore, it appears that Shady Shingles is my fate for the foreseeable future.

Mary Alice was at the airport to meet me. The fact that she showed up was proof positive that she could still navigate the Three Traffic Circles of Purgatory, so I let my initial anxiety about her driving at her age subside. On the other hand, her picking me up was not a pre-arranged thing, so what prompted her to make the impromptu appearance? She knew I would take the airporter, as I had done on other trips.

"Welcome home, you Latin wanderer! I hope you weren't loading up on Cuban rum in the duty-free?" I could have taken her comment as an admonishment, but as a dyed-in-the-wool Bluenoser, Mary Alice could also have been dropping a hint. I believe a drop or two of bootleg Jamaican rum has been known to make its way to Nova Scotia. In the right circumstance, Mary Alice might be ecumenical enough to try Cuban rum.

"No, I bought sherry instead. Cubans are not famous for their sherry, but if you have US dollars, it's amazing what they have in stock in their duty-free store."

"It matters not. The main thing is that you made it back safely. And you don't even look sunburned!"

"No, that wasn't one of the goals of the trip. I enjoyed lots of sun, but I watched it from the shade. Speaking of shade, how is life at Shady Shingles?"

"Maybe we should make a stop in the coffee shop, if we're going to get into that." It would be unusual for Mary Alice to suggest socializing at an expensive airport coffee shop. Something was up. I grabbed my bag off the carousel and followed her to one of the java places.

"Oh dear, they don't give the stuff away, do they?" Mary Alice evaluates food establishments by how much higher their prices are than at Lucky Foods.

"Never fear, my dear. The coffee is on me because you have gone to all the trouble of driving out here to the airport." The age of chivalry is dead, but some rituals are required anyway. It also helps if the ritual doesn't cost too much.

"They don't make decent tea at these places, but I suppose I could have coffee for a change. Just bring me a cup of their medium roast." Mary Alice lowered herself gently at a table and kept watch over my luggage while I stood in line and did my humble servant routine. I came back with the requisite java.

"They only serve it in paper cups, no proper mugs or anything. Sorry." I could tell by Mary Alice's expression of disdain that airport coffee shop hospitality was not going to be up to her standard.

"Any port in a storm, Stanley. It'll have to do." When Mary Alice adopts an understanding tone, it's a sign that the worst is yet to come.

"Pray tell, my dear, give me the update on our beloved Shady Shingles." I wondered if maybe the roof had blown off or the house had been broken into.

"I don't want to alarm you, but Captain might be on his way out. I mean, he seems to have developed a terrible cough. I hadn't noticed, but Melody and Allison are there a lot more than I am, and they heard him. They visited some kind of vet at the college, but then they wouldn't tell me what he said."

I couldn't tell if the Dowager Empress was distraught because Captain might be seriously ill or because the girls were not deferring to her matriarchal authority. I suspected more of the latter than the former.

"Maybe they just didn't want to worry you. That news seems surprising because Captain looked perfectly fine before I left, and I don't recall him coughing. He sniffles sometimes, but that's when he's indignant about something—the TV is too loud or I've let the grapes get too old. Could be he's developed something just recently. I can check when we get home."

"And there's another thing, although I suppose it's not my business to be concerned." As you might suspect, Mary Alice often says the opposite of what she is actually thinking. There isn't much in the realm that is not her ladyship's business.

"Well, I may as well get the complete scenario while we're here. What else happened?"

"Far be it from me to cast aspersions on Cora's granddaughter, but I asked if she would like to come along to mass with me, and she said no." I had the distinct impression that my earlier hint about Allison's confessional loyalties was going to catch up with me.

"Her grandmother is certainly a good Catholic, and I know she raised her daughter that way, so I just assumed that Allison went to mass. But she told me that she hasn't been to church since she was sixteen. It must be Melody who is a bad influence on her! Those girls may not be as honourable as I thought."

"That might be so, but after all, we didn't interview them; you only assumed that Cora's granddaughter would be a younger version of Cora. Grandma wasn't Catholic, and you got along fine with her."

"But I knew your dear grandmother for forty years, and she was properly religious in her way. It's not the same thing at all."

"Well, Allison isn't even forty years old, but she must have some of Cora's genes; if you just live for another forty years, there's potential."

"I should have known better than to expect you to take me seriously. You're one of those agnostics or heathens or whatever yourself!"

"Ah yes, my dear. The world needs people like me, so people like you can have a project. I've been thinking of starting up a chapter of Heathens Anonymous. You could be our chaplain."

"Oh, Stanley, you're impossible!" Mary Alice laughed and wiped away a tear.

"That's what Jerome at the bank says too. But I think he means it in a different way. In any case, we should head out before we need a bank loan to pay the parking."

Mary Alice and I are often on the same page when it comes to saving money. We deposited our paper cups in the recycling bin and made our way out to the parking lot. When I offered to drive her car home, she didn't object. She obviously made it to the airport without mishap, but it doesn't pay to tempt the traffic demons too often in the same day. We made it through the Three Circles of Purgatory in one pass. I parked the car in front of Mary Alice's house. She has a garage, but it's too full of stuff to accommodate even a small car.

"Well, thank you for the coffee and the drive home. I hope you sort out what's happening with Captain. I know you're attached to the silly creature."

Mary Alice disappeared through the front door of her house. I dug into my pocket for my house key. Then I remembered I had put it into my wallet. I retrieved the key and made my way inside. It was still light, and Captain was on top of his cage, leaning toward the door. He can see through the front window into the porch, and therefore spot anyone who's coming.

"How's my favourite bird? Did you miss me?" I've never gotten an answer to such queries, but there might always be a first time.

Never mind the chitchat. Did you bring me anything? You owe me big time for abandoning me to amateurs! Captain bobbed his head up and down.

"It looks like they've been changing your papers, and your water is clean. You can't be too badly off. But what's this about a bad cough? Mary Alice made it sound like you were dying or something."

Captain tilted his head and eyed me intently. *Don't believe the Dragon Lady. At her age, she's closer to dying than I am. I just made a little parrot intervention while you were gone.*

"I can't tell if you're really thinking something or you're just hinting that you want a grape. Let me put away my suitcase, and then I'll check on the grape supply." I retreated to the bedroom. After I unpacked, I padded into the kitchen. I was pleased to see a small bowl of grapes in the fridge.

"Since this is a homecoming celebration, I brought you the entire bowl. You can pick your own grape." I held the grapes up to Captain, who quickly reviewed the contents of the bowl as if he were about to make a complicated move at bridge. He chose the biggest grape.

"Well, there's nothing wrong with your appetite. And I haven't heard any cough. Maybe whatever it was is gone now."

I don't need to cough for you. You should know what your own cough sounds like.

"I'd love to stay up and chat, but I'm tired after my trip. You would have liked Cuba. Still, it's good to be home and have my own bed." Captain dove down into his cage, and I covered him with the dark sheet. Strangely, it was still folded up exactly the same way as when I left. Usually, I would stay up and watch the late news, but the lure of sleep was too strong. I turned off the lights and retired.

When morning came, Stanley slept in later than usual. He didn't hear any of the tenants when they came home at their various times. Even when Melody and Allison came down for breakfast, he was still asleep in the back bedroom.

"Do you think Mr. McFadden came home last night?" Allison looked around for some sign that Stanley had returned.

"Look at Captain's cage. It's covered. We haven't been covering the cage at night, and I don't think Brian or Pierre would bother. Mr. McFadden is probably in his room, sleeping."

"Are you going to talk to him when he gets up, or are you going to wait?" Allison generally preferred caution to bold risks.

"Well, I'm not sure about the cough. I don't want to bring that up until I let one of my profs hear the recording. But I'm going to show him some pictures of my mum and me and see how he reacts."

"Are you going to tell the prof that they're listening to a bird? I'd love to see their face."

"No, it's more objective if they just listen to it at face value. The tougher part may be explaining why I'm presenting a recording and not a live person."

"Knowing you, you'll think of something convincing. When does this astounding diagnosis happen?"

"I have a class this afternoon, and afterwards I can find the right kind of prof in the faculty of medicine."

"Well, I hope it goes well. I'd like to hang around, but I have a class at nine, and I have to run. Catch you later."

Melody uncovered Captain, who was sounding restless under the sheet. He had heard them talking and wanted his morning routine to start.

"Just hold on. I'll change your dishes and get you breakfast. Are you glad Mr. McFadden is home again?"

Captain did his head-swinging ballet. *I'm glad he's back, but he's a slacker. Bring on the goodies. I'm hungry.*

Melody busied herself in the kitchen, carrying out a routine that was now familiar. Captain's water dish was made of stainless steel, and it clanged when she accidentally dropped it in the sink. "Damn. That thing is loud enough to wake the dead." Melody tried to get the rest of the routine done hurriedly. She heard stirring in the back room, and then Stanley emerged in his pajamas.

"Good morning, Melody. Thank you for the wakeup clang. I think I must have overslept." Stanley yawned and looked decidedly bleary-eyed.

"Sorry. I didn't intend to do that. I was just trying to look after Captain's breakfast, thinking you might want to sleep in after your trip. How was it?" Melody could be both cheery and apologetic at the same time.

"It was fabulous, actually. I was there with old friends. The weather was warm but not hot. The food was good, and we had a nice side trip to Old Havana."

"Did you get to meet any locals? What are they like?"

"I guess the hotel staff and the waiters were local, but we didn't visit all that much. Come to think of it, we were typical tourists. Probably for ordinary people, life doesn't have many extras. I think they have to struggle."

"Yeah, that's what I've heard. Did you bring back pictures?" The query sounded innocent enough.

"I don't take a lot of pictures, but I have some on my phone. Would you like to see them?"

"Sure. Why don't I make us some breakfast?"

"You do that, and I'll get dressed and join you in a few minutes."

Melody brought Captain his usual breakfast—mixed seeds, fruit salad, and a slice of boiled egg. She noted there was no coughing while he ate. She returned to the kitchen and prepared scrambled eggs and toast and coffee. Stanley reappeared and headed straight for the coffee pot. "Ah, this is great stuff. Why is your coffee so much better than mine?"

"Easy. I put twice as much coffee in it. You make dishwater."

"You realize you're beginning to sound like Mary Alice, don't you?"

"Somehow I think that's not intended as a compliment. I think Mrs. Macdonald is delightfully direct. Has she always been that way?"

"I don't know about always. But for the past twenty-five years at least she's not been one to sugar-coat anything. That's how long I've had this house. Before that my grandmother had the house, and she and Mary Alice were as thick as thieves. In a nice way."

"Well, here's breakfast, such as it is. I hope you like scrambled eggs."

"Excellent. Just sit down and enjoy breakfast with me while it's hot."

"Then I want to see your pictures. I think Cuba would be a fascinating place." Breakfast soon disappeared. Stanley brought out his phone.

"If I did this right, we'll see pictures. Oh good. Here's the hotel. These are a few shots of the beach. And these ones with the Spanish colonial architecture are in Old Havana."

Melody dutifully admired the pictures. "Hey, you're pretty good with the camera. Are your two friends in the pictures a couple?"

"Yes, they've be a couple for a long time, and they've been married since same-sex marriage became legal. Andy is a friend from university days."

"Allison and I want to get married too, but we're going to wait until we finish our programs and get more established."

"I thought you were a couple. Maybe you don't need to mention that to Mrs. Macdonald. She is a kind enough soul but a bit old fashioned about some things."

"You mean she would have trouble acknowledging we're a same-sex couple?"

"She hasn't said that, and I think she chooses not to see the obvious."

"What about you? Are you a gay man or just an old bachelor?"

"As you have probably inferred, I am a gay senior. 'Old bachelor' sounds like some kind of a failure. At this stage of the game, I prefer singlehood to any of the alternatives."

"Good point. Allison and I are going to try and make the relationship thing work, but I can see that people need to make whatever choice suits them. How does Mrs. Macdonald see all this?"

"We're both seniors but we don't quite come from the same generation. She was a close friend of my grandmother, more like an honorary niece. Both of them intuitively knew what was what, but their way of dealing with the politics of identity was to discreetly overlook what didn't fit the world they knew. Grandma Vi would say, 'Be yourself,' without elaborating. Mary Alice practices live and let live, as long as you don't ask her to change her views, which tend to be black and white."

"Do you have any pictures of your grandmother? She sounds like a trooper."

"I have a few. The oldest ones are upstairs—on the third floor. But I keep a few down here in an album in the living room. If you're really interested, I can show you."

Melody cleared away the breakfast dishes, and then they made their way to the living room. Stanley rummaged through a bookcase near his recliner chair. He soon produced an album and set it down on the wobbly coffee table. Melody sat beside him on the couch, and he flipped through to the middle of the collection.

"Here. This is a picture of Grandma Vi and Mary Alice together. I took this picture when my mother and I were here on a Christmas visit, maybe thirty years ago. We lived in Saskatoon at the time, so it was a big adventure to drive here."

Melody scrutinized the photo. "I see some resemblance between you and your grandmother, especially in the eyes. Mrs. Macdonald looks slimmer in this picture, but it's definitely her. They're both wearing dresses!"

"Yes, that was typical for women of their age. Younger women were starting to wear slacks, but neither of those two would consider such a thing, even in winter. Mary Alice keeps up the standard, even today."

"And what about a picture of you from back then? Did you wear bell-bottoms and beads?" Melody's intonation was whimsical.

Stanley turned a page and pointed out a somewhat faded colour photo of a young man with longish hair wearing bell-bottom trousers. His shirt was paisley, and he was putting up a Christmas garland of natural greenery in the porch. "Now I get Brian to put up a plastic garland and lights, but in the old days, Grandma Vi insisted that I hang the real thing."

Melody noticed a touch of nostalgia in Stanley's voice. She also remembered that she had a purpose in this stroll down Memory Lane. "I have some pictures of growing up in Saskatoon. Since you grew up there, maybe you'll recognize some of the same places. Would you like to see them?"

"I have a few things to catch up on, but I can do that, if we have some more coffee."

Melody disappeared upstairs while Stanley did a coffee run to the kitchen. By the time he returned, Melody was back with a handful of photos. "I have more recent ones on my phone, but I do have a few print photos from growing up. Here's one from my high school graduation. This one is of Allison and me on the riverbank trail. In this one, I got a mountain bike at the end of public school. And going way back, this one is of me and my mum when I was a baby."

Melody watched intently for Stanley's reaction. At first, he just stared without saying anything. He squinted and opened his mouth slightly, as if labouring to take in a breath. Then he faltered, "Uh . . . yes . . . that's a lovely picture. Your mother looks very proud of her new daughter. She even looks like someone I once knew. I . . . notice . . . your dad is not in the picture. Maybe I shouldn't ask, but . . ."

"Oh, that's OK. My mum was always a single parent. I never met my dad. Mum said he left the scene before I was born. I've asked her why, but she would only say that it was by mutual agreement. I don't know if they had a falling out or if he was already married or what. That part of my life has always felt very incomplete. And Mum won't say."

"I'm sure she has her reasons. You'll learn that as you get older. People have their reasons, and sometimes knowing the reasons wouldn't change anything about what we have to accept in life. We just have to carry on." Stanley was very deliberate and considerate of his words. And a little unsure of how far he should go.

"Yes, I suppose that's fine for my mum. And it sounds like for you too. But I always have to know more. I feel like part of me is missing."

Stanley shifted his position and looked at Captain, as if for guidance. Captain tilted his head and looked back at Stanley, his shiny black eyes not blinking. Perhaps the meaning of the human words was not clear, but Captain certainly sensed the tone of the conversation.

"I think that your showing me these pictures is no accident, Melody. We're talking around the real issue. Somehow you know that your mother and I have a history, and you've made it your business to find out what it is. Contrary to what you have said, has Angela told you about us?" Mary Alice was not the only one who could speak with an authoritative voice.

"No, not at all. My mum kept her word; she kept your secret. I have to make a confession. It wasn't my mum who said anything. When Allison and I got the second desk from that third-floor room, I snooped. I saw the old albums and looked through them. And I saw the picture of you and my mum, where you have your arm around her. She looked the same age as she does in my baby picture. It just seemed too much of a coincidence. Is it true? Are you my father?"

"Yes, I believe so. This is a lot to absorb. You shouldn't have been snooping, but now that you have, I guess we can't put the genie back in the bottle. I'm not sure how much I can say without breaking trust with Angela. But I know you want to know more, and you have that right."

"Why did you run away? Why couldn't I be told?"

"We were in another time, and maybe we didn't really think things through. Angela and I knew each other in university. We liked the same music, and we could talk about anything. I hadn't come out to everybody, but I did to her. She knew I was gay, and we hung out together a lot. I was older than her, and she was getting into her late thirties. She felt that her biological clock was ticking, but there was no straight man whom she wanted to settle down with and marry or be common-law with. We talked a lot. She felt that she wanted me to be the father of her child." Stanley paused and took a breath.

"Just at that time, I got word that Grandma Vi had died. I would have to move to Victoria and take over the house, if I wanted it. Your mum was committed to staying in Saskatoon to finish her schooling and to be close to family. She preferred to go it alone as a single mother. Because of the attitudes of the day, we felt it was better that she just say that a relationship didn't work out, and the father abandoned her. People would accept that more than the idea that the father was a gay man who was somehow in the picture but not in the household. If we weren't going to have that kind of future together, it made sense to make a clean break. She might meet someone suitable and change her mind about marriage. Or I might meet someone and have a fulfilling gay partnership. We did the deed, and she was pregnant before I left. The agreement was no contact whatsoever, so we wouldn't create emotional attachments that were unrealistic to fulfill. At times I had second thoughts, but by then you and your mum had moved. I couldn't really make inquiries without raising suspicions. So, I stopped second guessing and just accepted that life had to go on."

His coffee had gone cold, but Stanley took a sip anyway. Melody sat back and mulled over what she had heard. "That's a pretty incredible story. That's not how I imagined things at all. And what about now? What does it feel like to meet your daughter?"

"Well, I'm delighted that Angela has done such a good job raising you. I've tried to imagine what you might be like but never thought the day would come that I would meet you. I guess we can start from scratch, if you can deal with suddenly having a father. And then there's how your mum will feel. She may or may not want people to know our secret."

"For starters, I'm definitely OK with having a father. I do want to share with my mum what I have learned. Then she can react however she needs to react. Maybe for now just you and I and Allison will know. Brian and Pierre are nice enough, but this isn't their issue. Captain seems to be handling the news well. He's sleeping."

"I hope you're more than just OK." Stanley stood, and so did Melody. They embraced gingerly and then stepped back.

"For sure. This is very OK. But now I have to head off to class."

"You do that. And we'll both let this new reality sink in a bit. We can talk again later."

Stanley did the dishes and reviewed in his mind all that had just transpired. Cuba was pretty exciting, but it paled in comparison to this turn of events. He went through the motions of unpacking, but his mind was still back at the morning's conversation. There was mail to check over and emails to open. All that seemed mundane in light of the confrontation that Melody had precipitated over breakfast.

It seemed to Stanley that he was no longer who he thought he was.

18
A Double Dilemma

THE REST OF the morning passed quickly. Somehow it was noon, and Stanley felt pangs of hunger.

"Captain, my stalwart, I think I'll grab some lunch at the Piddler. Too bad you don't drink, or I'd invite you along."

At mention of lunch, Captain climbed down to his fruit dish, giving it a good once over. *I think there are probably too many strange birds at that Piddler place. You always come back with some great revelation that doesn't translate into more goodies for me. Be off with you, and join your flock.*

Stanley donned a windbreaker and walked hurriedly to the Piddler. He had become accustomed to warm Caribbean breezes, and now Victoria felt decidedly chilly. The giant chestnut tree by the house reached toward the sky with empty arms, its rough bark declaring it had endured many a winter. A row of shrub roses on the way to the pub was similarly barren, but hedges of Portuguese laurel and Irish yew stood defiantly green, as they did all year.

"Well, look who still walks and breathes! We thought you had died, and Mary Alice forgot to invite us to the wake." Shelagh was a long-ago transplant from Sligo, Ireland, who served tables part time at the Piddler. Clearly, she kept a mental file on reprobate locals, and Stanley was on her "Do not delete" list.

"Sorry to disappoint you, my dear, but you'll have to wait longer for that auspicious occasion. I have just returned from abroad." He was not sure that Cuba qualified as abroad, but there is a continent and a sea between it and Canada, so abroad it must be.

"Begging your pardon, your highness. I hope our humble establishment is still good enough for the Laird of Shady Shingles. The usual?"

"Yes, a pint of stout, but not that Irish muck . . . the Hoyne one. And I'll have an order of chicken wings." Stanley had developed a taste for the local brew, and he rarely deviated from that choice. The chicken wings were strategic because he could bring the bones home to Captain. And the wings always went well with beer.

Shelagh feigned great indignation over Stanley's slight of her homeland's stout. She strutted to another table to take their order before her final sortie to the draught taps. Stanley found his way to his usual spot, which, unfortunately, was occupied by an interloper. Go away for a couple weeks, and the riffraff move in.

"Over here, Stanley! You're here early today." Conrad was nursing a brew, chatting with another regular named Simon. Stanley joined them at their table.

"Good to see you, Conrad. And Simon, are you having any luck in straightening out the imperial Englishman here? You have a big task ahead of you." Simon had been a chief petty officer in the Royal Canadian Navy before his retirement.

"No, Stanley. That job would be above my pay scale. What have you been up to?"

"Actually, I just got back from two weeks in Cuba. Sun, rum, and Caribbean beaches." Stanley's summary was a bit of a gloss-over, but travelogues at the Piddler don't require much accuracy or finesse.

"It's always good to get a reminder of what the sun looks like," Conrad said. "Here the ducks have been jumping off cliffs because of the rain."

Simon and Stanley contemplated the probability of duck angst leading to mass suicide. Most of Victoria's ducks live in Beacon Hill Park, where the average cliff is four inches high. Simon decided the most cogent response to Conrad's observation on the apocalypse was none at all.

Conrad considered the silence to be a sign that he could move on to his next topic. "Stanley, are you home for a while now, or are you going to be galivanting about? I'm surprised the Dowager Empress gave you permission to go to Cuba."

"If you mean Mary Alice, I don't require her permission. She's just a helpful neighbour whose eccentricities I graciously tolerate." Stanley looked from side to side, as if he were checking to see if Mary Alice was within earshot.

Simon raised his eyebrows. "Brave words for a man who has to keep looking over his shoulder." He and Conrad chortled with glee, familiar with Mary Alice's fierce reputation.

"If you two know so much, I have a serious question for you. What would you do if you suddenly found out that you have an adult son or daughter whom you had never previously heard from? Would you be overcome with joy or just blown out of the water?"

Simon and Conrad looked at each other, equally befuddled. Occasionally, their pub banter dealt with weighty matters, but mostly they just pontificated about civic politics, sports, and their latest medical ailments. Stanley was introducing a subject category for which there was no ready-made script. Conrad squinted, and Simon grimaced.

"That depends. Would this offspring be looking for money or just filling in the blanks for their family tree?" Simon always came at issues with a strong practical streak.

Conrad was a man of the heart, more than the head. "If they're your flesh and blood, then you wouldn't have much choice, unless you knew the connection and they didn't. Either way, you'd be a different man than you are now. Why would you ask such a thing anyway?" Clearly, Conrad didn't know the particulars of his granddaughter's friend, and he didn't connect Stanley's question to who Melody might be. Or he was being coy.

Shelagh arrived with the stout. "There you go, love. You don't deserve it, but the boss pays me to be kind, even to ingrates. Another one, gents?" Simon and Conrad nodded their assent.

"Well, it's a long story," Stanley said after she left, "but at this stage of life, I have a daughter who has identified herself, and she is not looking for anything from me. At least not money. It's just new territory to figure out . . . for both of us."

Simon looked relieved. "You sly old dog, Stanley. We didn't think you had it in you, hiding a secret daughter all these years. Were you trying things on the other side of the fence, so to speak?"

"Actually, I've always been on the same side of the fence, as you put it. I was just helping out a friend who didn't want what she felt was the burden of marriage. And then I was out of the picture—I thought forever." Stanley sounded rather wistful.

"People get married forever, and then it's not forever. So, 'forever' is a relative thing for most of us. I'll forever be a father for my daughter and son. But I can die or they can die, and then it's not forever anymore." Conrad was misty eyed.

"That's a darker place than I had in mind, Conrad. But I see what you mean. We can intend certain things, but the context changes, and then we have to adapt to a new reality."

"Yes, you had a life in Saskatoon. Then your grandmother died, and you came here and took over the boarding house. I'll bet you didn't see that change coming. But you've made out all right, haven't you?" Simon was obviously of the school of thought that every problem can be fixed. What is most helpful to friends is to show them how to fix whatever challenge confronts them. Generally, men like to fix things, and women like to be listened to. Simon wasn't quite sure what category gay men fit into, even though he had known Stanley for a number of years. There should be a manual for such things.

"The jury is still out on that one. Jerome, at the bank, thinks Shady Shingles is on life support, and I think we get by nicely, Captain and me. But yes, the change to come here was a good one.

Somehow, I think this change is different, more personal, maybe more demanding." Stanley spoke with hesitation in his voice.

Shelagh arrived with the second round of beer and Stanley's chicken wings. Conrad sipped the newly arrived beer before speaking. "You don't need to overthink these things. Just follow your heart, and everything will work out in time. This new daughter probably has to sort out how she feels too. You can do it together. That's how Cora and I learned to put up with each other."

Stanley felt a newfound appreciation for Conrad's savvy insight into people. He dug into his chicken wings while the other two continued the conversation.

"And if you get into trouble, you can consult Conrad the Soul Whisperer here. The older he gets, the softer in the head he becomes." Simon subtly let it be known that he wanted the conversation to move on.

Conrad made a mock swipe at Simon's head. "He could do worse. He could listen to you, and then his ship would go down with no survivors for sure!"

The rendezvous continued as Conrad and Simon filled Stanley in on the events of civic politics and neighbourhood scuttlebutt that happened while he was gone. In due course, the chicken wings were denuded of meat, and the glasses were empty. Shelagh appeared with the bills.

"Will that be cash or credit card or a pint of blood?" she quipped.

"We've always suspected that you were a vampire, bleeding defenceless seniors of the very force of life that sustains them in their twilight years." Simon did his melodramatic best to humble Shelagh.

"I think it's too late, Simon. The life force abandoned you a long time ago. Just give me your credit card before they cart you away." Shelagh was undaunted by the repartee.

"And in honour of Stanley's safe return, and because I accidentally left him with the bill last time, I shall gallantly pay for his lunch and beer, along with mine." Conrad peered into the depths of his wallet, seemingly in search of the right change.

"Why thank you, Conrad. That's totally unnecessary, but I shall not decline your kind gift."

Conrad continued to root through his wallet, which seemed to contain everything but money. Finally, he extricated a credit card. Shelagh took it from him, put it into the portable reader, and waited as he cautiously tapped in his PIN.

"Conrad, they don't want your PIN in Roman numerals. Just use those little Arabic numbers, and we can all go home. Don't forget you have a tip option there." Conrad furrowed his brow at Simon's unsolicited advice. Shelagh smiled hopefully. Conrad covered the face of the reader with his hand as he entered the required information, then handed the device to Shelagh.

"And we're done. Thank you gents for coming in. Go home now, and have a nice nap." She cleared the table and made her way to the kitchen.

"Good seeing you fellows. I shall return to Shady Shingles with my precious chicken bones and see if Captain is awake. Until next time!"

They went their separate ways. Stanley felt fortified by both the beer and by the conversation. While he would still have to navigate the new territory of fatherhood, it was good to have voiced some of his concerns in the sanctuary of the Piddler. The fact that a couple of friends were privy to this sudden turn of events was somewhat reassuring. He would need some of that confidence when it came to breaking the news to Mary Alice. Better that she heard his version of events first than she accidentally hear something in passing from Cora or her granddaughter.

With all these things going on in Stanley's head, he took a wrong turn before he realized what he had done. The houses were of the same vintage as those on Orkney Street, but the street itself meandered along the edge of an old streambed. Many of Victoria's streets are simply paved versions of old horse trails and cow paths, changing directions several times before crossing some invisible municipal border and assuming a new name on the other side. The delightful logic of Victoria's streets never ceases to befuddle new arrivals from prairie cities, like Calgary or Edmonton. Those places are laid out in a square grid of avenues and streets, often numbered in sequential order.

Victoria has a Fifth Street but no First, Second, Third, or Fourth. Apparently, there was never any money to build the other four. Equally mysteriously, Jutland Road turns into Finlayson Street, which, after a while, turns into North Dairy Road, which dies ignominiously just before it reaches Royal Jubilee Hospital on Richmond. The hospital was evidently named to celebrate the Golden Jubilee of Queen Victoria in 1887. Once something is celebrated in Victoria, the locals never forget, seemingly in the belief that something worth celebrating may never come along again. Alas, Queen Victoria went on to have a Diamond Jubilee in 1897, and locals had to concede that event was worth celebrating even more than the first one. But they had run out of new hospitals by then, so they went back to giving different names to various sections of the same street. Like lawn bowling or curling, there is no logic as to why one would want to do this. Victorians just like creating the potential for a wrong turn.

Stanley's wrong turn was no great crisis because he knew the neighbourhood so well. Unlike the box-like edifices of new suburban neighbourhoods, each house seemed to have a different architecture, if not a hodgepodge of several. Some people's yards were immaculately landscaped, and others were overgrown with ubiquitous English ivy or quack grass. Every house has a story, both the building and the people who dwell within, but the stories are mysteries unless one is invited into it.

These thoughts occurred to Stanley as if he were looking at the street for the first time, wearing a filter of awareness that was out of character. Walking home this new way was like walking a labyrinth, each step leading him into a spiritual awareness of something life changing, hidden at the centre. A seemingly absent-minded error in choosing a wrong street paralleled an unexpected turn in Stanley's personal life. Melody was the one who had stumbled into the Shady Shingles labyrinth, but now both their paths might change. Would it be good to invite her into his present story, or did their stories only overlap at one brief chapter in the past?

It was still early afternoon when Stanley reached the front steps of Shady Shingles. Captain was napping until he heard Stanley turn the key in the latch. He woke up and arched his wings, as if ready to launch into a cross-country marathon. Then he settled into his attentive pose, in case Stanley had come home bearing gifts. Sometimes paying attention pays off.

I smell chicken bones. Don't just put your coat on the hook. Take the goodies out of your left pocket, and give them to me! Captain stretched in Stanley's direction.

"Don't worry, Captain. Let me unwrap these little skeletons. I know you're not very sentimental about your relatives' remains." Stanley pushed a couple of the bigger bones through the bars, and Captain took them in his beak before they fell into his food dish.

Good thing the humans don't know enough to crack these open. I guess they just don't have a very efficient beak. Stanley's loss is my gain. Captain munched contentedly, dropping the bone splinters to the cage floor.

"That's enough for now. We'll save some for later. I'm going to put these in the fridge. And then I'm going to practice my napping. You don't need any practice; you nap all day."

Stanley retired to his bedroom rather than his chair. Captain turned to post-lunch preening, since the bones were a bit greasy, and some of his feathers got matted.

❊ ❊ ❊

Melody was on a mission. After talking with Stanley, she had made her way to the university. Time dragged as she tried to keep focused on her biochemistry class. Her mind flitted to different possibilities, despite her best efforts. What she really wanted to do was seek out the right kind of specialist at the faculty of medicine. While Stanley's explanation of his relationship—or more correctly, his non-relationship—with her mother was a startling revelation, she had not raised an even bigger issue.

Was Stanley hiding an ominous respiratory condition or some other kind of serious illness? Captain was imitating a rasping cough that he heard from someone, and the vet professor was definite that the recording he heard was not from a bird. Had Captain perhaps heard the cough on TV or from someone passing outside? Hardly likely that he would start mimicking something that he encountered only once or twice. No, there was no other plausible conclusion—Captain was reproducing Stanley's cough, and Melody made it her mission to find out a diagnosis.

Stanley had not volunteered any information about his health, and during his two weeks away, Mary Alice hadn't mentioned anything that suggested she was aware of him coughing. In fact, Mary Alice seemed surprised when Melody brought up the fact that they had heard Captain coughing. If Melody was going to raise the issue with Stanley, she wanted to be reasonably sure of her facts before sounding the alarm. It could be that Captain had picked up on the sound from a time when Stanley had the flu and just kept repeating it long after the ailment had passed. At least, that's what Melody wanted to believe. But to put the matter to rest, she needed input from either an internal medicine specialist or possibly a respirologist.

It wasn't long before Melody's steps let her to the faculty of medicine. She was familiar with the building because some of her classes were there. A number of the resident faculty were involved in post-graduate research projects, so she did not know them, given her early stage of study. The best course of action seemed to be to ask at the front desk for someone who might be a specialist in the field she needed. She reached into her pocket to make sure she could feel her cell phone there; it contained that all-important recording. Once inside the door, she saw the receptionist, Mavis, at her keyboard, eyes fixed intently on the computer screen in front of her.

"Excuse me. Could I interrupt for a moment?"

Mavis looked up. She was in her early forties and always had a matter-of-fact expression that made her look more severe than she really was. A pantsuit in conservative grey was her virtual uniform. She had been the office administrator for the faculty for several years, and interruptions by students were par for the course. Her primary role was to support the dean, but fielding student inquiries was an expected part of the job, so the dean would not be disturbed any more than necessary.

"Ah yes, Melody, isn't it? What can I do for you today?"

"I was wondering if you could direct me to someone in the faculty who is a respiratory specialist. I need their advice on something." Melody tried to sound as clinical and professional as possible.

"Usually, second-year students would make an appointment with one of their professors, either by email or by contacting a department secretary." Mavis was patient and even-toned.

"Yes, I know. But this is a special case outside my own courses, and it's rather urgent that I see someone who can advise me." Melody's tone went from cool professional to pleading. Mavis was normally inclined to deflect and refer, but something in Melody's voice indicated an anxiety deeper than usual.

"We don't have anyone on the teaching faculty who is a respirologist because that's a post-graduate specialty."

"Oh." Melody looked crestfallen and couldn't begin to think of where to go next.

"However, some of our medical staff are working on collaborative research projects. I can't guarantee they're available to meet with students, but you can try. I believe Dr. Schwarz does research in respiratory technologies. He's in office four twelve, but he doesn't keep office hours, and I have no way of knowing if he's in."

"Thank you very much. That's very helpful. I wouldn't bother him if it wasn't something important." Mavis nodded and went back to her keyboard. Students might be needy souls, but Mavis also had deadlines. This was already the third interruption of the morning.

Melody felt that she was making progress and that Dr. Schwarz might be an approachable sort. Or not. As she walked deliberately down the hall to the elevator, she strategized about what to say. Was it better to be the helpless student in need of rescuing, or should she adopt her best clinical manner and approach him as a colleague? In the end, it seemed wise just to wing it because she wouldn't be able to decide until she had at least a first impression of him.

Melody exited at the fourth floor and found her way to office 412. She hesitated and then knocked gently. There was no answer from within and no sound. She knocked again, this time more forcefully.

"Just a minute. I'm coming." The voice sounded slightly annoyed. She heard footsteps, and the door opened halfway. A man in his fifties and wearing a lab coat looked out. He had salt-and-pepper hair and a skewed expression as he looked her up and down.

"Hello, Dr. Schwarz?" Melody didn't want to launch into her spiel if she had the wrong person.

"It is I. What can I do for you?" He had a slight German accent and a precise manner of speaking.

"You don't know me, but my name is Melody, and I'm a second-year student in the pre-med program."

"That's very interesting, but I'm not involved with teaching, and I'm very occupied in analyzing some research data. Perhaps you have been misdirected?" It was more of a statement than a question. So far, he was even less accessible than Mavis.

"Actually, I have a research question that might make a huge difference in someone's well-being. And I think you might be the only person who can answer it. Can I trouble you for just a few minutes, please?"

"It appears that you a determined young lady. And I am intrigued that you could have such a research question at your level of study. Come in and be seated."

The office had the usual desk, and a couple of chairs were located in front of it. Crammed within were shelves of books and journals as well as a long counter with various pieces of equipment linked to laptops and monitors. The office was smaller than a classroom but larger than a regular professor's office. The atmosphere was functional rather than friendly. Melody read the situation quickly and decided to chuck the helpless student approach. She sat down in one of the chairs offered.

"I can see you're busy, so thank you for seeing me. As you know, I am not far enough along in the program to be dealing with patients. However, I would like to play a recording for you and get your opinion of what it might mean. I think the subject—my landlord—has a disturbing cough, and I doubt he'll seek medical help unless I can convince him it's very serious. And I don't know enough about respiratory disorders to recognize if that is really the case."

Melody left out the part about the recording being of Captain, not Stanley. She inferred that the distinguished Dr. Schwarz might not be willing to listen to a bird.

"Actually, it's not quite that simple. Just hearing a cough can tell me something, but a proper diagnosis requires listening to the patient's chest and possibly an X-ray or a CT scan, measuring blood pressure, or even inserting a miniature camera down the bronchial tubes. I don't know what your recording is like, but in itself, it would not be conclusive of anything. Understood?"

"Yes, I understand. But for now, I just want to know if I have enough grounds to force a conversation, or if I should just mind my own business and say nothing."

Dr. Schwarz smiled. "I think you have a remarkable amount of concern for someone who is just your landlord. In any case, you are here, and you need to play me this recording."

Melody pulled out her phone and started the recording. It was several seconds of the same cough being repeated twice. She watched Dr. Schwarz's face for any clues of what he might be thinking. He tilted his head to one side and scribbled some notes as he listened.

"Well, what do you think?" Melody waited anxiously for his verdict.

"I have heard this cough before, but there is something slightly mechanical-sounding in the resonance. It's as if this cough was recorded through a thin door or is a secondary recording of the actual cough. How exactly did you make this recording?" Dr. Schwartz gave Melody a suspicious look.

"My landlord didn't know he was being recorded. Actually, the recorder was his parrot. I recorded the parrot—his name is Captain—because he was making this cough after my landlord left on vacation. I was worried that Captain might be sick, so I made the recording and took it to one of the doctors in the veterinary assistant program. He explained that Captain was probably fine and that the cough was not a bird cough at all. All he could say was that this recording is a human cough and that the parrot has probably reproduced very accurately what he has heard. Sorry not to tell you that right away, but I thought it might make me look silly."

"I must say, young lady, that you have very unusual research data indeed! At least you have explained one curious aspect of what I heard. Perhaps your parrot is not absolutely flawless in his replication of this cough, but clearly the 'data' is impressive, albeit unorthodox in its origin. As I mentioned, I cannot make a conclusive diagnosis on the basis of this recording, but I can say that your landlord should be referred to a respirologist by his family physician as soon as possible. For now, I have a few questions. Has he recently or even a long time ago, worked at an asbestos mine or in home renovations or demolition of older buildings?

"Well, my mum knew him about thirty years ago in Saskatoon when he was working for a contractor doing house renos. I suppose some of the houses were old." Melody couldn't see the connection between the recording and work on old houses.

"And do you know if this coughing is long-standing or something that has become apparent just recently?" Dr. Schwarz seemed to be on the trail of something.

"I think it's fairly recent because the next-door neighbour sees my landlord a lot, and she's never mentioned hearing any cough—from him or the bird."

"And weight loss? Has he been experiencing weight loss?"

"I can't say for sure. He looks thinner now than in pictures that I have seen of him when he was younger. And it's not because he does a lot of exercise. He's quite sedentary, actually." Melody was basing her observation on the prime location of Stanley's throne in front of the TV.

"I'm afraid to say this wheezing cough is almost uniquely associated with pleural mesothelioma—a rare cancer of the lungs that can follow from asbestos exposure. Mesothelioma is unique in that it has a long latency period, which is the amount of time between the initial exposure to asbestos and the appearance of noticeable symptoms. The latency period for most symptoms caused by mesothelioma ranges from ten to fifty years. Your landlord may have seemed fine for a long time, but eventually, symptoms will occur. I would guess he experiences fatigue regularly and that he probably likes to avoid stairs or any aerobic exertion. Given the depth and resonance of his dry cough, he may have, or he will also develop, chest pain."

Melody was stunned by the news. Perhaps the doctor was wrong. Maybe an in-person examination by a specialist would produce a different diagnosis. But deep down she knew that Dr. Schwarz was a cautious and methodical medical researcher who did not make mistakes.

"How long can someone live with that condition, and what is the treatment?" she asked, her voice shaky as she fought back a tear in her right eye. "Mr. McFadden, my landlord, is probably in his late sixties or early seventies."

"That depends on several factors. Sometimes surgery helps. Radiation and chemotherapy can improve the patient's quality of life, as part of palliative care. We don't know how far along your Mr. McFadden is. And actually, you should not suggest to him that this is a diagnosis. He may, in fact, have something else, possibly a pulmonary fibrosis condition called asbestosis. But for now, he should visit his doctor, so a thorough examination can be made. You need only stress that you're concerned about his cough, and that alone should be cause for a medical appointment. I'm telling you all this only to underline that you are well advised in stressing to him that the cough is serious, and he should not put off medical evaluation."

"The problem is, I haven't heard him cough. His bedroom is on the main floor, and I haven't seen him use the stairs. All I have is the parrot's word!"

"You have two choices. Simply play your recording for him, and confront him with the evidence. He's not likely to take revenge on the parrot, is he? Or insist that he come upstairs to do something for you that only he can do, and you will hear this coughing firsthand. Either way, you will be in a position to make your point. Whether or not your landlord heeds your warning is up to him. Family medicine is twenty percent science and eighty percent persuasion. That's why I prefer research!"

Melody smiled ever so weakly. Dr. Schwarz was helpful, in his clinical and matter-of-fact way, accentuated by his slight German accent. Really, he couldn't do any more to help her. Now she wished she could put the genie back in the bottle. Had she discovered her father, only to lose him to a disease that she had never heard of?

"Thank you very much for your time and your insight. You've given me a lot to think about, but I have taken you away from your work." Melody got up and retreated toward the door.

"I think this Mr. McFadden is more than just a landlord for you, no? You see, I observe everything, which is what a good doctor must do. But I regret that I could not give you better news. Do not worry that I have lost some minutes on my work. My research is ultimately aimed toward helping people like Mr. McFadden. And now it is for you to do what you are able, and to recognize also what you cannot do. That is my advice to a young, aspiring doctor." His tone suggested he was more aware of Melody's dilemma than he let on.

"You are very kind, Dr. Schwarz. I'll try to remember what you have said. Goodbye."

Melody walked slowly down the long hallway to the elevator. Her steps, like her heart, were heavy. She would share her discovery with Allison before deciding what to do next.

Dr. Schwarz returned to taking readings from his instruments. At such times, he wished he could be wrong, both for Stanley's sake and for Melody's. But medical science, like people, must carry on in the face of unpleasant truths. Tough work, this carrying on.

19
Reluctant Confessions

IT WAS MIDAFTERNOON, and Stanley was wakened by Pierre's rapid footsteps coming down the stairs.

"Salut, Monsieur Stanley. Sorry to disturb your afternoon meditation. Me, I overslept a little, and I need to hurry down to the garage tout-de-suite. No time to eat. I go, and you can go back to sleep with the corporal dere. I t'ink he was meditating, just like you."

Pierre's appearance was like that of a small tornado: a flurry of sound and commotion when it set down, and then it took off in a few seconds. The only difference was that Pierre left no obvious path of destruction behind him. In particular, there were no dirty dishes deposited in the sink. For this, Stanley was thankful. He heard the front door close behind Pierre. Indeed, it seemed prudent to follow Pierre's advice and return to the land of nod. Perhaps he could finish his dream about living in a palm-lined retirement villa in Cuba. It was worth a try.

Captain turned his hea backwards and rested his beak in the middle of his back, between his wings. The sun sank lower in the sky, and the house was completely in shadow.

Stanley heard the front door open. He awoke with a start. Captain had assumed his Mary Alice pose, glaring at Stanley out of the corner of his eye.

Enemy tank approaching at twelve o'clock. You should have woken up when I chirped, you lazy pigeon. Now you're going to get plucked!

Stanley used his arms to launch himself into a vertical position, as if he had been busy doing something important. Experience had taught him to wait a few seconds before walking to the kitchen; otherwise, his fluids wouldn't be flowing through his chassis, as Tony the mechanic had once cautioned him about his car. Unfortunately, that meant Mary Alice was already entering the door from the porch while Stanley was still idling.

"What are you standing there for, man? You should have had the kettle on by now. It's getting on to four o'clock, and we'll all perish before dinner if you don't get a move on." Mary Alice was her usual congenial self.

I tried to tell him, but he gets harder to wake up as he gets older. Parrots don't get older. Why are humans so clueless when they wake up?

Captain returned to his stand-at-attention pose. There might be a collateral benefit to a Mary Alice visit, because she was carrying a round tin box, and it smelled of shortbread. If the tank could be encouraged to give up its cargo, a morsel of treasure might be available for a savvy parrot.

"Sorry, my dear. I didn't realize it had gotten so late. No doubt we can find something in the kitchen."

Stanley led the way, all the while considering if it was the right time to bring up his new role as a father or whether to consider the further implications in his own mind. As an introvert who had once studied psychology, he knew his preference. But this was Mary Alice—an extrovert who had little tolerance for other people's secrets. That day's script would no doubt play out like the script of all previous crises, and the tea ritual would give a framework to what must pass between them.

"Don't look too hard for something edible. I didn't bring shortbread while you were gone because the tenants would likely pillage it. But now that you're back, I brought a wee bit to keep you going. With the price of butter, I don't know how much longer I can afford to keep making it. So, enjoy it while you can." Mary Alice was not shy about sharing her martyrdom.

Stanley filled the kettle and retrieved the teapot from its shelf. Mary Alice put her shortbread on a small china plate, because civilized people don't eat out of a tin. The plate, which had a heather pattern, was one that she had given to Vi some fifty years previously, and Stanley knew its significance. Actually, he was terrified of breaking it, and he always warned the tenants not to touch it. But if Mary Alice handled it, the sacred vessel would be treated reverently by the high priestess. And if she broke it, he would be off the hook. Following the established liturgy, Stanley primed the teapot, and Mary Alice chose the "good tea" to scatter in the bottom of the fragile vessel. A few minutes later, they proceeded out to the living room, where Captain was dancing from side to side.

Before you get to nattering, don't forget the parrot is here. Shortbread ration urgently required!

Stanley took a piece of shortbread and broke off the corner. Captain was on top of his cage, leaning forward to gingerly grab it from between Stanley's thumb and index finger. It was a long-established protocol in which both parties knew their place. Captain retreated into his cage, so he could hold the shortbread over his seed dish. When the crumbs fell, they would be easier to retrieve later. Parrots know a thing or two about fine dining.

"Wasting good shortbread on that bird is a travesty, Stanley." Mary Alice shook her head in disapproval, although she was secretly pleased that her shortbread was so highly thought of, by Captain if not by Stanley. Stanley seemed preoccupied and didn't even mention how pleased he was to receive the shortbread. Something was up.

"Ah, yes, we need to savour something so exquisitely made lest a butter famine descend upon us. On behalf of Captain and myself, we thank you for what is indeed so precious and tasty." Stanley thought it wise to lead with something that would appease Mary Alice.

"When you get flowery, I know you're hiding something. Out with it. What's going on?"

Stanley had hoped for a smoother transition to the subject of his fatherhood, but this strategy had already foundered on the rocks of Cape Breton, so to speak. Better to proceed full speed ahead, come what may.

"Since my return from Cuba, I have gotten to know Melody much better. In fact, we had a rather intense talk yesterday."

"And how is that a bad thing? She's a lovely girl, and I'm glad that Allison has such a good friend, although I can't say I entirely approve of that sort of friendship, if that's what you're trying to break to me. I wasn't born yesterday, you know." Mary Alice sighed.

"Actually, that's not where I was going, but I'm pleased that you seem so accepting of their being a couple. If I might be so bold, how did you come to this perspective on things?"

"Cora and I talk, you silly goose. I did happen to drop in a few times when you were gone, and I had bits of conversation here and there with the girls. They seem to care for each other greatly, and Cora noticed the same thing. It was pretty obvious. It's not how I was brought up; however, the world is changing, and I don't necessarily want to change with it. But times change anyway. And I wouldn't want Cora to feel that I think ill of her granddaughter. So, I'll just accept what doesn't concern me and trust others to do the same."

Stanley tried not to show his shock at this progressive new strand in Mary Alice's worldview. Perhaps it was the Cora connection. Or maybe it was an indirect affirmation of how she viewed his own status as her best friend's gay son. In his memory, they had always danced around that issue, although he inferred tacit acceptance.

Captain tuned in to the emotional tone of the conversation. The shortbread was gone, but he sensed it was not the time to ask for more. *The humans are flock bonding. I can tell.*

"I think that's a commendable way of approaching a sensitive topic. I don't know if their relationship is a forever thing, but maybe 'forever' isn't the measure of what's a good relationship anyway.

We know lots of straight people who are divorced or separated. Some people are on their second or third relationship, for whatever reason. My immediate concern is about *a* relationship but not *their* relationship."

Mary Alice looked blank. She had expected to seize the agenda and perhaps be commended for her acceptance of something new. Now Stanley was alluding to something else. She took a slow sip from her tea.

Methinks there is a disturbance in the Force. These two seem to be dancing out to the end of a limb, and neither of them has wings. This is still not a shortbread moment. Captain shifted slowly from side to side.

"And what relationship are we talking about exactly? Are you trying to say something about our relationship? What's on your mind?" May Alice eyed Stanley cautiously.

"Well, no. I mean, we have a relationship . . . a friendship relationship, and that's something I've always appreciated since taking over Grandma's house. What I mean is, I find myself in a new relationship."

Before he could go further, Mary Alice interrupted. "All right, who is he? I hope it's not one of those reprobates down at the Piddler. You can do better, you know."

"To be sure, but it's not a male relationship. And before you think I've changed horses, I'm talking about a father-daughter relationship.

Mary Alice held back from asking if Stanley was thinking of becoming someone's daughter. In this day and age, one never knew. "Would you mind explaining how you could suddenly have a daughter, and I wouldn't know such a thing? Were you smoking something while you were away in Cuba?"

"Cuba was intoxicating but not in that way. No, this happened after I got back. That's the conversation with Melody that I started to tell you about. I am ninety-nine percent sure that Melody is my daughter, albeit from a relationship long ago."

Stanley waited for the import of his statement to sink in. Perhaps it would have been a good time for Vi's "special tea," but he couldn't very well add the gin with Mary Alice right in front of him. Mary Alice's eyes widened, her mouth partially opened, and then she closed it again. She looked at Captain and at Stanley. "And pray tell, how can you be so sure? And when did this relationship happen?

"The year before Vi died I became a good friend of a woman who knew I was gay, but that didn't matter because she wanted to remain single anyway. Angela also wanted to have a child, and she didn't want anyone else to be the father, except me. She said she would rather be a single mum than be coupled with someone, because relationships are so complicated. When Grandma Vi died and I decided to move to Victoria permanently, that was perfect. Angela would explain to her daughter that her father had just packed up and left before she was born. It didn't make me look good, but that wouldn't matter because I would not be in their lives, and it was what Angela wanted. I kind of liked the idea of leaving a human legacy in this world, even if I couldn't marry like straight people and do the socially approved thing. Nowadays it's possible to do things differently. Gay couples adopt children, or lesbian couples can have a sperm donor. But that was then, and we both kept our part of the bargain for our own reasons." It was Stanley's turn to sip some tea and wait for a reaction.

"I had no idea, and I don't think Vi did either. She just spoke fondly of her only grandson, who lived so far away. Just when you think you know someone. This is all a bit much for a lass from Cape Breton." Mary Alice paused thoughtfully. "And how did all this come out, if Melody didn't know about you and you never made any effort to learn about her?"

"I felt honour bound to keep my word to Angela, and I didn't want to risk undermining whatever she set up. It was Melody who did the sleuthing. While I was gone, she and Allison went through some old photo albums that I had stored up in my office."

"You mean that junk room on the third floor?"

"I prefer to think of it as my invention office, but whatever. I gave them the key, so they could move down an old desk. They must have noticed the photo albums and were curious enough to look through them. Melody saw a picture of me with my arm around Angela from twenty-five years ago, when I still lived in Saskatoon. She rightly concluded that her mother and I knew each other. She wouldn't have to be a medical major to guess that I was likely the man who fathered Angela's child. It seemed pointless for me to deny what happened and that I really am her father. And I don't know that I would want to deny it anyway. She's an adult, and she doesn't need to be protected from the truth any longer, if the truth is out. So, what do you have to say to all that, Mary Alice MacDonald, wise woman of the world?"

"Well, I think it was very bold of those girls to go snooping where they shouldn't be snooping. And I think you and this Angela were naïve to think you could just bring someone into the world and not give the child a proper home. What goes around comes around." Mary Alice was just building up a head of steam. "That being said, it seems that Melody has turned out all right. But I have no idea how you're going to sort this thing out now. Does she even want a father after all this time? And can I picture you becoming the adoring father of someone who doesn't really know you?"

Can Stanley handle a parrot and a daughter? That's the real question here. I'm only in favour of a daughter if the parrot is still number one. Captain bobbed his head, as if to enter the conversation.

"Those things have certainly crossed my mind. I don't have a master plan at the moment. Maybe there is no master plan. Maybe things just evolve, and we'll know what to do at the right moment, when the right moment comes along. For now, I just wanted you to know where things stand."

"Well, I suppose I should thank you for mentioning this little update to me. Let it not be said that life around here is humdrum. Is there anything else I should know, or should I just quietly go home and have my heart attack there?" Mary Alice began to get up.

"I think that will do for now, unless Captain has any dire secrets that he wants to share." Stanley's query was rhetorical, but Captain turned and looked out the window.

Wouldn't you like to know. I've shared the big one, and it's about you. But I can't look at you in case you're smarter than you look. A guilty parrot is a very sad thing. Poor me.

"Hmmph. That bird has no secrets because he barely has a brain. He's looking out the window at nothing, and he's as happy as can be."

Mary Alice could warm to a dog or even a cat, but birds did not figure prominently in her constellation of intelligent pets.

"You can go ahead, Mary Alice. I'll look after these dishes. The tenants will soon be coming home, and the kitchen will get busy. I'd best eat something now before the vultures descend."

Mary Alice made her way to the door. Captain gave up on getting more shortbread, and Stanley busied himself in the kitchen. Routine is sometimes a marvellous therapy in the face of chaos.

20
Who Will Bell the Cat?

MELODY AND ALLISON arrived within minutes of each other at the Java Hut. Aside from being one of the ubiquitous coffeehouses found almost everywhere in Victoria, it was on the bus route that connected the university and the trades college to where they lived. Indeed, it was only steps from the stop where they would get off to walk to Shady Shingles. In their short time in the city, it had already become their favourite haunt.

Even though it was January, the outside tables still had people sitting at them. For many Victorians, winter attire consists of a sweater or a light jacket, complemented by a funky scarf or possibly a headband. It's also the requisite attire for the average dog in the Cook St. Village, but it's pretty much the same dress code for people. The only difference is that people usually have an umbrella hidden away somewhere; dogs usually wear little rain capes strapped around their torsos. In sheltered locations on a calm day, the sweater or windbreaker is enough outerwear for people to cope with the elements.

If there happens to be a breeze from the ocean, locals will seek outside tables near a heat lamp. On those rare winter days that bring in winter storms from the Pacific, the wind and the driving rain force people inside. As bad as that might be, at least they don't have to shovel what falls from the sky, though they might have to dodge a severed tree branch or even the entire tree. But snow is a four-letter word that shall not be spoken. Maybe that's why Victoria drivers are so befuddled when they encounter it.

That particular day warranted a thorough tête-à-tête at the Java Hut. Melody and Allison did talk at home, but if the subject of the conversation was the goings-on at Shady Shingles, it seemed more prudent to debrief elsewhere. They had never bumped into Stanley or Mary Alice at the Java Hut, so they considered it a safe place to catch up on Melody's latest findings. Whatever was to happen required them to read from the same script, though Melody was not yet sure what that script should contain. In her earlier text to Allison, she had only said, "Big nuz. Meet me @ the Java @ 4."

After getting their coffees inside, the two women chose a table on the patio. It was quiet enough that they could hear each other easily and far enough from other tables that they would not be easily overheard.

"Melody, you seem out of breath. Did you have to run to catch the bus or something?" Allison was one to notice people's body language more than their attire.

"Ah, no. It's just that my conversation with the respirologist was more 'educational' than I had planned." Melody's voice had a distinct shakiness.

"What do you mean? Out with it. What did your expert say about the cough?"

"Well, he said that he couldn't be sure because it was only a recording, and he would need to do other tests with a patient in person if he were to give a conclusive diagnosis. But aside from all that caution, he seemed fairly certain that Captain was imitating the cough of someone who has advanced pleural mesothelioma. It's a type of lung cancer that comes from cumulative exposure to asbestos fibres."

"That sounds pretty bad. Can this doctor do anything to help?" Allison's preferred response to a crisis was to move toward fixing it as soon as possible.

"Dr. Schwarz is a researcher, not the kind of doctor who sees patients. There are treatments that can help, but he advised me to encourage Mr. McFadden to tell his own doctor about his symptoms, so a definite diagnosis can be made. It may be that he has something less serious, and the symptoms just look similar." This latter observation was more Melody's hope than an objective clinical assessment.

"Strange that you still refer to him as Mr. McFadden. If he's your father, why aren't you calling him dad or father or even his given name?"

"It just seems natural to call him that because that's how we were introduced." Melody hesitated. "And maybe I feel safer if he's Mr. McFadden and not 'Dad.' I mean, I could lose him if this illness is what Dr. Schwarz thinks it is. And if I get too close, it's harder to lose someone."

Allison nodded, not quite sure what to say. Clearly, her partner was somewhat in shock, and clear thinking alone was not going to fix things. "That may change, but for now, surely you have to do what the respirologist suggested. We have to get our landlord to go to the doctor, and he'll want to know why we are suddenly leaning on him to do that."

Melody took a deep breath and collected herself. She knew Allison was right, but sometimes being right is unsettling. "I guess this is not something that can be put off. I'll have to own up to making the recording and letting doctors hear it. As long as you can be with me, we'll invite him to have tea as soon as we get home. Anything important in that house seems to happen over tea."

"How about we invite Mrs. Macdonald over? She and Mr. McFadden are pretty thick. He would probably listen to her."

"Maybe later. But for now, I think this is something he needs to hear alone. And then it can be his choice if and when he tells her. In fact, I'm concerned that one of the other tenants may come in while we're talking. This may be pretty intense."

"No problem. I'll sit out in the porch reading, and if Mrs. Macdonald or one of the others comes in, I'll head them off with small talk." Allison was more than happy to assume this role, especially if it meant she didn't have to be part of what was going to be a family scene.

"Aren't you the noble one. That leaves me to bell the cat. But I suppose that makes sense. I think we have our plan. Let's go."

They didn't finish their coffee, but java infusion was not really a priority at the moment.

It took only a few minutes to reach Shady Shingles. Allison took up her post in the porch, and Melody ventured inside to find Stanley. The house smelled of bacon and beans. Captain was daintily shoving some canned beans into his mouth, sauce running down the sides of his beak. He was torn between eyeing Melody and licking the sauce off his toes.

You're too late for supper. The good stuff is already gone. Captain was getting to the stage of wiping his beak sideways on his perch.

Melody proceeded into the kitchen where Stanley was drying the last of his supper dishes.

"I take it that you and Captain had a feast of beans and bacon for supper?" The question seemed rhetorical, but she had to start the conversation somewhere.

"Yes indeed. Captain doesn't get bacon, but he loves a table-spoon or two of beans. Since I'm a good boy, I get both."

"You two are not exactly poster material for healthy eating, but I guess you could do worse. If you're all done there, perhaps I can make us some tea?" Melody wanted to move the gig along before she lost her courage.

"Mary Alice and I had some just a little while ago, but tea after supper is something I won't turn down. Is Allison going to join us?"

"Uh, no. She really needs to read something, and she's out in the porch . . . getting in a few chapters before it turns dark."

"We do have electricity, you know. She could turn on a light inside, and I won't raise the rent excessively." Stanley wondered a bit at Allison's sudden frugality. The woman took bubble baths, and now she was concerned about the energy conservation of a reading light?

Melody busied herself with the familiar ritual of making tea, careful not to dip into the tea reserved for Mary Alice's visits. When everything was ready, Stanley helped her carry the teapot and accessories into the living room. Captain had finished eating and was in his post-supper preening stage, listening carefully as he groomed his plumage.

"This is all very civilized, Melody. I'm sensing that maybe you want to continue our conversation from this morning?" Stanley had long ago learned that he could direct the conversation if he started it. At least it worked with Mary Alice. It might also work with a newfound daughter.

"Not exactly. But I do need to tell you about another thing that happened while you were away." Melody was unsure of where to begin.

"Oh dear. You are determined to bring some drama to my life, aren't you?" Stanley had no idea how prescient his comment was.

"Actually, I had help from Captain. Oh, nothing bad happened to him. He was fine except that I heard him do this awful cough. I thought he might have caught some serious virus but I didn't know how to transport him to a vet."

"He seems fine now," Stanley said. "If that happens again, there's a carrier kennel in the basement. It's for a small dog or a cat, but it also works for a parrot. You drop a towel on him, and he's passive enough while you put him in the carrier. Then off to the vet you go. Next time I'll leave you the info for the small-animal hospital."

"That's good to know. But the cough sounded really bad, so I recorded it and took it to one of the vets at the veterinary assistant program at Allison's college. When he listened to it, he said it wasn't a bird cough at all and that Captain was imitating a human cough. Since you're the one who is around Captain the most, I assumed it must be your cough."

Stanley looked a little flustered. "Well, yes, I cough sometimes. All old people have some kind of cough or other, especially in winter."

"But this is not some casual dry cough or even a cough from a cold. It's really harsh." Melody was even toned but insistent.

"I've not heard Captain give a dramatic cough; he just sniffles now and then. Can I hear this clandestine recording that you're basing all this on?" Stanley wanted to give the impression that he was more skeptical than he was.

"Actually, I have it right here. Just listen, and then tell me that I'm imagining its severity." Melody played the recording on her phone. Stanley's brows furrowed. His expression soured, and to Melody, he looked like a speeding motorist nabbed by highway patrol.

"I've never heard him do that, but yes, it's me. That recording just sounds worse than it really is. He's exaggerating!" Stanley glared at Captain, who had developed a sudden interest in scraping the grape juice off the bars on the far side of his cage.

Busted. It was such a weird sound that I had to see if I could repeat it. Damn near perfect, I would say. Don't pluck the messenger. I got it right; you got it wrong. The parrot is right. The parrot is right.

"You've been pretty good at hiding that cough. Let's hear it live, and we'll see how accurate Captain's imitation is. I'd like to see you walk upstairs to the room where the photo albums are. You can show me any other photos you might have of you and my mother."

"That's a bit much to ask. After all, I'm tired after my trip, and that's a lot of stairs." Stanley tried to sound aggrieved and frail, but it was Melody's turn to look skeptical.

"Let's pretend I was an investor wanting to see one of your inventions up there. I'll bet you would soon find the energy to take him upstairs."

"Pity the poor patient who has you for their doctor. They'll surely be driven to expire!"

Despite his protestations, Stanley got up from his chair and led the way to the stairs. He gave one more backward glance at Captain, who was bobbing his head too contentedly to look very repentant. Melody followed, confident of her strategy. Stanley slowly started up the stairs, as if to conserve energy for the interminable steps ahead. Halfway up the stairs, he stopped and coughed, sounding much like the recording, but the cough was not quite as rasping or deep.

"See? I'm just a bit short of breath. It's not nearly as bad as that recording. Can we go down now?"

"That was only a few steps, and that was a minimal exertion. Keep going to the top, and we'll see what happens." Melody was not about to be diverted.

Stanley continued for another three steps and then coughed twice. The sound was much deeper, each cough ending with a gurgling resonance.

"I hope you're happy now."

"Keep going." Melody was not about to ease up on her test subject. The same coughing bout happened twice more before Stanley reached the landing and made his way to a chair in the hallway. He dropped into the chair with a sigh of relief.

"There, I hope that's enough for you. I really don't want to tackle the third floor without a bit of a breather in between."

"That's all right. Point made. The more you exerted yourself, the more those coughs sounded exactly like my recording of Captain. Maybe you don't hear yourself like we do, but that's how you sound to others." Melody tried not to sound too victorious.

"It's really not a serious problem. I cough when I have to go upstairs, but otherwise I'm fine. The problem is that Shady Shingles has lots of stairs, and I'm old. So, stairs get harder to handle. And that's just part of being a senior in an old house."

"So you say. But I didn't finish telling you about my research. I also took the recording to a respirologist at the university's faculty of medicine. He's a researcher who works exclusively on respiratory technologies. Dr. Schwarz was very definite that whoever had this cough should see their doctor immediately."

"Indeed. It so happens that I already see my doctor regularly, once a year, whether I need to or not. He knows me better than your Dr. Schwarz."

"And has he heard your cough?"

LARRY SCOTT

"Well, no. I go up to his office in an elevator, and I only cough when I have to climb stairs or Mt. Everest. It didn't seem relevant to mention, if he didn't ask."

"How convenient that he didn't ask. If he heard this recording, I think he might be more curious than you would like to admit."

"Has anyone ever told you that you're like a dog with a bone? Or a parrot with a bone, for that matter? My philosophy is that if you don't go looking for trouble, it won't find you."

"It's a wonder there are any men still alive in the world, given that seems to be the creed of most of your ilk. In this case, trouble is already there, and it won't go away if you just try to ignore it."

"And what makes you think my humdrum cough is actually 'trouble,' as you put it?"

Melody thought carefully about how much she should say. Dr. Schwarz had been clear that a clinical diagnosis could not be given on the basis of a cough soundtrack. But she had to say enough to convince Stanley that it was urgent enough to warrant a visit to his doctor. Any relevant tests that flowed from that visit would tell the tale.

"Dr. Schwarz could not say conclusively what would cause your cough, other than the fact that he has examined other patients with precisely that cough, and they were found to have respiratory conditions related to asbestos exposure."

"There you go. I may have been exposed to some asbestos long ago when I was doing house renovations in Saskatoon, but I've done nothing like that recently. And the cough only started up in the last couple of years."

"With conditions like pleural mesothelioma or asbestosis, for example, the exposure can be long ago, but the symptoms don't present until decades later. At the beginning of the lung irritation, the cough only happens during periods of heightened aerobic activity, like jogging or climbing stairs. That's why you don't cough all the time."

"Never heard of 'plural miserable,' or whatever you said. Maybe even my doctor has never heard of it. You're sounding a bit

234

melodramatic for something that is probably very ordinary." With that, he got out of his chair.

As she followed Stanley back downstairs, Melody considered what kind of argument would counter Stanley's denial of what seemed like objective facts. It was time to bring out the big guns.

"I think it's definitely time that Mrs. Macdonald and I get together for a good heart-to-heart talk over tea. I have a feeling that she would be very interested to hear about your coughing episodes and the fact that you refuse to go to the doctor. Don't you agree?"

Stanley reasoned that he could plausibly set aside Melody's amateur speculations about his health, but the prospect of her teaming up with Mary Alice was a whole other ball game. Mary Alice believed in taking no prisoners if she thought she had righteousness on her side. If hell hath no fury like a woman scorned, it is also true that hell hath no suffering like being on the wrong side of a matriarch who considers herself right. Stanley had been down that road before, and the possibility of escaping unscathed was nil. It might be better to yield and fight another day when the odds were better.

"It would appear that you are fixated on this issue. I don't want you making Mary Alice anxious for nothing, so I'll go ahead and make a doctor's appointment, if only to lay the matter to rest. While I'm at it, I should make Captain go to the doctor too. Maybe there's a cure for meddlesome parrots." All the latter was said in Stanley's most ominous tone as he stared at Captain, who seemed to be taking in the conversation, head tilted to one side.

Stanley has to go to the people vet. He's been a bad boy. I'm a good bird. Good birds get treats from the vet.

"I think you should thank Captain for being such a good nurse. He just wanted somebody to know something was wrong. Look, he's studying you even now."

"Indeed. He's studying me to see how much trouble he's in. That's a guilty parrot if ever I saw one."

They heard voices in the front porch. Allison was talking to Brian, who had just come in. She spoke loud enough to ensure Melody and Stanley could hear.

"Hello there, scholar. Have all your courses started already?" Allison tried to think of something that would make Brian stop and chat.

"Uh, you're not talking to Mr. McFadden, you know. I'm not hard of hearing. By the end of the week, I'll have had them all. This afternoon it was just Post-Revolutionary France."

Melody smiled. She could make out Brian's much quieter reply, but she inferred that Stanley didn't hear what he said.

"Allison is talking to someone; it must be Brian or Mary Alice because Pierre already left a while ago," Stanley said. "I guess we'll have to postpone the rest of this discussion. Never fear, I'll follow through and visit Dr. Chan. He may even still remember who I am."

The living room door opened, and Brian entered, looking mildly perplexed after being ambushed by Allison.

"Hi there, Captain. You must be throwing a party here. You've got Mr. McFadden and Melody waiting on you. Parrots have it too good!"

You're not one of the sharper thumbies, are you? I've been on trial here, and you think this looks like a party. On the other hand, you're a useful interruption. So, speak and let Stanley forget that I'm here. Captain shook himself and dropped his skirt feathers over his feet, as if he were deciding to take a nap.

"I would agree that this parrot has it too good, and I have a mind to do something about that." Stanley cast a disapproving glance at Captain, who blinked and pretended not to notice the veiled threat. "I think I should leave him with Mrs. Macdonald the next time I go away."

Captain lurched slightly but decided it was better to feign sleep than vocalize his horror at the prospect of being under Mary Alice's care. There might be a price to pay for this caper.

"Didn't I do a good job this time? It's no trouble for me to look after Captain." Melody pretended to take slight at Stanley's chiding of her avian ally.

"Indeed. You and Captain seem to have developed a chummy rapport. I'm sure he didn't suffer under your care while showing off his talents."

Brian looked puzzled, suspecting a conversation was going on at two levels, and he wasn't privy to the secret. First Allison was suddenly interested in his studies, and now Mr. McFadden was making odd comments about his parrot. "Nice chatting, but I need to put my stuff away and check out the kitchen. Anyone going to be using it just now?"

Stanley got up and collected the tea mugs. "I'll just put these away, and the kitchen is all yours."

Allison finished pretending to read and came in. Melody glanced at her. "We're not eating just now, so go ahead." Both women retreated upstairs.

Being dumb can be very hard work. On that note, Captain went to sleep for real.

Later in the evening, Stanley wished he could do the same. Carrying on sometimes happens best in sleep.

21
Between a Rock and a Hard Place

IT WAS WITH mixed feelings that Stanley set out for his doctor's clinic. He could have driven or taken a bus, but he hoped an invigorating walk might help him sort out what he felt about this upcoming visit. He would have preferred to put off such medical scrutiny. But when he called the doctor's office for an appointment, the receptionist said there was a cancellation slot available at eleven, if he could come. It seemed prudent to say yes and get it over with. If he didn't go, there would be nothing to find, and life could go on as usual. Life can be remarkably satisfactory if one ignores what is bothersome and only deals with what is necessary. On the other hand, he was aware of so many seniors who had ignored initial symptoms and ended up taking an extended nap at one of the city's fine funeral homes. Now there was the added pressure of Melody's sleuthing. She would certainly have shared her findings with Allison, and she, in turn, would likely natter to Cora, her grandmother. And the pipeline from Cora to Mary Alice was a short one, given their daily chin wags. It would be far better to head them off at the pass and visit Dr. Chan before Mary Alice joined the crusade. Then there would solid evidence that Stanley's cough was normal for someone of his age. Or not.

The problem with doctors is they don't always say what their patients want to hear. Politicians are more reliable that way, even if they don't always tell the truth. Doctors tend to come up with more tests and referrals to other doctors. This explains why so many seniors fill their social calendar with medical appointments. The pharmacists make a good living off them too.

As Stanley walked along the various streets leading to the clinic, he passed all sorts of people whom he knew nothing about. It's not obvious from appearances who has a chronic disease, who is facing surgery, or who faces some mortal challenge known only to them. In that sense, he didn't feel alone because other people at that moment would be dealing with the unknowns of their lives. And yet Stanley's own unknown weighed upon him with unique significance. One's mortality seems more relevant the older one becomes.

There was no more time for further musing because Stanley had reached the clinic where Dr. Chan practiced. He entered cautiously and approached the receptionist with his health card.

"My name is Stanley McFadden, and I'm here for an eleven o'clock appointment with Dr. Chan."

The young receptionist looked skeptical. "I don't see your name on our online booking chart. Are you sure you have the right day?" Clearly, she had more than a little experience with confused seniors.

"Yes, I had a call from somebody who said there was a cancellation, and I could see Dr. Chan if I could come on short notice at eleven."

A second receptionist interrupted. "I was the one who contacted Mr. McFadden this morning. I didn't get a chance to update the entry. My bad. Just have a seat, and we'll call you presently."

Stanley smiled victoriously and then made his way to one of the chairs. The stack of outdated magazines did not look promising, so he fixed his gaze on a west coast landscape on the wall. After a few minutes, another woman in a turquoise pantsuit ushered him into a sparse consultation room. There the only art was an anatomical chart. *"One would think that Dr. Chan should have memorized human anatomy in Medicine 101 without ongoing need of a visual aide for finding vital human organs,"* Stanley thought to himself.

Stanley seated himself and waited for his audience with Dr. Chan. Presently, there was a knock at the door, and the doctor entered briskly. A receding hairline and touches of grey at the temples confirmed he had reached his early forties. Dr. Chan had been Stanley's doctor for several years.

"Good day, Stanley. How are you doing today?" Dr. Chan would never win an award for social chitchat. He was always civil, though on the taciturn side.

"It may be a false alarm, but over the past year I have developed an occasional deep cough. It's not related to a cold or the flu, and it happens only when I go upstairs or up a steep hill. Otherwise, it doesn't bother me, but I need you to check it out, because my daughter has become aware of it, and she's worried." Stanley was of the view that doctors should be given the sordid details right off the bat.

"Well, two things. You have never mentioned this cough before, and you have never mentioned that you have a daughter. Did you only notice this paternal fact now, or have I missed something?" Although clinically oriented, Dr. Chan had his own droll sense of humour.

"Actually, my having a daughter isn't a medical problem. Her mother and I parted company at her birth, and she chose to raise Melody alone. I moved to another city and only recently did Melody and I meet. Melody became aware of my cough, with the help of my parrot. That's another story. In any event, she is in pre-med, and she believes the cough is bad enough that I should tell you about it."

"Interesting. It sounds like she is beginning her medical career early. She is at least right to the extent that we need to have a look at you. Can you cough for me?"

"Well, I can cough, but it's not like what happens when I'm going upstairs or when I carry something heavy."

"For now, I just want to listen to your chest." Dr. Chan used his stethoscope on Stanley's back and front while asking him to breathe deeply. "Hmm . . . there are some crackling sounds in your lungs that are not usual; also, there appears to be some fluid there."

"Does that mean I've got Rice Crispies in my lungs, doc?" Stanley considered it a challenge to put a chink in Dr. Chan's clinical armour.

"There is no snap or pop, so we can assume the crackle is indeed a solo interloper. Breathe, don't talk." Dr. Chan continued to listen to various parts of Stanley's torso. "We need to send you off to do a stress test at a medical lab. They'll put you on a treadmill and monitor your heart and lungs. Some X-rays are also in order. After that we can better say if you have something we need to treat or if you're simply aging. You're sixty-seven not thirty-seven, you know."

"Maybe it's not worth bringing up, but my daughter thinks I might be at risk for something called pleural mesothelioma, because I did renovation work in the past. There was quite a bit of asbestos dust around, but that was thirty or so years ago, and I only did that work for about five years. I've been fine until just recently."

Dr. Chan raised his eyebrows and remained quiet for a few seconds. "That part of your history is indeed of interest, but I think it might be premature to make a diagnosis at this stage. A chronic cough can have many causes. Mesothelioma is one option, and asbestosis is another one related to inhalation of asbestos fibres. But the cough could derive from any of a number of respiratory reasons, some benign and some not. I've going to fill out some requisitions, and you should take them to the diagnostic lab at the hospital. It's open till five o'clock today. I'll call you in when the results come back."

"Should I be doing anything different in the meantime?" Stanley considered asking if he should lay off the Rice Crispies but thought better of it.

"Not much. Try walking more, but avoid the stairs until we know what's happening. If per chance you should have chest pain or notice a fluid discharge from your lungs, let me know immediately. I'm not saying that will happen, but those are symptoms to heed, should they develop. Take these requisition forms with you. I've checked off what's needed." He shook hands with Stanley, then exited.

Stanley felt a little dazed. He had hoped for a routine examination and then Dr. Chan to tell him there was nothing to worry about. This visit seemed inconclusive. Nor did Dr. Chan's comments give him the ammunition he wanted in dealing with Melody, and potentially Mary Alice. In fact, the need to have more tests suggested there was something to test for. And Dr. Chan had mentioned watching out for chest pain and fluid from his lungs. He wished he had asked Dr. Chan more about asbestosis and mesothelioma, but the doc rushed off before Stanley could formulate his questions. There must be a special course in medical school about how to give the slip to patients who wanted to know too much too soon. Dr. Chan obviously needed no upgrading in that department. Either he didn't want to say what he really thought, or he had so many patients that he had no time for bedside manner. Perhaps the best thing was to get the tests done, so his next visit with Dr. Chan could happen as soon as possible. Meanwhile, there was always Dr. Google to consult, if he were brave enough to be informed of gory details.

Since Stanley was already downtown, he decided to catch one of the buses that went by Royal Jubilee Hospital. He could drive, but Victoria hospitals appeared to be financing their latest MRI machines by charging heart-attack prices for parking. If people didn't feel bad before they drove there, they certainly did afterwards. That was another improvement that he should write to the prime minister about. Or maybe the premier of the province was able to read too; it might indeed be the province that let hospitals charge so much for parking. It wouldn't hurt to spread one's good advice around. There was no reason why the prime minister should derive all the benefit from Stanley's wisdom. And besides, the ungrateful politician hadn't answered his last five letters.

Stanley found a bus stop and boarded the #14 that connected the city's two acute-care hospitals. Depositing two bus tickets resulted in his receiving an all-day pass. It pleased Stanley that he could ride all the way to the hospital and return again, then go for an extra joyride at no extra cost. Unfortunately, there was no second place that he wanted to go. Riding the bus just to see the variety of other passengers was entertaining enough, but it didn't count toward the doctor's prescription of "more walking." It would be necessary to get off the bus a few stops early if he were to accomplish that mission. For the moment, it would be sufficient just to get to the hospital and find the right department.

The other passengers were a mix of mothers with infants, college students plugged into their iPhones, and seniors. Stanley wondered how many would get off at the hospital.

After a dozen stops, they reached the entrance to Royal Jubilee. Stanley was the only one to exit. Once inside, he stopped at the information desk and was directed to the correct department. If there was any ambiguity about the verbal directions, it was mitigated by brightly painted arrows and stripes on the walls, indicating the location of various medical Nirvanas. Eventually, Stanley ended up at another reception desk where a clerk behind a computer monitor took his requisitions and his health card.

"Just go down the hall to the first waiting room on the left. There are lockers and hospital gowns there. Please change into one and then take a seat, Mr. McFadden. The radiologist will call you in shortly."

It was a good thing the efficient lady did not say, "It could be a while," because that would have implied an overnight vigil. As it was, a chap with a large ring inserted in each earlobe came out about thirty minutes later. "Is there a Stanford Fadding here?"

In such circumstances, it is unwise to quibble about accuracy. One could only hope the chap's skill set for operating medical machinery exceeded his ability to read English.

"That would be me."

Stanley was ushered in by the young man, whose nametag said, "Shawn." The various tests happened in quick succession. The imminent one that caught Stanley's attention was a treadmill with variable slope.

"I guess it's more accurate to use that machine than it is to follow me upstairs with wires attached to me." The harried technician stared blandly at Stanley, apparently incapable of visualizing the scenario. Or more likely he did, and it wasn't a pretty sight.

"They should have told you to wear running shoes, but we'll see how you do with those leather dress shoes. My dad has a pair just like that." Stanley thought he should feel better because Shawn was accustomed to dealing with ambulatory specimens from another era. Probably this was payback for Stanley's stair test suggestion. He hoped Shawn wouldn't be the one choosing his father's nursing home.

Stanley stepped up on the treadmill, and Shawn attached various leads to his chest as well as an oxygen "clothes pin" to his index finger. Then he started the machine slowly, on the level. That didn't last but a few steps. Stanley felt the slope increasing and the belt going incrementally faster, at ten-second intervals.

"You can hold on to the crossbar for balance. If you start to feel chest pain, let me know right away."

It didn't take long before Stanley felt tired and a bit lightheaded. He coughed once. Then, as the machine kept increasing slope and speed, he coughed several more times as he tried to keep up. Admittedly, they were the kind of deep coughs that bothered him on the stairs at home. Sanguine Shawn said nothing, but his eyebrows furrowed a couple of times as he watched the readings on the monitors.

"Does that cough happen at other times or just during aerobic exertion?" His tone was matter-of-fact and clinical.

"I don't go jogging, but the cough does happen if I walk briskly for an extended period or if I need to go upstairs. It's not a constant thing." Shawn slowed the machine down and stopped it. That happened none too soon from Stanley's perspective.

"Your chart doesn't say you've had bronchitis or double pneumonia in the recent past. You might have that kind of cough as an after-effect of one of those. But you're sure those are not part of your medical history?"

"I think I would remember those things if I ever experienced them. Definitely not."

"I just wanted to be clear on those points. It's not up to me to provide diagnoses, but we will send this data to your doctor, and he will have the results in a couple of days. The X-ray and the blood work will also help him assess your respiratory condition."

"You said 'respiratory condition.' What does that mean precisely?" It never hurts to try to pry some information out of the hired help.

"Well, obviously, you have a hacking cough, and your breathing is laboured when engaged in aerobic activity. You know that yourself. The doctor needs to make a diagnosis before any measures are taken to mitigate your discomfort. 'Condition' is just a general term for whatever medical issues are affecting your health."

"It sounds to me like you have a future in the prime minister's communications office. That's a very eloquent way of revealing next to nothing."

"I consider that a compliment, sir. Diagnoses are above my pay scale." He smiled ever so slightly. *Shawn will be a hospital administrator before he's thirty-five*, Stanley thought.

Stanley concluded that further prodding would result in nothing, so he made his way to the exit. Shawn had said very little, but in a way, he revealed much by what he didn't say. Generally, this kind of statement is easily understood by people who have been married for a long time. Stanley had no intention of getting married to Shawn, but their brief interchange had some of the same dynamics around what is said and left unsaid. Clearly, Shawn knew more than he was telling, and it was a reasonable assumption that what he knew wasn't good.

Stanley decided to take the bus partway home and make a side trip to Beacon Hill Park. There would be no doctors or bankers or Cape Breton matriarchs there because they would all be busy with their daytime routine elsewhere.

Mallard ducks and turtles congregate in abundance, without asking questions. At least for the ducks, there is only interest in people if they happen to be dispensing a seed mixture or, on a bad day . . . bread. That day they snubbed Stanley because he just sat on a bench, staring at the water of Goodacre Lake. As with most things in Victoria, the name is grander than the thing itself. Goodacre Lake is a large pond of shallow water, patronized by resident ducks and several Canada Geese, plus a few turtles that bask on a tethered log, when the sun it out. It's a great place to be lost in thought, and casual strollers will not interrupt, because they are there to do nothing too. Squirrels pretend to be doing something by scurrying about, but actually nothing is on their rodent agenda. They can retain their cute image without doing much work. The same public perception does not apply to pensive seniors sitting on park benches. To anyone observing, Stanley was doing nothing. But in his nothingness, he was brooding on several "what if" questions. What if the tests revealed he actually had mesothelioma or asbestosis? And what was the difference? Was one more treatable than the other? What if he had something for which there was no treatment? What if there was a treatment and it was worse than the disease? What if his new relationship with his daughter was short-lived?

Doing nothing can be terribly hard work because of what's going on underneath. The ducks also seemed to be doing nothing, just paddling around in circles or drifting along. Perhaps they secretly think about ducklings—the ones that survived last year's season, the ones that didn't, and the ones to come. It would be several months before little ducklings scurried across lily pads and chased invisible insects. Still, it's all about the ducklings, this carrying on and appearing to do nothing. The Goodacre Lake community continues, even if many ducklings won't make it. The parents have to carry on, so they can begin again next year.

When Stanley got up, the afternoon was more than half-gone. If he upped his pace a little, he could make it to the Piddler to claim his seat before some interloper arrived. In any event, it was time to go, because his doing nothing had born fruit. Many questions swirled in his head until he decided to suspend the questions and watch the ducks paddling gently. Carrying on is not about knowing all the answers. It's about *carpe diem*.

22
The Eggshell Waltz

MELODY AND ALLISON made it to the Java Hut by midafternoon.

Melody had wanted all morning to call her father, but she remembered what Allison had said when they parted at the bus stop that morning, "Your dad is used to doing his own thing, and he'll tell you when he's ready. You can't make him be close."

She had classes to attend and an afternoon lab to distract her. Time went slowly. She had tried to imagine the conversation between Stanley and his doctor, but that didn't make the day go faster. Now she and Allison could debrief in their favourite haunt. The coffee was good, and they could talk without running into anyone else from the house. They chose a table outside, close enough to a heat lamp to be cozy and far enough from the locals that they would not be casually overheard.

Allison unwound a loose-weave woollen scarf from her neck. "Well, did you hear from Mr. McFadden today?"

"No. I stopped at the house before coming here, but he wasn't home. Hopefully, that doesn't mean he got hospitalized right away because he has something serious! I thought of asking Mrs. Macdonald if she had seen him, but that might arouse her suspicions. He was pretty clear that he wasn't ready to tell her anything yet. For that matter, I'm not sure how much he will tell us."

"If he's in the hospital, that would hardly be something he could keep secret from Mrs. Macdonald. Actually, we could find out by calling the hospitals and saying we want to visit Mr. McFadden. If they say they have no patient by that name, then he's not a patient."

"Not necessary. It's only late afternoon, and sometimes he goes to that pub where he and his buddies hang out. I wonder if they talk about anything real or just tell war stories."

"My reading is that he doesn't come to our coffee shop, and we don't go to his pub. I doubt even Mrs. Macdonald goes there. I think her hangout is the seniors' activity centre."

"For one thing, she is of the teetotaler persuasion and wouldn't be caught dead there. She probably doesn't come here because she can make cheaper coffee at home. And clearly, she makes tea at Shady Shingles. Somehow I think there'll have to be a big tea discussion very soon."

"And you want to be in on it. That's also clear!"

"And why not? If it turns out that major decisions are in the wind, Mrs. Macdonald's opinion will probably count for a lot, and she is not likely to be put off by wishy-washy excuses from my father. He might delay telling her something, but I can't picture him leaving her out of any life-and-death update."

❈ ❈ ❈

The Piddler had its cast of regulars, plus a few interlopers, when Stanley walked in. He wasn't looking for anyone in particular, but it was a pilgrimage site when he needed solace. Some people might head to their church or their Tai Chi class, but Stanley felt spiritually sustained among those imbibing spirits. It was more the setting than the beer per se, although the latter usually helped the conversation go in the right direction.

Stanley settled on his usual stool by the bar. Susanne brought his Porter's even before he could nod in her direction. Piddler patrons are a predictable lot. It was 3:45 p.m. Therefore, the #3 had just deposited Conrad by the front door. That too was a given for that time of day. Stanley wasn't sure if he wanted to seek Conrad's counsel because his wife was so connected to Mary Alice, and how to keep Mary Alice at bay was one of Stanley's troubling dilemmas.

"Hail, Stanley! Are you keeping your head above water?"

"Well, I'm treading water, if not exactly making progress. And you?"

"Can't complain. Cora does all the complaining for me, so I've been relieved of that burden."

Conrad laughed at his own joke, and Stanley nodded. Stanley believed small talk was often a useful distraction in the face of small-time worries, but that day it would take more energy than he could summon. He stared abstractly at some imaginary focus point on the far wall.

"Stanley, my man, you don't seem to be really here today. Where are you exactly?" Conrad could do small talk with the best of them, but he could also discern when it was appropriate to go fishing. Stanley had learned to appreciate him for that reason.

"Well, I've been to see the doctor, and the news wasn't what I was expecting."

"Indeed. In general, you shouldn't expect too much from doctors. The ones on TV are pretty inspiring, but the ones we actually deal with are a mortal lot. Did this one cause you particular grief?"

"It's not that he did anything wrong. I went to see him about a cough that I sometimes have, and he referred me for tests at the hospital lab. I was expecting him to prescribe cough syrup and tell me it was just something routine that goes with aging."

"Is this the cough you have when you came upstairs from the basement washroom here at the Piddler? You were hacking for a bit a week ago."

"Ah, yes. Probably. It happens mostly when I'm coming up stairs."

Susanne arrived with Conrad's Rickard's and set it down in front of him. Conrad took a sip and thought for a couple seconds. "Are you bothered because you think the doc is asking you to do something unnecessary, or are you bothered because you knew something was wrong, and he didn't set your mind at ease?"

It was Stanley's turn to sip some more draft and consider what Conrad was suggesting. "I guess I've known that the cough probably means something. And it doesn't seem to go away. If I were brutally honest, I would have to admit that I know something is wrong. And then my mind races to what the possibilities could be and the decisions I may have to make."

"Is one of the decisions about telling Mary Alice what's going on?"

"That's one factor, yes. And more recently there's a new factor— the daughter I told you about. Lots of people cough, but Melody thinks I could have a condition related to asbestos contamination from years ago. I'm awaiting test results, and if I have such a thing, I don't know how long I can continue with Shady Shingles or what kind of treatments I'll have to endure."

"When will you know the results of these tests? You seem sure of all this without having any real confirmation."

"The doc wasn't very specific, but the radiologist thought the results would be ready in a couple of days. Then it depends on how fast Dr. Chan's office contacts me."

"Well, I hope it's all a tempest in a teapot, but I don't think it's wise to try and conceal the facts from Mary Alice, such as they are. Melody will want to hear your update, and women being women, she'll surely talk to Allison about it. That's already three other people, including me, who know your secret. Guaranteed Mary Alice will not be happy about being left out of a secret. You may as well spill the beans."

Stanley sighed. "Whatever happened to 'what they don't know won't hurt them?' But I suppose you're right. It takes a lot of energy to lie convincingly, and my track record on that is not great."

"Your news may not be quite the dramatic revelation you think. I actually mentioned your cough to Cora a week ago, because it sounded so bad. And as you know, she and Mary Alice tend to be in touch. I wouldn't be surprised."

"Well, that clinches it. I may as well call a press conference and invite them all. Then I'll only have to give my report once."

"I believe a press conference at Shady Shingles is known as a tea party. Since you and Mary Alice have a template, you may as well use it."

"It would be an even better tea party if you came and helped deflect the interrogation. I don't want to do the eggshell waltz alone. How about some moral support, my beloved and learned friend?"

"Ah, Stanley, my lad, this is a solo mission. I survived WWII, but I don't want to push my luck. I can't be your wingman on this one. I don't navigate eggshells well. And this is about you, not me."

❋　❋　❋

Allison and Melody reached the house before Stanley. They put their backpacks away and came downstairs again. Captain was dancing on top of his cage.

This place has been a morgue all day. Let's have some action!

"Look, Allison, Captain must be in a good mood. He's dancing up a storm."

"Either that or he's running on the spot to keep fit. I don't think Mr. McFadden taught him that."

"I'll get him a grape. He seems to have finished what he had in his dish this morning."

While Melody was in the kitchen, the front door opened, and Mary Alice entered. She wheezed as she walked, and she looked a little frailer than usual. "I saw the lights on, and I thought maybe Stanley had come home. Have you girls seen him? I think you know why I want to talk to him."

Melody returned with a Red Flame and passed it through the bars to Captain, who took it from her daintily.

A grape is better than popcorn. Let the show begin.

Melody looked to Allison for a subtle sign of what to do. Allison raised her eyebrows and nodded. Captain continued to nibble his grape while paying attention to the conversation.

"Would you like us to leave or should we stay?" Melody wasn't sure where they stood in Mary Alice's eyes.

"You can stay because this concerns you too. I know you're Stanley's daughter and that you got him to go to the doctor. I've known for a while that's he's not quite up to par. But I knew he wouldn't pay me any heed if I suggested something. A woman's intuition isn't enough to sway a man, especially a stubborn man like Stanley. He would listen to that parrot before he'd listen to me!"

Captain bobbed his head vigorously without losing grip of his half-eaten grape. *He would do well to listen to me, but actually, I listen to him. And I can repeat what I hear to the right person. Humans don't say much that's worth repeating, but every once in a while, they make an interesting sound . . . like a cough.*

"Oh, I think my father takes your opinion into account a lot more than you realize. Probably he's just been waiting for the right moment to tell you about his health issue. He went to the doctor today, so maybe he'll have something to report. Perhaps you can show me your technique for really good tea, and we can have some ready when he gets here."

Stanley went to the people vet? I wonder if he got a peanut treat.

"That sounds like an excellent idea. The world looks up when you have a proper cup of tea in your hand."

Mary Alice was plainly pleased to have her expertise recognized. She led the way into the kitchen where she introduced Melody to the hiding place for the good tea. The rest of the ritual followed.

"The secret is to bring the water just to a boil and then pour it over the loose tea leaves after you have primed the pot."

Melody carried the tea back into the living room. Mary Alice followed with a plate of shortbread. Before they could set their treasures on the table, the front door opened, and Stanley walked in.

"Good afternoon, ladies. I hope I'm not interrupting a private gathering."

"Allison and I were actually waiting for you, and Mrs. Macdonald decided to join us."

"You were waiting for me, or you were lying in wait?"

Mary Alice folded her hands in her lap. "Stanley McFadden," she said in a deliberate tone, "we were concerned about your visit to the doctor, and we are hoping you might be willing to tell us how it went. We can't be of any help if we don't know what's going on."

"Actually, I was intending to invite you all to tea, so this little gathering saves me the trouble. I indeed have a troublesome cough when I do strenuous activity, like climbing stairs. I wasn't able to reproduce the cough in the doctor's office, but he sent me for tests at the hospital lab. I certainly had reason to cough on their tread-mill, and the technician fellow took measurements of everything, as well as X-rays of my chest. Dr. Chan will get the results and tell me what all that means. So, there you go. That's what I know."

"Oh dear. That sounds like it might be something serious. Didn't the doctor give any hint of what he diagnosis might be?" Mary Alice's voice trembled unmistakably.

"I don't know about the diagnosis, but the medicine that would work for me right now is a cup of that tea and a piece of Cape Breton shortbread."

Allison poured Stanley a cup of tea, since Mary Alice seemed temporarily immobilized. Captain's head followed the piece of shortbread that Stanley picked up.

Not a bad con attempt, but your delivery needs work. While you're coming up with something better, pass me a piece of that shortbread you're in danger of dropping.

"There you go, Captain. You know that a piece of shortbread is more interesting than doctor stories."

Captain retreated to the farthest part of his cage with the short-bread, dropping it into his seed dish for safekeeping. Threat of a shortbread-recall is not to be taken lightly.

Melody was hoping to change Mary Alice's mind about Captain's usefulness. Mary Alice looked sceptical. Melody really wanted to grill Stanley more closely about whether or not he had asked the doctor about the possibility of respiratory distress related to asbestos exposure. It would be tactful to ask that question after Mary Alice had gone.

"And can we count on you to tell us what diagnosis the doctor decides on, when he does?" Mary Alice was folding and unfolding her hands, looking earnestly at Stanley.

Stanley nodded. "I shall not keep you in suspense. As soon as I know something definite, I shall summon the tea council. Meanwhile, don't fret."

"I don't know if I can promise that, but I suppose we have to carry on until we know more," Mary Alice said. "I still have to prepare something for the parish potluck tonight, so I need to be on my way. Maybe you'd like to come to the potluck, Stanley?"

Stanley glanced at Melody, suspecting there would be a round two at the tea party after Mary Alice was gone. Melody nodded slightly, confirming his intuition.

"Uh, my heathen presence might taint the saintly feast. And besides, I need to rest up from that ridiculous treadmill. Another time, my highland lass. But thank you anyway."

Mary Alice got up, steadied herself, and headed for the door. "Suit yourself. I'm away."

After Mary Alice closed the front door behind her, Stanley turned to Melody. "Thank you for not bringing up your asbestos theory in front of Mary Alice. It's not necessary to introduce her to that idea unless Dr. Chan confirms mesothelioma or that asbestosis thing."

"What did he really say when you were there? Did he advance a tentative diagnosis?"

"He's close-mouthed at the best of times. After he listened to my chest, he commented about some crackling sound and then named off a bunch of tests that I should have before he would say more. The lab fellow at the hospital kept asking if I ever had double pneumonia or bronchitis. But when I said no, he wouldn't elaborate."

"You were lucky the hospital lab could take you so quickly. Are you nervous about getting the results? Two days could seem like a long time when you're waiting for a doctor to call you."

"Actually, no news is good news. If it takes him more than a couple of days to get back to me, the news isn't urgent. If he calls me in the day after tomorrow, I know it's likely not a good sign."

"You sound so matter-of-fact. You can't really be that cool about the whole thing!"

"I'm not cool. I'm worried, to a point. I also worry about the big earthquake they say is coming anytime. We're supposed to have an emergency kit by the door and be ready to flee on a moment's notice. Even with all that early warning stuff, lots of us will die because we're at the wrong place at the wrong time. And truth be known, it's a natural thing for all of us to die at some point. Some people know it's going to happen, and they die slowly. Other people just have a massive stroke or get hit by a semi—instant death. At my age, death is more than an abstract possibility. If I don't die from some asbestos condition, it will be from something else that I didn't expect. In any case, living forever is not one of the available options. That may seem macabre to you because you're young. For me, carrying on is what I'm called to do, until that's no longer possible. Maybe religious people believe they're going to carry on in heaven or in some other spiritual real estate. But I carry on at Shady Shingles with Captain here. I've always hoped I could look after him as long as he lives, but he may outlive me. And he will have to carry on with somebody new. Perhaps that could be you when the time comes?"

Sensing the gravitas of the moment, Captain crouched forward, as if parsing Stanley's words. Melody's eyes were moist, and Allison turned her head away. A pause ensued.

"Of course, I would look after Captain if you were gone," Melody said, her voice trembling. "But that's not a given. There are treatments for those conditions that I mentioned. And there are always new research developments that can make a difference."

"No doubt. My suspicion is that those things just prolong the inevitable. There's always a chance that the good doctor will come up with something less serious. But for now, I guess this is a reminder that I should make some decisions and review my will, just in case. I decided that earlier in the day while I was sitting in the park."

"I was worried you wouldn't take your cough very seriously, but I see you have been pretty thorough in thinking through what it could all mean."

"Thank you for your concern. Let's leave things be for a while. No one needs to walk on eggshells. The facts will be what they are, and then we can meet them head on. Now I really am tired.

"I understand you've had a big day. Allison and I will head upstairs and leave you to your evening ritual. We can grab something to eat later."

Stanley nodded, and the two women returned the dishes to the kitchen before going up to their room. The laird of Shady Shingles made himself a sandwich and then watched the evening news but without really taking in the import of the events reported. He covered Captain and retired early, knowing the new day would come all too soon.

23
The End of a Reign

THE DAY STARTED like any other. Then came the news.

Mary Alice's daughter knocked at the front door at 7:30 a.m. It wasn't a gentle rapping but an insistent pounding. Stanley wasn't accustomed to early morning visitors, and all who knew him were aware of that fact. Agnes would normally heed her mother's warning not to bother Stanley before 8:00 a.m., but that day was a huge exception.

Agnes's loud knocking awakened Stanley. The annoying sound didn't stop, so he got up and grabbed his housecoat, putting it on as he headed toward the front door. He had half a mind to scold whoever was responsible for his rude awakening. Then he saw that it was Agnes, and she looked distraught. Her eyes were red, and she spoke rapidly, as if she were out of breath. "I'm sorry to get you up so early, but I felt it was very important to speak to you."

"Come in, come in. Don't stand out there in the cold. What is it that could put you in such a state, Agnes?"

Stanley had an ominous premonition of what it could be, but he hoped he was wrong. Only one thing would prompt Agnes to be sitting on Stanley's couch at such an hour.

"It's Mother, Stanley. Cora called her at seven this morning, as per usual. There was no answer. And Mother had not said anything to her about being away. Cora was alarmed and called me right away, and I rushed over. I rang her bell, but there was no answer. I used my key to get in. She wasn't downstairs, so I went up to her room. She was in her bed, and she wasn't breathing. I felt for her pulse, but she was cold. She must have died during her sleep. I called 911, and the paramedics came, but without the sirens. They're there now, waiting for the coroner to come before they move the body. It's all so awful. I just can't believe she's gone. I thought you should know right away."

"You're quite right, my dear. You did the right thing. I'm so sorry your mother is gone. Let me get you some tissues."

Stanley retrieved a box of tissues from the bathroom, as much for himself as for Agnes. They both needed to wipe away some tears. Captain looked on with some anxiety, since both humans seemed to be exhibiting intense emotion. He sensed fear and danger, but he couldn't see the cause of their distress. Clearly, something was not right. Stanley and Agnes were not looking at him; therefore, something else must be the cause. Humans can be very puzzling creatures at times.

"I think I need to go back now," Agnes said. "The coroner will ask questions. And I'll soon have to contact the funeral home. And there are all those relatives in Cape Breton to contact. Mum handled all these things when my dad died. And now it's me."

"Would you like me to go back with you? Anyway, I want to see Mary Alice one last time, before all the rest of it happens."

"I would appreciate that. Mum left a checklist for when this moment came. So, I sort of know what she wanted. She wasn't one to leave loose ends."

"That's an understatement. I'm sure you don't need me for advice, especially since Mary Alice has laid out what's to be done. She didn't leave a similar list with me, but I know she would want me to be there for you, at least for this first little bit. Just let me leave a note on the table for the girls. They might wonder where I am."

Stanley didn't stop to give Captain his breakfast. He left a note and asked Melody to do it, noting the sad reason why. She would see it on the kitchen table.

Is Stanley running off with Agnes? Why are they leaving without giving me my breakfast? Stanley always gives me my breakfast.

Captain watched through the front door window and saw Stanley and Agnes go into Mary Alice's house.

This behaviour seems very strange, because Mary Alice always comes here, and Stanley never goes there. For some reason, it must be a very stressful thing to go into Mary Alice's house. Both the humans were very sad and afraid before they went in.

Stanley and Agnes encountered the coroner, Margaret Walker. She had already spoken to the paramedics, who confirmed that Mary Alice was deceased when they arrived. They estimated the time of death to be approximately 2:00 a.m., give or take a couple of hours.

"You are Mrs. Macdonald's daughter?" she asked Agnes.

"Yes, that's correct. I'm also my mother's executor."

"That's helpful. When was the last time you saw your mother?"

"I took her to a parish potluck at her church last night. She had baked a casserole, and we went together. We finished a little after eight, and I brought her back here."

"Did she say anything about feeling unwell or was her behaviour unusual in any way?"

"Usually, she would have washed the casserole dish as soon as she got home, but she said, 'Leave it for now. I'll wash it when I do the breakfast dishes in the morning.' That was unusual because she would always do that kind of thing right away. She seemed a bit distracted."

Stanley decided to interject. "I'm Stanley McFadden, Mrs. Macdonald's long-time neighbour and friend. She may have been distracted because she learned about some medical tests that I had yesterday, and she was concerned about what the outcome might be."

"Mum told me about that, because we had tea after she came home. It's true that she was concerned, but I didn't get the sense that she was panicky or overly anxious."

"Probably that's not what is most relevant. Did she complain of any radiating pain or perhaps acute shortness of breath?"

"Mum has been kind of tired for the last while, and her breathing hasn't come as easily as it used to. She did see her doctor regularly, and she took her prescriptions. "

"And they were?"

"Meds for high blood pressure. And I think she had recently been diagnosed with type-two diabetes. She thought she could manage that with diet."

"And her age?"

"She was ninety-two last August."

"I'll need to inform her doctor, but I think we can assume that she died almost instantly from a major heart attack. This can happen with little obvious warning, especially for older people with diabetes and a history of high blood pressure. While this sudden event is a tremendous shock for you, it may be a small consolation that she died in her sleep, and there would have been no suffering. This event was very quick."

"Thank you for coming so promptly. And for telling us what happened."

"I'll authorize the funeral home to remove the body. Is there a particular establishment that your family uses?"

"When my dad died, it was Camosun Memorial Home. And Mum wanted the same place, in the directions that she left."

"I'm glad that you and our mother had that kind of discussion. Lots of people are not prepared at all. I'll notify Camosun when I leave, and they should be able to come shortly. Is Mr. McFadden going to stay here with you?"

Stanley nodded. "Yes, I am."

Margaret took her leave. The paramedics indicated they would stay until the funeral home staff had removed the body.

"I always thought Mum would live until she was really old. And she would say the rosary. And a priest would come and give her Last Rites. And it would somehow be very peaceful."

"We can assume that she will give St. Peter a piece of her mind. But in my experience, death is not so idyllic. We can imagine how it will be, but it's not something you get to vote on. Somehow I don't think Mary Alice would have wanted a lingering death where she faded away and people pitied her."

"No, if she couldn't be in charge she wouldn't want to be here."

"Probably she would have liked a visit from Father Kawolski, but she no doubt got admiration for her casserole at the parish potluck the night before she died. That's pretty close to a sacramental goodbye."

Agnes smiled and nodded. "You and Mum knew each other pretty well. I'm surprised she didn't turn you into a good Catholic boy."

"Your mum certainly got a lot of strength from her Catholic roots. I always admired that, but a long time ago we came to an understanding about faith and doubt. She would look after the faith, and I would look after the doubt. And it seemed to work."

"Will you come to the funeral mass, or is that asking too much? She would want you to be there, if that doesn't violate your principles."

"Yes, indeed. I'll be there to say my goodbyes. And all of Orkney Street and probably the local Cape Breton diaspora and your father's people and the Catholic Women's League as well. You should also have bagpipes. That will annoy the hell out of Father Kawolski. It will be Mary Alice's revenge for him not visiting her, even though he didn't know she needed visiting."

"Now I know why you and Mum got on so well. Deep down, you're both evil!"

They both laughed. Then they cried some more. And they laughed. And the funeral home staff came. Agnes gave them the dress that her mother said she wanted to be buried in. It was plain white with a Macdonald tartan sash.

After the funeral home took the body away, Agnes and Stanley hugged. Agnes locked the door on the way out and then drove away. Stanley lingered at the front door of Shady Shingles and then went in.

Captain was on top of his cage, and his food dishes looked full. He bowed his head, and Stanley wandered over to give him a head scratch.

"She's gone, Captain. There's no more Mary Alice. No more shortbread lady. Gone for good. What do you think about that?"

I didn't know humans could be gone for good. Sometimes you're gone, but you always come back. Mary Alice always comes back. But now you say she won't come back. I don't like this change. I was always kind of afraid of Mary Alice, but she brought me grapes.

Stanley wandered to the kitchen. Melody had penned something at the bottom of his note. "So sorry to hear the news. Allison and I have classes this morning. Will talk later. CU this evening."

It was noon, and already Stanley was tired enough for an afternoon nap. Whatever he had been thinking about his own medical woes seemed remote and irrelevant. What he really felt was fatigue. Yes, it was physical fatigue. But at a deeper level, it was a fatigue of the spirit. Sometimes too much happens on too many levels. All Stanley wanted was some sleep before explaining the day to Melody and Allison, and probably Brian and Pierre too. He retired to his room and to the unmade bed that he had bolted from that morning. Mary Alice would be appalled that he had left the bed unmade. And now he could claim that his negligence was her fault. She would scold him if she were there.

If she were there . . .

That was the last thought Stanley remembered before falling asleep.

※　※　※

The rest of the day was a blur for Stanley. The girls came home, and he filled them in on the morning's events. Brian and then Pierre came in while they were talking. Everyone expressed surprise about Mary Alice dying so suddenly. They offered their condolences to

Stanley. In truth, he wasn't sure what he should be feeling. He felt numbness and loss and anger. He also felt regret that he never got to say the kind of goodbye that he would have liked. He imagined that Mary Alice would be the one to carry on, and he would be the one to initiate a goodbye, given his likely illness. Now it fell to him to carry on. And he wasn't sure what form that should take.

❈ ❈ ❈

The funeral mass happened on the third day after Mary Alice's death. Stanley attended, and all the people whom he predicted were present too. Melody had offered to come with him, but he preferred to go alone, in case he decided not to stay for the entire service.

Father Kawolski didn't allow the bagpipes inside the church, but the piper played on the steps outside as people entered. He also played a lament at the cemetery. All the cemetery's occupants must have been truly dead, because no one got up to complain. That was always Mary Alice's line when one of her Celtic kin was laid to rest. There was no danger of anyone in Cape Breton getting buried when they were just napping. Those folks make sure the deceased was thoroughly dead. Only the severely hearing impaired could sleep through the sound of bagpipes.

When Stanley came home from the funeral in the late afternoon, Captain was agitated, and a voicemail was waiting.

"This is Dr. Chan's office. The doctor would like you to come in for an appointment tomorrow morning at ten. Please call back to confirm."

"Well, Captain, it appears this will be the news that I haven't been waiting for. Clearly, they have found something, and it's just a matter of telling me precisely what it is. Doctors don't usually invite people in on short notice to discuss the weather."

Maybe the people vet will be able to help. You've been sounding kind of broken when the other humans aren't around. You should go get fixed.

"It must be nice to be a parrot. Birds don't know enough to worry about anything—they just eat and poop. Come to think of it, I have friends in a nursing home who do pretty much the same thing. I don't think Mary Alice would have been happy in a nursing home. Well, maybe if she were the director of nursing or something, but otherwise I think she went the way she preferred. The only part that would have upset her is that no one made the bed after the funeral home people carried her out. They wouldn't have done it right anyway. I hope Agnes has made the bed by now, or there will be hell to pay. Then again, I guess it doesn't matter."

Captain did his figure-eight head swing, and Stanley returned to the moment again. He knew it was his cue to get a short section of millet spray. Captain was an impatient duckling. After going to the kitchen and coming back with the requested treat, he called the doctor's office. The receptionist answered on the sixth ring.

"Dr. Chan's office. How may I help you?"

"This is Stanley McFadden. I'm calling back to confirm my appointment with Dr. Chan, tomorrow at ten."

"Thank you for returning my call. We'll see you then." Her voice revealed nothing.

Stanley looked at the clock and decided to make tea. The girls would likely be home soon, and he could tell them about the funeral and the doctor's appointment. He made his way to the kitchen and started the familiar routine. When he looked in the cannister that held the good tea, he saw there wasn't much left. Time to make a trek to Murchy's on Government Street for a new supply. Then he heard the front door open and the sound of Melody and Allison talking. Allison was the first to enter the living room.

"I wonder if he's back yet. The door was unlocked, but maybe Brian or Pierre forgot to lock it on their way out."

"No, Allison. I can hear the kettle rumbling in the kitchen. He's here."

Melody proceeded into the kitchen while Allison made space on the cluttered table. When Melody arrived, Stanley had his back to her as he got the "everyday" teapot down from the cupboard.

"Here, let me help with that. I'll get the cups down. Don't forget to prime the pot."

"It appears we won't be dropping the standard for proper tea. Mary Alice trained us well."

Soon the tea council assembled in the living room. Captain kept an eye out for any stray shortbread but didn't drop his millet spray. Both women looked expectantly at Stanley.

"Well, it was an eventful afternoon. The funeral went well, if one can say that about such a ritual. I stayed for the entire thing, including the reception in the parish hall after the family and I returned from the cemetery. Mary Alice would probably have been pleased at the turnout. The only thing out of place is that she didn't come back for tea. I guess I'll have to get used to that."

Melody and Allison looked at each other awkwardly. Melody took the lead. "I wish she could be here. But I think she would be glad that have carried on—with tea, that is. She would be concerned as to how you will manage."

"I take it you're talking about more than the tea? Indeed, carrying on is what life is all about. I fully intend to carry on, maybe with some help from you two?"

"That's a given. We'll definitely be here." It was Allison who spoke, but both she and Melody nodded.

Melody decided to press on. "And what would you like help with, in particular?"

"Actually, I listened to a message from my doctor's office before you came in. He wants me to come in tomorrow morning at ten, and I'd like you to come with me."

"Oh, for sure. I don't have classes until the afternoon." Melody silently calculated the significance of an appointment so soon after Stanley's tests.

"You can meet him, and you can also remember some of the details that he will likely tell me. Sometimes I don't think of the right thing to ask until I'm gone, and then it's too late.""I'd be glad to do that if you don't think it's an invasion of your privacy." Melody wasn't sure of her new status in Stanley's world.

"I think we both know that Dr. Chan would only be acting this quickly if there was something serious to report. And since you are, in fact, my only immediate family, it may fall to you to make some decisions, eventually. Better to be in on the game now than parachute in later. You can say no, of course, but I'd like you to be there."

"Understood. And I'm quite willing to be a kind of advocate, if that's alright. I just didn't want to step beyond my place when you're hearing all these things."

"I don't want you to take over his role, but I would value your opinion when it comes to considering options—assuming there are options."

"Well, let's wait and see what he says first. And then we can always ask Captain for his opinion when we get home."

Captain heard his name and stopped munching the millet. *Hey, I've done my bit. Now it's your turn, Florence Nightingale.*

"Captain has many talents, most of them relating to manipulating people into giving him his favourite foods. On the other hand, he makes a good pretense of listening to whatever you say, and that's more than most people can pull off."

"Well, I'll try to learn from the master, especially when I get along further in my medical training. Point noted."

"I didn't mean you. I just meant that people in general like telling more than listening. I think that's why pets can be so comforting."

Allison decided it was time to chime in. "Sounds like subject matter for somebody's thesis someday. But I don't think I'll take that on. My thing is more building things."

Melody noticed that her father was looking restless, glancing at his watch and then at the tea dishes. "Thank you for your update," she said. "This must have been a full day for you. What time should we leave tomorrow, for your appointment?"

"There's a bus at 9:25 that will get us there early enough. Let's leave the house at 9:20, if you're amenable to that."

"Sounds like a plan."

Melody and Allison looked after the tea dishes and left Stanley to his devices for the evening.

24
Onward

CAPTAIN WAS PLEASED that he heard morning sounds earlier than usual. At that time of year, he had to wait patiently for Stanley to remove the cover sheet from his cage. He always woke up with the dawn, and that was fine in December, because Stanley's getting up coincided with the arrival of ambient light in the living room. Now it was a month after the winter solstice, and Stanley's appearance was falling behind the morning light. A good squawk might remedy the situation, or produce a scolding. That morning there was no need to fret, because his lordship was up early.

"Up and Adam, Captain. You get to stay here, but Melody and I are off to see the wizard. I can see that we need to do some cage cleaning. But breakfast comes first."

Stanley found it reassuring to go through the usual routine of looking after Captain. The morning news might be a litany of disaster, and Mary Alice might be gone, but that morning would have to start like any other. Stanley cleaned Captain's dishes, changed the newsprint at the bottom of his cage, and brought back an assortment of cut vegetables and fruit to augment the mixed seeds that were Captain's staple diet.

Rapid steps on the stairs indicated Brian's arrival. "Hi, Mr. M. You're up and on the job early. Can I butt in and grab an apple from the fridge?"

"You may indeed. No eggs Benedict for a diligent scholar?"

Bryan made an expression of mild disgust. "Too much time. That's for old-timers like you. I'll grab something later on campus."

Brian rifled his way to the bottom of the fridge and found a Golden Delicious. He started munching it on the way out the door. "Catch you later."

Stanley busied himself with his own breakfast, half paying intention to the morning news on the TV. It was -30 in Winnipeg, and the Maritimes were being buried in a blizzard. In Victoria the city council had reached an impasse over the expansion of further bike lanes. The world was unfolding pretty much as it should.

Stanley had started on cleaning some of the gooier bars on Captain's cage when Melody and Allison came down. They both had fruit and yogurt before Allison left. Stanley had made coffee, so Melody poured some and joined him in the living room.

"I see that Captain can be quite a messy fellow. He's lucky to get his house so thoroughly cleaned."

"I won't do it all just now. I go at it in stages. He probably wonders why I bother because he's going to mess it up again in short order."

"I have a friend who talks about her children that way."

"Having a parrot is like having a two-year-old permanently. The difference is that this two-year-old stays a two-year-old, whereas your friend's children will likely grow up. On the other hand, I know where Captain is every night, and he doesn't treat me like a mobile ATM."

"I hadn't thought of it quite that way. I almost feel that he should come to the doctor with us because he's family. But I guess his place is here."

"Yes, let's not overload Dr. Chan's family practice with too much family. I'll be ready to leave in just a few minutes. Finish your coffee first."

"No problem. I'm ready when you are."

The two left the house together and chatted intermittently as they rode the bus downtown to the doctor's office.

They arrived at the waiting room about ten minutes before the scheduled appointment. As usual, it was full as people came and went. The receptionist ushered them into an examination room and closed the door. Presently, they heard a gentle knock, and the door opened.

"Good day, Mr. McFadden. I see you haven't come alone."

"Yes, I brought my daughter with me. I spoke about her last time. She'll remember the things that I'll probably miss. I'd also like her to hear directly what you have to say."

"Very well. I think that's probably a good idea. I guess we can get down to business then." Dr. Chan looked ill at ease, which was not his usual demeanour. "I have your test results, and they indicate something more serious than a chronic cough or a simple viral infection. The X-rays show fibrous material in both lungs, reducing the capacity of your lungs to oxygenate your blood supply. This defect is aggravated by pleural effusion—meaning you have a buildup of fluid around the lungs. These things were also very evident from the readings made when you were on the treadmill. You had shortness of breath and chest pain during that test. There is also weight loss since we last recorded your weight, and this is not due to rigorous exercise or a change in diet?"

"Uh, no. I haven't been dieting, but I haven't had as much of an appetite of late. I just assumed that was because of a bit of stress about money matters. And my neighbour, Mary Alice, died just recently."

"Sorry to hear that, but I think the appetite issue is more than a reaction to life's usual worries. There is weight loss to consider, but your fingertips are also wider and rounder than normal. We call this clubbing."

"You mean fat fingers is a condition?"

"Well, no, but they are a symptom among the other symptoms that I have noted."

"I think the doctor is describing a differential diagnosis, in which he considers a cluster of symptoms that point to a particular condition as opposed to any one symptom by itself that could be explained by a variety of causes."

"Indeed. Well done, young lady." He turned to Stanley. "All this leads me to conclude that you have a moderately severe level of mesothelioma. Your exposure to asbestos fibers was several decades ago, but unfortunately, the damage may not present itself for a long time after the fact."

Melody clenched and unclenched her hands. She gasped audibly and looked to Stanley.

"And what does 'moderately severe' signify?" Stanley asked. "What does it mean for my future, and what can be done?"

"Well, the damage cannot be reversed, and there is no cure per se. Mesothelioma is a relatively rare type of cancer induced by asbestos fibers, and those fibers do not dissolve or exit from your lungs. The treatment is to slow down or mitigate some of the effects of the disease. You have some fluid around your lungs, but you don't yet present with fever or night sweats. The condition is severe enough to affect parts of your lungs, but it shows moderate progress in that there is no sign of tumours or spreading to other organs. Also, it would seem that your chest pain is episodic with exertion, but it's not constant. I will need to refer you to a special oncologist for measures like surgery, radiation, and chemotherapy. Those are the usual treatments for mesothelioma."

Melody could see that Stanley seemed overwhelmed by the volume of information. She decided it was time to interrupt. "How would surgery help with something so well established in his lungs?"

"The purpose would not be to remove the fibrous contamination but to take biopsies that would indicate how far the cancer has spread. That information is then used to establish a treatment plan for the radiation and chemotherapy that follow. If only small parts of the lung are fibrous, sometimes surgery itself can be not only diagnostic but also curative."

"If doctors do all those things, how long would I live?" Stanley's voice was calm and devoid of obvious emotion.

"Without the biopsies, it's just a guess. I can say that in severe cases, patients live from six months to a year after diagnosis. However, about a third of patients live beyond a year, and there are new developments in treatments all the time. So much depends on what the lung biopsies reveal. I can only tell you in general terms that you have the disease and that there are treatment options."

"But I could go through all those things and not be cured?"

"That is correct. But if optimal measures are pursued, it could mean that you have at least several more years in which the worst symptoms are mitigated. This is perhaps something that you and your daughter would like to talk over and then get back to me. I recommend an appointment with a specialist oncologist at the cancer clinic. That person would organize the biopsy process with a surgeon and then consultations would follow from there. That is my recommendation, but the decision is yours."

"Thank you, I guess. I knew you would likely find something, but I wasn't quite prepared for this. Melody, is there anything else you think we should ask before we head home?" Stanley was uncertain and more than just a little dazed.

"No, Dr. Chan has been very thorough, and now we just have to digest what he's said. I think that home is the next thing on the agenda. Thank you, Dr. Chan."

Dr. Chan offered a perfunctory handshake to Stanley and Melody, then left. If being the bearer of this kind of news bothered him, it didn't show.

Melody and Stanley made their way to the waiting area and the exit. Once outside, they walked slowly to the bus stop. Stanley was the first to speak.

"You can know something at an intuitive level, but when it's all laid out like we just heard, the reality of it is quite a blow. Maybe if I had said something sooner, more could have been done. As things stand, it sounds like the outcome is pretty bleak."

"You shouldn't blame yourself. You couldn't have known what the effect of that renovating work was going to be. And as Dr. Chan said, the symptoms can take a long time to present, and people can easily think that what they're experiencing is aging or indigestion or the flu."

"Part of me wants to do nothing and ignore it. But as the symptoms get worse, I guess ignoring them won't be an option. It's all about how long I get to play the game, even if there's no chance of winning."

Melody thought that sounded fatalistic, but she resisted the temptation to contradict her father. She wasn't sure herself what authentic hope looked like in that scenario.

They continued walking, falling into silence as each thought of what the discussion at home might be like. Stanley would miss a tea debriefing session with Mary Alice, but he was also glad that she would not be burdened with worry about him. Melody might worry, but she was younger and had more energy for the future. And now his own future would require some decisions that also involved a caring daughter and a precocious parrot.

Stanley thought back to the ducklings on the railway track. They might have been run over by a train, but they carried on down the track, because ducklings don't think about the future. They live purely in the moment. Sometimes, against all the odds, the train stops, and someone lifts them over the rail. Or not. In either case, they won't live forever; that's not what the game is about. What they do know is how to carry on and be ducklings, vulnerable as they might be. They carry on. And therein lies the hope for any duckling household.

Printed in Canada